More from Wyvern's Peak Publishing

Charlie Sullivan and the Monster Hunters:
The Varcolac's Diary
Witch Moon
Council of the Hunters
The Dragon Gate

Coming Soon:

Rise of the Ancients

The Recalcitrant Project
by Lauren Lynne

The Butterfly Stone
The Stones of Power, Book 1
by Laurie Bell

Halloween Games:
Terrifying Tales of Young Adult Horror
by D.C. McGannon

Charlie Sullivan and the

MONSTER HUNTERS

Book 1: The Varcolac's Diary

Charlie Sullivan and the

MONSTER HUNTERS

Book 1: The Varcolac's Diary

by

D. C. McGannon & C. Michael McGannon

WYVERN'S PEAK PUBLISHING

An imprint of The McGannon Group, Ltd. Co.

Charlie Sullivan and the Monster Hunters:
The Varcolac's Diary

Written by D.C. McGannon and C. Michael McGannon

Cover design by Matthew D. Smith – www.mdsmithdesign.com

Published by Wyvern's Peak Publishing. 2018
An imprint of The McGannon Group, Ltd. Co.

Charlie Sullivan and the Monster Hunters: The Varcolac's Diary / by D.C. McGannon & C. Michael McGannon – 4th ed.

Summary: Five friends in a quiet town gather to discover the cause behind recent disappearances, uncover the truth about the town's history, and confront the ancient evil that lies behind it all.

4   8   12   16   20   24   28   32   34

ISBN-13: 978-0-9854088-2-4

www.WyvernsPeak.com

For Michael.
My son. My friend. My co-conspirator in all things creative.
I love you and am honored to have labored with you in this.
It sounded good . . . are we there yet?

D.C. McGannon

For my parents.
Couldn't have done it without either of you (literally, with this
story!). Love you guys more than you know.
And, no. But . . . we're halfway there!

C. Michael McGannon

Prologue

T he Dark Prince towered above Hunter's Key, eminent and brazen. He looked down from the mansion's tallest tower, eyes glowing like coals from the belly of Hell. Five stood between him and the town below. He would eliminate them, and collect what he came for. Nothing would stop him from completing the ritual.

Charlie could see himself standing there, one of the five. Who were the others? They seemed familiar, but he couldn't remember why. He felt a kinship among them, though he didn't know them. At least, not yet.

In a torrent of fire and violence, their world began to fall. One of the five was ripped away and now only four remained. Together they would face the darkness and its Prince.

Death consumed them. Sorrow opened wide its embrace to welcome them. Who was taken? What happened? Charlie's vision was blurred, distorted. Someone blocked his sight.

Static. Noise. Until. . .

The Dark Prince descended from the mansion's tower, his shadow spreading like a disease over the town. His eyes burned holes through Charlie's mind, and Charlie fell under the weight of it all. As his vision dimmed, he felt the blackness reach deep into his soul. His breath separated from his body as he reached for something, anything, to break his fall.

Nothing.

He couldn't save them.

He couldn't save himself.

It was finished, and he could only watch as the world burned.

Charlie sat up, tangled in his sheets, gasping. Tears streamed down his cheeks.

Another nightmare.

He got out of bed and cracked his bedroom window, breathing in the fresh air before heading to the bathroom. In his experience, going back to sleep after a nightmare was not a good thing to do.

Charlie splashed his face with cool water and checked his eyes in the mirror. They were getting worse.

The nightmares brought the worst headaches and bloodshot eyes. *I look terrible*, he thought. *Wonder if I should see the school nurse? But then mom and dad would hear from the school and freak out.*

He shrugged. It wasn't that bad. His eyes were just a little blood-shot at night, that was all. Charlie was sure they would get better, as soon as the nightmares stopped.

If they stopped.

Charlie heaved a deep sigh and flicked off the bathroom light, then slipped back into bed.

I'll be fine, he thought. *Winter break is soon and I won't have school to stress me out. I'll be able to sleep without these dumb dreams. The stress is causing the nightmares, I'm sure. Everything will be okay.*

Charlie was right about one thing. He wouldn't have to worry about school for much longer.

But everything was not going to be okay.

Chapter 1

Few dared venture into the woods of Hunter's Point. Perhaps the only people who did without fear or hesitation were one Fish McCollum, and one Wardley Dink. The past couple of years had been hard, and frightening, but life went on.

For Fish and Dink, life was best spent scouting through the woods searching for the best fishing spots. Such scouting was accomplished in the wee hours of the morning, as soon as the first rays of sunshine began to weave their way through the treetops. If they had any say in the matter, the fishing was done for as long as there was light left in the sky.

"Downright snippy, if I do dare say." Dink pushed the collar of his thick coat up the back of his neck.

"Problem is, Dink, you 'do dare say' too much," quipped Fish. "And I do dare say I wish you would just up and shut your trap sometimes."

"Sure, sure," Dink said, unoffended. Snow and frozen twigs crunched under his boots.

It was late fall in Hunter's Grove, an aptly named town known for its quaint charm and hillside country allure. The air was crisp, and snow was starting to tumble in its wintry pageant. Leaves were dark and brittle, congregating to dance lightly on the wind over streets and sidewalks. The small town was picturesque, and a favorite resort for people who enjoyed a quiet, rustic escape from a hurried and noisy world.

Or so it used to be. Hunter's Grove was still charming and scenic, but there was something that hung heavy in the air, making it feel oppressive and isolated from the rest of the world. Fear tugged at the thoughts of local residents. Each year, snow fell a bit earlier and ice imprisoned the waters faster and faster. The sun hid a little longer out of sight with each new coming of Spring. Hunter's Grove was content to slumber, rather than risk waking to the horror that had besieged its peaceful existence.

Dink opened his mouth to speak, having already forgotten Fish's complaint, when a branch snapped in the distance. Fish held up his hand and they both stopped.

"What is it?" whispered Dink.

Fish scowled and shook his head. He wasn't a coward by any means, but he was a careful man. Many in Hunter's Grove thought Fish a few steps short of his destination, mentally speaking, but in truth Fish was one of the most informed individuals in the nostalgic little town. The same was true for Dink.

A few moments passed before Dink slapped his old friend on the back.

"Aw! A squirrel got you again, that's all! It ain't for worrying about."

"We don't know that, Dink. Can't take anything for granted these days. Especially after last night."

Dink nodded, a sadness sunk deep lines into his face.

Fish listened, looking around the woods one more time. Rubbing the rabbit's foot hanging from a hand-cut leather strap around his neck, he ventured farther in, with Dink tight on his heels.

Several feet away, a diminutive cloaked figure listened to their conversation. Its heart hammered a mad beat in its clammy chest. Clinging to the trees, it waited for the two men to pass until it moved back toward the human town — to Hunter's Grove.

Jack Sullivan picked up the first copy of THE GROVE DAILY, which was more of an every-other-day-or-so paper, as editions were delivered twice a week, if Hunter's Grove was so lucky. One came on Sunday for sure; that was never missed. And one was delivered on Wednesday, or Thursday, or perhaps Tuesday if there was enough news to bother printing. Mr. Sullivan flipped open the snow-damp copy and read the soggy print, bracing for what he might find.

He found it. And he dreaded every word. It wasn't the main headline, of course. Front page news, but not the headline for THE GROVE DAILY. It was decided long ago, by the Mayor himself, to never make these events main headlines.

2nd PERSON MISSING IN AS MANY WEEKS; SUSPICIONS TURN TO HUNTER'S POINT

As if the air suddenly got colder, Mr. Sullivan pulled his coat tighter. The sunlight seemed to tuck further behind the gray, pre-winter clouds.

Back inside the warmth of his kitchen, Mr. Sullivan wilted as he continued to read. The missing person was a local boy — Bobby Muldor. Old Mrs. McBranson had disappeared the week before.

Two years ago, people started to go missing at an alarming rate, at first once a week, but then doubling in number. The Grove Disappearances, they called it. It was the town's dirty secret...the skeleton in the closet.

The activity had stopped for a spell, but now the disappearances were starting again.

The strange thing—the really strange thing—was that the police hadn't been able to find a solid connection between any of the missing persons. No trace. No clues. Nothing. They were there one day, and the next day...a secondary headline in the town's meager newspaper.

That makes ten, thought Mr. Sullivan. *Ten people gone in two years.*

Charlie burst into the kitchen.

"Dad! We're going to be late!"

Jack put the paper down, relieved to do so, and turned to his son. Charlie had just walked out of the bathroom, his hair still a disheveled case of bed-head, and a dingy, pen-and-pencil-drawn backpack hanging loose from one shoulder. He squinted in the morning's light, and Mr. Sullivan noticed Charlie's deep-set, bloodshot eyes.

He ruffled the teen's light brown hair and grabbed his coffee-filled tumbler. "Well, get to the car then. We can still make it on time."

"I hope so," Charlie muttered gravely as he headed for the door. "I've got to get to homeroom. If Mrs. Pinkerly marks me tardy one more time, I'm doomed."

Darcy shivered in her autumn coat. She stepped onto the welcome landing of TAVERN'S QUICK-N-GO next to her father, Mayor

Witherington. Stooping next to one of the weather-beaten rocking chairs lining the porch, she picked up a bundle of snow-crusted newspapers. The ink was smudged from slush, top and bottom papers lost to the effect.

Mr. Witherington was a well-rounded fellow that resembled an upright light bulb. Patting his pockets, he huffed in his clumsy effort to open the door for Darcy. They both moved inside, shivering from the biting cold. The thawing newspapers found their home on the checkout counter, left of the door. Darcy smoothed back her tussled, blonde hair and breathed over her fingers for warmth.

Tavern, the store's owner and namesake, stood behind the quick-serve breakfast buffet. "Thanks, Darcy. Morning, Mr. Witherington! You two drop in for some breakfast?"

The mayor scowled at the morning's edition of the local news, the sodden sheets crumpled in his shaking fists. He looked up, startled, when Darcy tapped him on the shoulder.

"What? Oh, yes. Yes indeed, Mr. Tavern."

Darcy and her father walked to the right side of the QUICK-N-GO — a building which featured a convenient store on the left, and a diner on the right — and seated themselves at an open table, scanning the menu.

Tavern, a square-shouldered, sturdy man who looked as if he had been a lumberjack in a previous career, approached the Witheringtons moments later. Tavern knew the mayor liked to give a thorough looking at the menu, though he ordered the same breakfast every morning without fail. *Country Omelet Supreme, extra cheese, hold the onions,* Tavern recited in his head before asking, "What can I get for you?" He produced a notepad and pencil from his apron.

Darcy folded her menu and handed it to Tavern. "Blueberry

pancakes for me."

Mr. Witherington peered over the top of his menu. "Are you sure, dear? Those can be quite . . . *sticky*."

Darcy withheld her exasperation and continued. "Extra whip. And one of your caramel macchiatos. Those are so yummy!" she added with a grin.

Tavern nodded. "And for you, Mr. Mayor?"

But the mayor wasn't listening. "Darcy! Coffee, again? So much sugar and caffeine. It's not good for a young woman, and it certainly hasn't been helping your studies lately."

Darcy crossed her arms. "Whatever."

Tavern looked between the two, unsure of what to write down.

Mr. Witherington took one last, studious look over the menu.

"I think I shall go with the Country Omelet Supreme today, Mr. Tavern, extra cheese, and cup of your freshest coffee, black. And, ah, if you could hold the onions on that omelet, please."

Darcy rolled her eyes and shared a grin with Tavern, both escaping Mr. Witherington's attention altogether.

"One order blueberry pancakes, one Country Omelet Supreme, extra cheese, comin' right up! Holding all onions, of course."

Charlie made his way to his locker, lost in thought, unaware of who or what was going on around him, as usual. Perhaps he had not been paying enough attention to his classes lately, but such was the teenage mind, to the dismay of his teachers and administrators.

That mind was absorbed in thought about his nightmares. In almost every nightmare he could recall, Hunter's Key made an appearance. It struck him odd that so many of his dreams came back to the Key. He had never gone up there, and . . .

Charlie didn't see Donnie Wickles until it was too late. The two collided, sending up a flurry of books and papers.

Of course, Donnie had been aiming for Charlie.

"Hey, doofus!" he called. "Watch where you're walking!"

"Sorry," muttered Charlie, picking himself up.

Donnie grabbed the lapel of Charlie's jacket and tapped his knuckle on Charlie's forehead. "You always stuck up in that head of yours?"

Charlie didn't answer, which infuriated Donnie. He needed a reaction of some sort, especially this morning.

"Of course you are, loner freak."

He shoved Charlie away and moved on, looking for someone who would put up a fight.

Charlie's face burned, but he kept quiet, focusing instead on picking up his books. He tried to ignore those staring at him, diving deeper into his own thoughts.

Each morning after breakfast, Mr. Witherington would drop Darcy off into the waiting arms of her devoted followers. And each morning, unbeknownst to Darcy, he carried a box in his pocket, meaning to give it to her. He was waiting for the right moment.

Mr. Witherington patted his coat pocket, feeling the long, thin box.

"Darcy, wait!"

Darcy huffed. "Yes, Daddy?" She waved to her friends.

"I wanted..."

She leveled an impatient glare, and he hesitated. That look hit Mr. Witherington deep, stirring old feelings of fear and guilt. He would give the necklace to her another day. Perhaps a day when people stopped vanishing into thin air. A day when he was stronger.

"I just wanted to say, be careful, dear."

"Was that all?" Darcy asked. She sighed, opening the door to her adoring fans.

Mr. Witherington patted his pocket again, as if that would bring Darcy's mother back. He watched his daughter walk up the school steps and then drove away.

Darcy tried to forget the disappearances in her own way, which is to say discussing the latest school gossip with her gaggle of chattering friends. One by one, the girls split off toward their respective classes, until Darcy and Caitlin walked shoulder-to-shoulder through the hallway.

"Creepy," Darcy whispered, scrunching her nose. "That's what I think. They're creepy!"

Caitlin nodded, pigtails bobbing with enthusiasm. "I know, right! It's like something that should be cool, like from a book or . . . a movie, only it's in real life, so it's totally not cool. Just—"

Darcy rolled her eyes. Of all her friends, Caitlin was the worst at subtle gossiping. "Shhh! Keep your voice down or they'll hear you," she said.

They were talking about the Vadiknovs. The school's one and only set of twins, and an enigmatic pair at that. A host of rumors drifted around school about the two, some of them true. The twins were said to run a paranormal consulting service, but no one would admit to using said service. No one was desperate enough to ask

Lisa and Liev Vadiknov for help with the paranormal.

Or anything else for that matter.

Caitlin, who had become concerned that the Vadiknovs heard her gossiping, ducked behind Darcy and tried her hardest not to look at the twins. "How can they hear us from here?"

"They just can," Darcy explained, lifting her chin. "It's part of their creepy witch powers."

"They're WITCHES?" shouted Caitlin. Lisa and Liev turned to look at her, then turned away dispassionate.

"I don't know," said Darcy, "but I'm sure if they heard you, you're cursed! First, you won't be able to talk, then all of your fingernails will rot and fall off. Then . . ."

Caitlin feigned a hurt look. "Darcy, stop it! I just got my fingernails done. You know, you are so . . . mean sometimes."

"Shush. Or I will put a curse on you."

"Wait . . . You can do that?"

Darcy rolled her eyes. "You're impossible."

The two hurried to their classes, leaving the subjects of their chatter standing by the school stairwell.

Lisa and Liev could often be found standing aloof near the stairs, or perched on the cement-stepped planters outside the school courtyard, or on top of the stone half-wall lining the walkway between the main building and the athletic complex. They never seemed to talk to anyone else, and few saw them move between classes. They seemed just to be here, or there, or nowhere at all.

Lisa wore her raven hair in a ponytail. Her pitch black clothes and lustrous, black fingernails were routine. Even her eyes looked black, enshrined in masterful application of goth-inspired makeup.

Liev was a striking contrast of his sister, with his platinum-silver hair and lightning-gray eyes. He wore clothing so white that when he stood next to Lisa, one tended to think of opposing pieces in a game of chess. Still, they shared a sense of style many secretly envied, and that few could pull off.

Both had strong, angular features and the mystique that came with their Russian blood. They were a collective oddity, and a fascination, to their schoolmates.

Donnie Wickles produced several not-so-nice expressions and gestures toward the twins as he walked by them. Liev watched him with his eyebrows raised in quasi-interest. Lisa didn't seem to notice at all.

After inciting the twins proved futile, Donnie scanned the crowd, eyes landing on someone trying to make his way quickly through the hall. Nash Stormstepper.

His grin dripped with venom. If Donnie could pick a fight with anyone, it was Nash. He moved on, leaving the Vadiknovs to their enigmatic silhouettes and shadows.

The school bell rang, and the twins simultaneously stood and walked to Mr. Switzler's class for first period.

"What do you think it was this time?" Lisa asked her brother.

"Well," said Liev. "I think it was something with an appetite. Maybe a pricolici . . . or maybe the giant purple people eater!"

Lisa elbowed her brother in the ribs.

"Be serious. We have to figure this out."

The twins had been following the recent disappearances of the townspeople with scrupulous attention, and this resurgence of activity piqued their interest. Something was off, and the Vadiknovs were more willing than most to admit it might not be the work of human influence. Even they had been stumped by the kidnappings, though. Lisa decided it was time for some research.

The two walked into their classroom, the already present students turning to stare at the tardy pair. Mr. Switzler peered over his flat-rimmed frames, pointing without words toward the two adjacent seats universally recognized as the Vadiknov seats.

"Then again," whispered Liev as they sat down, "it could be Mr. Switzler. He could be a grumpy werewolf!"

"What was that Vadiknov?" called Mr. Switzler.

Liev brightened up with his whitest smile. "I was just saying how delighted I am to start the first day of my week in your class-room, sir!"

Mr. Switzler pointed a trembling finger at him.

"Keep it up, Mr. Vadiknov. Good grades only go so far."

Liev smiled. The clock indicated mid-morning, and he was already pushing people to exasperation.

Chapter 2

For Charlie Sullivan, the day continued the same as any other wet, cold, overcast Monday. No teenager liked having to start the week at school, let alone with dreary weather. It made the droning at the front of the classroom, at best, difficult.

As far as Charlie could recall, Mondays had been wet, overcast, and downright miserable ever since the mysterious visitor appeared in Hunter's Grove two years ago. It began raining the day he arrived, on a Monday, and the clouds had been thicker since.

Some people, at first, gave life to the speculations that the obscure visitor was the cause of the missing people. Others, like Fish and Dink, were deliberate in hanging their old world charms on both person and property. Of course, in attempts to shake any notion of bewitchery, many had resolved that the stranger's appearance was coincidence.

Charlie's father was one who believed it was a coincidence. Charlie, on the other hand, did not.

However, they both agreed about the grave condition of Mrs. Pinkerly's hair, and her mismatched shoes . . . and socks. How could someone look so . . .

Oh, thought Charlie, stricken with terror. *She's glaring at me.*

"CHARLIE!" screeched Mrs. Pinkerly. Every student in the room let loose an inner cry of sorrow for their wounded ears. "Did you throw that pencil at me?"

Charlie sat up and began to plead, "Not me . . ."

But it would do no good. It never did.

Mrs. Pinkerly's heavily painted eyelids squinted sans mercy as she leaned forward.

"Then would you care to explain to the class what I was talking about? And don't you dare look at the board!" she instructed, lips pinched into a thin line of disturbed flesh and badly plucked moustache hairs.

Just thinking about Mrs. Pinkerly's hair and eyes and lips were enough to erase Charlie's memory.

"Um . . . I . . . you were talking about . . ."

Charlie hadn't the slightest clue as to what Mrs. Pinkerly was discussing. His mind was crowded with thoughts of Hunter's Key, his nightmares, the dark stranger . . .

He caught himself drifting in thought again and snapped out of it. His classmates snickered at something Mrs. Pinkerly had said.

"What?" he asked, fearing he already knew the answer. "I'm sorry, I was — "

"Not listening, I know! Charlie Sullivan, get yourself to the principal's office. *Now.*"

Charlie groaned. He could not afford the principal's office again. Embarrassed, he flung his backpack over his shoulder, took the *You're in Trouble* note from Mrs. Pinkerly and dragged himself out of the classroom, toward the office of Principal Adams. A collection of giggles and disapproving glares followed him out.

On his journey to the administrator's office, Charlie's vision was drawn beyond the hallway windows, and toward Hunter's Key. The three tallest towers of the mansion sat like a crown on the grandest of all the mountains surrounding the town: *Hunter's Point.*

If the stranger was a mystery, the Key was a riddle all to itself. Sitting high above the town, surrounded by thick forests and shrouded by low-hanging clouds, Hunter's Key was the centerpiece of the town's heritage, and yet the most forbidden. It was the mayor's ceremonial residence — like the White House, or Buckingham Palace. But the mayor didn't live there, and he denied any knowledge or association of the person that took up residence there when people began vanishing. Charlie wanted to know why.

He knew others would laugh at his theories, so he kept them to himself. He wondered whether the stranger now living in Hunter's Key was some sort of eccentric scientist, a reclusive widower...or a deranged kidnapper. It might explain the missing people.

The idea grabbed hold of him. Was this "stranger" causing the disappearances? Charlie had to find out. But how?

He was so immersed in his thoughts he didn't realize he had entered the waiting area to the principal's office. Nor did he hear the principal's secretary tell him to sit and wait.

He walked straight into Principal Adams' office, where a girl — Darcy Witherington, he recognized — stood prim with an accusing finger pointed at a boy with dark skin and polished black hair: *Nash Stormstepper.*

Nash was the school's only Native American student, and a loner like Charlie. Standing in the role of the accused, Nash was hunched at the shoulders, fists clenched and arms bulging. He looked like he'd just been in a fight and was ready to start another one, right here in Adams' office.

"...Nash was pounding him when I got there," Darcy said as Charlie stood in the doorway.

Charlie noticed the third person standing in front of Adams' desk. It was the bully, Donnie Wickles. He stood off to the side, acting hurt, wringing his threadbare baseball cap between his hands.

It took less than a second for Charlie to realize what was happening. Darcy was reporting Nash for a fight Donnie Wickles likely started.

Principal Adams stood red-faced, glaring at Charlie. Following the principal's lead, everyone else turned to stare at him.

"Young man," said Adams, "*get out.*"

"Right," said Charlie. "Sorry."

Heart thumping, he hurried to close the door and sat in the waiting area. The secretary raised her eyebrows as if to say *I told you so.* Charlie felt his cheeks flush.

Five minutes later, Darcy Witherington walked out of Adams' office with her chin held high, victorious. Nash stormed out shoving past her, his knuckles white over his backpack straps. Charlie imagined he could see veins bubbling across his forehead. Last to exit the office was Donnie Wickles, still acting like a wounded pup, holding his arm just so.

Charlie shook his head at the injustice of things.

"Principal Adams will see you now," the secretary said.

Charlie wondered what was in store for him. The word *DETENTION* hovered in his mind, right next to *GROUNDED.*

He entered the office and sat down in the single and uncomfortable metal chair facing the principal's oversized, authoritative desk. Principal Adams stood looking out the window over the school parking lot with a commanding measure of regulatory disdain. Very principal-like. He turned around at the sound of squeaking echoing from Charlie's chair.

"Mr. Sullivan," Adams questioned, weary, "weren't you here just Friday?"

"Thursday, sir."

"Right. And what is it this time?"

It was a rhetorical question—they both knew what Charlie had been sent to the office for, and by what teacher. Adams held his hand out for the disciplinary note Mrs. Pinkerly had written. Charlie fidgeted while the principal read it.

"Well," said Adams.

The principal's face held a steady shade of red, but he made an effort to articulate the word. Charlie braced for a lecture, reminding himself to focus on the chief task at hand, which was being terrified of detention.

"I don't know what you expect out of this school, Charlie, but it is not an amusement park. Your lack of attention is a continuing problem, and seems to be getting worse. Am I right so far?"

Charlie hesitated. There was only one answer he could give. "Yes, sir."

"Of course I am. I've been lenient so far. But this negligent attitude, your slipping grades, and recent tardiness—along with your rather impolite intrusion earlier—forces my hand. Detention."

"What?" Charlie moaned. It came out in a whisper, though he didn't mean for it to come out at all.

Still, Adams heard it, and, upon hearing it, steamed a beet shade of red.

"Do not backtalk me, young man. You can spend an hour's detention in the library. Be there, tomorrow, after school. That's the end of it. And Charlie?"

Charlie withered into a deeper slump. "Yes, Mr. Adams?"

"You'd better take care in the future. I'll consider suspension the next appropriate step."

Adams thrust the detention slip at the level of Charlie's eyes. Charlie accepted it with regret and a painful lump in his throat. Mrs. Pinkerly was making his school year a hellish experience.

Later that day, Charlie slogged out to the school yard where the last remnants of his peers piled onto the final bus. Its doors closed before he could catch the driver's attention.

He walked home, alone.

Midnight had made its call some time ago, and the people of Hunter's Grove were tucked and tidy. A black car with blacked-out windows prowled along Certifus Street before turning left onto Frederickson. Moments later it vanished into the shadows of the trees.

The driver of the car scowled as he jostled to and fro in his seat. Frederickson Street was nothing more than a fancy name for a dirt road that trailed the side of the large hill. It was a bumpy ride, slanting upward so the driver experienced the sensation of falling backward through the seat. The drive was, at best, uncomfortable.

Behind the wheel, the stranger refused to retract his scowl, or the words that slipped from his tongue at every bump and jolt.

The ground evened out after some time and the driver parked amid a cloud of up-ridden dust, throwing open his door. Scanning the immediate area as he exited the vehicle, he hurried to the large, black, cast-iron gate that stood foreboding across the width of the road.

The gate had turned many people, mostly adventurous teens, away through the years, as it gave whoever approached a spine-tingling sense of being watched and frowned upon with an angry vehemence.

The man wielded a large skeleton key and unlocked the padlock that held the gate's chain together, heaving its doors open wide. This was not light work, but the dark stranger was stronger than he appeared. He drove the car through, stopping again to close the gate and relock the monstrous chain.

Leaving a trail of angry dust behind it, the car drove on as if complaining about the disrepair of the road.

Through the tops of the wild, gnarled trees the stranger saw the three tallest spires reaching for the night's collection of clouds. The trees soon gave way to the courtyard of Hunter's Key.

The Key. A citadel of strength and refuge that seemed out of place and time amidst the quiet town at its feet. Dwarfing the old feudal castles of Medieval Europe, this relic radiated a life of its own. Through the stillness of the forests surrounding it, its voice seemed to lift and carry on the perpetual, gentle breezes that circled its grounds. Hunter's Key was an incomprehensible vision to be studied in portion, with an air of ancient pride.

The dark stranger continued up the driveway, circled the dry fountain anchoring the center of the courtyard and turned toward the nearest of the large stable-like garages. He glanced up at the titanesque gargoyles perched on the spires, smiling at their watchful presence as he opened the old garage door by hand.

The grinding of the metal chains was loud, but not so loud as to drown out the slight rustling of trees several feet away. The stranger peered vigorously into the blackness of the trees.

Nothing. No movement. Not even the chirp of a cricket.

Maybe he was imagining things. Perhaps he was at last giving way to paranoia.

No, he thought. Paranoia or not, he could not chance letting any trespassers violate the property. The hour had grown dangerous. The time to finish his job shortened with each passing day, and each day was more threatening for it. The stranger stalked into the trees, like a cat hunting for a mouse.

Half an hour later, he was skulking back toward Hunter's Key. After a thorough search, it was clear he wasn't going to find anything.

The very thing he'd been looking for moved on, as quick as it was discovered. It moved silent as the night itself, with purpose and direction.

That direction was Hunter's Grove.

Chapter 3

C harlie looked around his room in a daze before zoning in on the alarm clock. 6:45 am.

He groaned and threw his legs to the floor.

Another nightmare plagued his sleep. Out of morbid curiosity, Charlie tried to remember it. He remembered himself — or was it? — running through a forest, scaling a mountainside steep. He also remembered finding a treacherous book.

Then someone dying, three times.

Charlie shivered and reminded himself that he needed to get ready for school. He didn't want to be late again. Detention would be bad enough without any more of his usual blunders.

Catching a glimpse in the bathroom mirror, Charlie frowned at his reflection. His eyes were scarlet, like a vampire from some cheesy horror film. He blinked a couple of times and they returned to normal. As normal as a severe case of bloodshot eyes can be. He let the cold water from the shower shock his overactive imagination out of last night's dreams.

I need something to keep my mind occupied. Maybe I should get a job or join an after-school club . . .

The sudden idea of sneaking up to Hunter's Key after school woke him up more than the ice-cold shower. He pushed it out of his mind. It was crazy.

Cold, wet, and miserable enough to face the school day, Charlie shut off the water.

After surviving another day at school, including an incident- free yet painful dose of Mrs. Pinkerly's class, Charlie hoisted his backpack and walked to detention.

Detention was held in the library, which was on the far opposite side of the school. To students, the library always seemed to be on the other side of the school, no matter which side you were on. Students often suspected the school's architects had laid the library toward the far end of Limbo on purpose. That purgatorial walk to the library — and detention — therefore was named *"The Eternal Walk of Mortal Penance,"* or *"The Penance Walk,"* for short.

As Charlie stepped along "The Penance Walk," he could see the Towers at Hunter's Key looming in the clouds. He frowned. Although Charlie had managed to stay focused enough to avoid the attention of his teachers, only one thing had really occupied his mind today: Hunter's Key.

The possible connection between the mansion and the disappearances seemed obvious. And what of his dreams? The Key was a relentless haunt arresting his nightmares.

Charlie didn't know what it was, but something strange was going on in that place, and he needed to find out. It was more than a curiosity. Feeling a little crazy for thinking it, Charlie knew it was all connected — the Key, the missing people, his insomnia.

But then, most would pass it off as a series of coincidence and superstition. Or daydreams.

Charlie shook the thoughts from his mind, pulled the strap of his bag tighter, and hurried along toward detention. *Detention. Nothing like after-school detention to bring a person back to reality*, Charlie thought.

The tall oak doors of the library appeared, and Charlie was so tired of walking that he strode into a jog to cover the remaining distance . . . only to be met with the reprimand of Mrs. Nutterwicke, the librarian.

"Charlie Sullivan!" she reproached from behind her desk. "No running in this hall. You should know that, young man!"

"Yes, ma'am," Charlie said, sheepish.

He handed her the detention slip with a smile. As far as the school staff went, Mrs. Nutterwicke wasn't too bad. She was nice, even if strict and eccentric.

"Caught woolgathering again?" asked Mrs. Nutterwicke, peering over her half-moon spectacles. The faintest hint of a smile touched her thin lips.

"Something like that, yeah."

"Alright, then. Head on over to the wall. You'll have company today, at the least."

Charlie crossed the creaky wood floor, past rows of bookshelves that stood like somber guardians. He had been here before — often enough, to his dismay — and knew where he was going. He paused when he reached the desk chairs facing the library's infamous, boring brown wall. Someone else was there indeed.

Charlie chose a seat two chairs away from Nash Stormstepper.

"Hey," he said, trying to be friendly.

Nash turned to look at him, but said nothing. Charlie got the hint. With nothing better to do, he stared at the brown wall.

Several generations before him had been forced to stare at this very wall. His father shared many horror stories about his own experiences in front of this wall, and Charlie had lived more than his share of them to date. The dull, indifferent effect of the brown wall was setting in.

This is going to be one very long hour.

The Chief of Assistants fussed and fumed in hushed and muted rants, hoping the humans walking on the street wouldn't notice. Occasionally, he would peer out from behind the dumpster to make sure no one was coming.

The contents of his sack were poured out in a scattered mess before him. Nervous, he wrestled the leather sack itself between his long, thin fingers. His behavior was most unlike any in the Dark Prince's circle of assistants, especially for the Chief of Assistants.

Abbreviated in height, this chief servant conferred the presence of a grayish-green devil, nix the horns and pitchfork. Not a slight of menace, except for his razor-sharp teeth and black eyes that furrowed deep beneath a swollen, crevassed brow. Wiry strands of hair dotted his otherwise bald and beady head. And yet, adorned in ceremonial robes reserved for authority, the ghastly little monster was regal.

Today, however, his behavior betrayed his respected title. He was pathetic, beside himself and, in fact, afraid for his life.

The Dark Prince's diary was no longer in his sack. It was lost. It was lost, and he had to find it. And if he didn't find it . . .

He felt his master begin to enter his mind, encroaching upon his thoughts. It was like someone had opened his skullcap and began rummaging through his brain at will.

The Chief of Assistants scrunched his eyes tight and recited ancient words, beating his head against the brick alley wall in a struggle of will and concentration. The resulting headache only made things worse.

His master's presence recoiled and abruptly exited his mind. The servant collapsed onto the ground. He knew full well, there would be repercussions for keeping secrets from the Dark Prince.

Consequences would be more severe if he could not find the diary.

The Chief of Assistants gathered to his feet, sack still wrung between his hands. His face a mask of abject horror, he stared at all of his tools scattered before him.

He had to find the diary. The Prince's plans depended on it, as did now the little servant's life.

Thinking himself into action, and with the intense motivation of self-preservation, the Chief of Assistants retraced his steps in his mind. He had come from the woods, beside the old hunters' castle and into the town.

Next, he remembered, he had been to the gassing station, where humans filled their metal carriages with some acrid liquid that was as noxious as any evil spell he had ever cast. While there, the impish servant had marked a female human with her metal carriage-load of human fledglings for collection.

From there he scouted from the single radio-wave tower for tomorrow's Collection. Following that he stopped to watch humans go in and out of a marketplace, which was also some sort of food-place, he knew. A popular place, he noted, always full of humans.

Lastly, he recalled making his way to the school, where children were arriving. The idea of marking a fledgling sickened the Chief of Assistants — even if it was human — but he dared not disobey the master. His master needed a fledgling's blood for the Ritual — the final and most important step of the Ritual. The master's appetite had grown fierce with the recent lesser rituals. Humans were becoming more suspicious due to the increased disappearances, and all this was making the job of collecting more difficult.

It was when he reached the center of town that he realized the master's diary was no longer in his possession.

The Chief of Assistants dried his large eyes on his robe and, sniffling, repacked his sack with care. He clambered up on the dumpster and climbed onto the roof of the building, setting off in the direction of the gassing station first. He had completed his official tasks for the day, and Hunter's Grove would soon be a few degrees colder for it. Now he had to find that diary, and fast. His master would be calling soon.

Ten minutes had passed and Charlie was already losing his mind. How was he supposed to last an entire hour?

He glanced at Nash, arms crossed, and leaning back in his desk chair. The front legs of the chair hovered a few inches off the ground, and Nash's angry stare wasn't much higher than that.

"So what are you in for?" asked Charlie.

"What?"

"You know, detention. What happened?"

Nash's jaw muscle twitched when he gritted his teeth, but he didn't answer.

"I saw you in Adams' office. Looked like they had the wrong guy."

"They did have the wrong guy," Nash said, setting his chair down with a bang. "And if the mayor's brat had kept her nose to herself, Wickles would have been mashed to a pulp, and I wouldn't be sitting here."

"So Wickles started the fight?"

"Uh," Nash faltered, "yeah. Well, technically I threw the first punch, but he deserved it."

Charlie raised an eyebrow.

"Wickles was mouthing off about the missing people. You know."

"I do." Charlie nodded, somber. It was one of Donnie's primary ways of getting attention — or a fight.

Nash continued. "This time, it was about Bobby Muldor. Saying he was just another dim wit who got lost in the woods. And then he started talking about Mrs. McBranson."

He didn't need to elaborate. Most knew Nash helped Mrs. McBranson around town from time to time. They went to the monthly pay-per-view Mixed Martial Arts events televised at Tavern's. He would help her with everything from groceries to small repairs at her house. In return, she taught him martial arts. She was an odd woman, with odder tastes still, which Nash loved. He always felt a sense of peace around her. Her presence and the time spent helping her calmed him.

"Oh. You were friends with Mrs. McBranson, weren't you?"

Nash nodded. Today they would have been kickboxing.

"I'm sorry you had to hear that," said Charlie. "You know why Donnie talks about the missing people like that?"

"I know why. Doesn't make it right, though. I just shut Wickles' mouth for him, since he wouldn't. I guess this is worth it," he added, pointing at the brown wall.

"Better reason than dozing in class," Charlie mumbled.

"I just wish I knew what happened to them all," Nash continued. "It's not like a kidnapper could hide out in Hunter's Grove. Too many people like to talk in this town. And who would want to kidnap Mrs. McBranson?"

Charlie stiffened in his seat. He thought again about the Key, and about sharing his theory. But he didn't want Nash to think he was crazy.

He coughed. "Well . . ."

Nash eyed him. "What?"

"There is one way to hide in Hunter's Grove."

"Yeah? How's that?"

"Hunter's Key."

Nash frowned and stared at the wall for a few seconds, rolling Charlie's idea around his thoughts.

"Hunter's Key. That actually makes sense."

"There's a black car that drives up there a lot. I've seen it, always coming from Certifus street and turning onto Frederickson. And it's not the mayor's car."

Nash sat back, and for a moment there was silence. Then he stood.

"I'll be right back."

"Wait, where are you going?"

"Nowhere."

"We're in detention," said Charlie.

"I'm in detention because of an idiot and a snob-nosed brat. I've got better things to do."

"Well, what're you going to do?"

"I think you might be right," Nash said with a sigh. "About Hunter's Key, I mean. So I'm going to check it out."

"Well then," said Charlie, standing up, "I'm going with you."

Nash crossed his arms. "No."

"It was my idea."

"You can't go with me. I'm always in trouble with someone, whether it's my fault or not. You hang around, the same will happen to you."

"In case you hadn't noticed, I'm in detention too. Look, I need this. I need to know what's happening at Hunter's Key."

"Why?"

Charlie rubbed his arm. He wasn't ready to reveal his nightmares about the Key. "It's just something I need to do, okay?"

"I'm sorry, but I can't let you go with me."

"Fine," said Charlie. He was miffed, but he tried to hide it. "Then I'll figure it out on my own."

The two stood staring at each other for an awkward moment before Charlie nodded, walking away.

This is a library, Charlie thought, *there must be books on Hunter's Key somewhere.*

He tried to ignore Nash walking away as he found the direction he wanted to go, and took the first step to learning the truth behind Hunter's Key.

Desperation was setting in. The Chief of Assistants had gone from the gassing station back to the radio tower, which had been difficult in broad daylight. His master's diary was nowhere to be found.

Back at the food-place, he skulked across the roof, looking everywhere. He even plunged his head into the small metal chimney, mustering hope that it somehow found a home there. The only thing he found was a sudden poof of hot steam from the kitchen below, scalding his already twisted face.

Spewing and gasping from the steam, the Chief of Assistants whimpered and surrendered to the fact that it wasn't there. He scratched at his bald head with long, labored fingers. Only two more places to search. He looked to the horizon for the next target, finding the school's steeple.

The sun was sinking. Sick with worry, he began to run.

Charlie scoured the bookshelves, careful to avoid Mrs. Nutterwicke's desk and her line of sight. He kept a close eye on his watch, praying he would get back to his seat before she came to announce detention was over. If he was caught sneaking around the library during detention, Principal Adams would suspend him for sure.

Still, this was something Charlie had to do.

The library had a healthy collection of classic literature — required reading for several classes. There was also a Hunter's Grove history and records section — this was the section he was looking for. The town hall didn't have the space to accommodate much of the historical documents for Hunter's Grove, so a section of the school library had been commissioned for this purpose years ago. He dove into one aisle and started searching, trailing his fingers along dusty spines.

The shelves were old; he could tell by the rough, aged wood. These keepers of the books seemed to have a life of their own, almost as if they could speak if someone were to ask. Most of the books bore well-worn leather binding, though some were so old the covers were torn and eaten by time, if they had covers at all. Stagnant whirls of dust trailed the books Charlie picked from the shelves. He struggled to keep from coughing and giving away his position.

Charlie put them back one by one, unsatisfied. Nothing screamed "Hunter's Key!" covering instead many other aspects of the town's history. He had to be close, though, and kept searching.

A shadow of a figure passed by the bookshelves, startling Charlie. His heart pumped faster, and gooseflesh pricked at his arms and neck.

Charlie almost called out. But then, he was supposed to be sitting in detention.

Any unknown figure prowling the library, scared the bejeebers out of him.

Charlie inched his way forward until he came to the end of the aisle. Before him stood a rough stone wall. Dead end. Right or left were his only options. From where he stood, peeking around the corner of the shelves, both directions seemed endless — endless, silent, and eerie.

Swallowing his fear, Charlie turned left and followed the direction the shadowy figure had gone, imagining wild confrontations with the stranger who lived in Hunter's Key. Instead, he saw Nash perusing the next aisle over. Charlie almost laughed in relief.

Almost.

Nash was facing away from Charlie, shoulders tensed. In front of him stood two figures, dressed in white and black. Charlie quickly noted that Nash and the Vadiknov twins seemed to be in a standoff.

"I need that book," Nash said, pointing to the large, black book that Lisa Vadiknov was pulling from the shelf. It was still wedged among the other books, her pale fingers gripping the spine.

The twins shared an almost telepathic look before turning back to Nash.

"Sorry," said Liev Vadiknov. He was carrying a tall stack of books. "We need it, too. Not to worry, though! We'll put it back in a few days, and you can have it then." He flashed a gleaming, borderline sarcastic, smile.

Charlie glanced at his watch. He was running out of time, and so was Nash. With caution, he approached the others, catching the title of the book as Lisa pulled it the rest of the way off the shelf.

HUNTER'S KEY: The Legendary Beginnings and Strange Histories of the Fortress on the Hill.

This was what he was looking for.

Lisa saw Charlie first. She squinted her black-lined eyes, glaring between him and Nash with growing suspicion.

"Hey," said Charlie, "I kind of need to see it, too. Maybe all of us could sit down somewhere and take turns?"

Nash turned, surprised, then angry.

"Have you been following me?"

"No! I think we had the same idea in mind, which makes me think we should be working together."

Nash grunted, unimpressed.

"So what about it?" Charlie asked the twins. "This is important."

Lisa tucked the book under her arm.

"Deepest regrets," said Liev politely, "But we work alone. I mean, together, the two of us, but just us, you know."

Nash took a step forward, fists clenched, but Charlie put a hand on his shoulder. He pointed to his watch, and Nash understood. They were out of time.

Nash gave in and backed away with Charlie. They nodded to the twins, who returned a solemn nod, before racing back to the brown, lifeless detention wall.

The twins looked at each other.

"What was that about?" wondered Lisa.

"Not sure. That was Nash Stormstepper, wasn't it?"

"Yeah, but who was the other guy?"

"Charlie Sullivan, I think. He's the one always getting on Mrs. Pinkerly's bad side."

"Ah." Her eyes softened a little. "Poor guy."

The twins walked to the counter to check out their selections.

"You think they've come to the same conclusion we have?" Lisa asked.

"Doubt it. They're two bored teenagers in this oh-so-exciting town. Rather like us, I'd imagine."

Lisa frowned at her brother. "Looks can be deceiving. They seemed to know something. Charlie most of all."

Liev nodded, scratching his chin on the top book in his stack.

"We'll watch them, then."

Meanwhile, Nash and Charlie were, not too quietly, scrambling to get back to their seats. Charlie didn't know if Nash was close to suspension as well, but the look of desperation on his face told

43

Charlie it was likely.

What neither of them knew was that the twins were delaying Mrs. Nutterwicke with their tall order of books at the checkout desk.

When Mrs. Nutterwicke *did* come, Charlie and Nash were sitting at their desks staring at the horrid brown wall of eye-watering insipidity, hands folded on their desks like dutiful students.

Mrs. Nutterwicke, who was a shrewd woman, eyed them over her spectacles with blatant suspicion.

"All right, you two. Your sentences are up and you're free to go."

They wasted no time standing and gathering their belongings to leave.

"Thank you Mrs. Nutterwicke," they chimed in chorus, scurrying from her presence like they were fleeing the Devil himself.

"No running," she called out in her loudest possible whisper. "You two had better slow it down!"

They waited to speak until they had passed the oak doors, when Nash grabbed Charlie's sleeve, pulling him to the wall.

"Don't ever follow me again," growled Nash. "I told you, I'm trouble."

Charlie's ears felt hot. "I didn't follow you. I was looking for a book on Hunter's Key. But for the record, you don't seem that bad, and two heads are better than one."

"Whatever. Just keep to yourself."

Nash let go of Charlie's jacket and stormed off, leaving Charlie to glare at his back. After a few steps, Nash rounded the corner and was out of sight.

The scene in the library made Charlie confident that he was on the right track. Not only had Nash gone looking for answers, but the Vadiknov twins were a step ahead of both of them. If the

Vadiknovs were on to Hunter's Key, then Charlie had no doubt that something was going on in that mansion. He was close to answers, but he needed help.

Warning or no warning, Charlie jogged after Nash.

The Chief of Assistants peered over the top of the school as he perched on its roof. His search once again proved fruitless. He watched the sun disappearing in its early winter course.

Winter. A season when his master was at his strongest.

Something below, on the school steps, caught his attention. His big round eyes narrowed as he leaned in for a closer look. Trouble was brewing.

The Chief of Assistants liked human troubles.

Chapter 4

N ash, wait up!"

Charlie caught up with Nash, too much in a hurry to see the figures waiting on the steps. Donnie Wickles and a few of his lackeys stood off with Nash. When Charlie appeared, calling after Nash, the bully took interest.

"Look at this, it's a loner gathering! What's up, recluse?" motioning to Charlie.

"Back off!" Nash warned, trying to move past the gathering. "Remember what happened last time my fist met your face?"

In fact, Donnie's left cheek *did* have a nasty shiner bubbling up. He flinched as Nash raised a heavy fist.

Below the steps, a small crowd of students gathered to watch the afternoon's brewing entertainment.

Among the crowd, Darcy stood with her hoi polloi of followers. Caitlin stood next to her, ears plugged with pink earbuds blasting the latest pop anthem. She blathered on about the new flavor of gum she found at Tavern's QUICK-N-GO.

Darcy had tuned her incessant chatter out some time ago, but she stopped pretending to listen when she heard the other students whispering and pointing to the standoff between Donnie and Nash.

"So, what is it?" Donnie asked, looking between the two. "You two starting the Loner Society, or the Detention Club? Oh, I know, it's the Grandma's Scouts Club, am I right?"

Nash grabbed Donnie's jacket lapel and raised his fist, ready to instill a healthy dose of fear into Donnie's skull. It made his day better to see Donnie quiver and try to shield his face. Even more satisfying was noticing that the bully's gang of followers made no move to stop Nash. A few from the football team took to chanting: "Fight! Fight! Fight!"

Nash felt a hand on his arm, and his nostrils flared. Rage was visible in his eyes. He turned to see Charlie shaking his head. Charlie wasn't holding him back—they both knew Nash was the stronger one here. It seemed Charlie was reminding him more of where he was.

Caught between aggravation and gratitude, Nash lowered his fist and shoved Donnie back with a sneer.

"You're not worth the trouble again," said Nash.

"That's right, coward," said Donnie, backing into his group of fellow ruffians. "Even you couldn't take us all on. And loner freak over there isn't going to help you," he scoffed, pointing at Charlie.

That's when Darcy made her move.

She felt bad about reporting Nash the day before. He had backed into her by accident while fighting, and she had used her influence as the mayor's daughter against him. It was a habit that she was known for, and one that made her few friends.

Nash had thrown the first punch, but she knew it was Donnie who really deserved detention. She knew how Donnie badmouthed anyone who'd gone missing, and she hated him for it. She was not willing to make the same mistake again.

Darcy marched up the steps.

"Shut it, Wickles!"

Donnie, not to mention Charlie and Nash, turned with dropped jaws in surprise. The entire crowd went silent.

What was Darcy Witherington, the hyper-socialized and caffeine-infused mayor's daughter, doing sticking up for two of the school's decaffeinated loser class?

Donnie recovered, pretending to be ashamed.

"Sorry, Witherington. Am I making fun of your boyfriend? Which one is he?" he asked, pointing his fingers between Charlie and Nash.

Darcy felt a sudden rush of awkward, with a dash of feeling silly. Her cheeks flushed hot in the brisk afternoon air, but she wasn't about to back down.

When everyone was sure they had the best gossip for the next day, the school doors opened again to let pass a certain set of black-and-white twins with piles of books in their arms. The Vadiknovs noticed the crowd and saw the standoff between Darcy, Donnie, Charlie, and Nash. They gave a long, deliberate stare—Lisa glaring, Liev smiling—at each in turn.

"Oh," said the white twin. "Hello, again."

His sister elbowed him in the ribs.

Everyone knew that detention was served in the library. Everyone also knew that Charlie and Nash had emerged from detention moments ago, which made it interesting to see the twins stepping out of the library loaded with books, yet staring with indignant suspicion at the two detentionees. Darcy's place in the crowd of students only added to the tension and bewilderment of the whole situation. What was in it for her?

This was turning out to be an interesting Tuesday, indeed.

A sound cut through the excitement in the air. They heard it. They all heard it.

Somewhere far off — but not far enough — a woman screamed.

The horrifying thing about the scream, was that it had been cut short. Muffled. Silenced. And everyone knew what that meant.

The next victim had just gone missing.

Every student standing in front of the school held their breath, goose bumps creeping up their arms and the hairs on the back of their necks raising a shuddering chill. The twins looked and nodded at each other before pressing past Charlie and Nash, Donnie and his posse, Darcy, and the rest of the crowd below.

Their departure shook the feeling of dread and caused the crowd to snap back to the present and disperse. Even Donnie Wickles seemed in a hurry to get home. The students scattered toward the parking lot, the bus line, or the sidewalks, chattering about everything and anything that could keep their thoughts occupied. Everything, except the scream. And nobody left alone.

Charlie's face went pale as he caught Nash's gaze. They shared an understanding, and had figured out which direction the scream had come from. Terror was afoot in the woods surrounding Hunter's Point — Hunter's Key sitting like a crown jewel of horror, watching. *Waiting.*

"Two heads are better than one," said Charlie. "And safer."

Nash looked at the ground, then at Charlie, and nodded. "Together then."

"It has to be tonight. We can't let anyone else be taken."

Nash nodded, solemn and anguished.

Darcy watched the two walk away before she realized she hadn't apologized to Nash. It was the reason she got involved in the hoo-ha to begin with.

Nash had been right to shut Donnie Wickles up the day before.

Donnie had been in the wrong—a dirty, sickening wrong. And that made her wrong for what she did, too. It was a foreign feeling for Darcy, and not a comfortable one.

Disappointment tugged at her, seeing that Charlie and Nash were already a good jaunt away, and she saw her father's car turn in to the pickup lane as well. She didn't want to apologize to anyone, but this guilt would nag at her until she did.

It would have to wait. The two "loners" had turned a corner, and her father's car now obstructed her view. Bothered by her own inaction, Darcy waved goodbye to her friends and jumped in the passenger seat, pulled her knees up close, and buried her face.

Hiding on the crest of the roof, tucked behind weathered stone statues, the Chief of Assistants had been watching the scene unfold with interest, until he, too, heard the scream.

It was done. He allowed himself a smile for a job well done. But it was a broken smile, tarnished by despair and longing for a way out.

Hopes and fears aside, he turned his attention back to the human fledglings. He was scouting for new targets, even if he didn't like his job. He knew if he didn't complete his tasks, the master would have his skeleton for one of his many trophies.

Worse, if he didn't find the diary, the master might have his bones anyway.

The Chief of Assistants turned his gaze from the departing fledglings. There was one last place to look, and that was in the woods surrounding Hunter's Point.

He hoped it was not there. The tangle of brush and trees in those woods, and the magic that swirled through them, would make it hard to find anything, even for an expert tracker like him.

Then again, he hoped it *was* in the woods, and that he would find it, since it had not been anywhere else he'd looked.

Either way, it would be dangerous, and no fun whatsoever, to be so close to Hunter's Key.

He scratched his small head and, with a swift eye, marked a new human for the Collectors to gather, guilt turning his stomach. Shuffling away from the edge of the school's topside, his eyes grew wider in the setting sun. The air was growing colder, as was his hope for finding the master's diary.

He jumped from the rooftop, careful to avoid human eyes, and set a rapid pace toward Hunter's Point.

Chapter 5

H ello?"

Charlie cradled the phone to his ear. "Hey Dad."

"Hi Charlie. Did you just get out of detention?"

"Uh, yeah," said Charlie, cringing at the D-word.

Charlie's mother had been livid about his sentence at the library's brown wall again, but his father had intervened. After all, Mrs. Pinkerly had been his father's teacher, too.

"Alright, sport, see you in a minute then."

"Well, actually. . ." Charlie looked over his shoulder to where Nash stood, who was impatient and tapping his foot. "I was going to hang out with some friends. I mean, if that's okay."

"Friends?" asked Mr. Sullivan, surprised. "You're meeting friends?"

Charlie waited for his father to tell him no.

"Well, your mother's still upset about detention, but I'll hold the fort down here. You go have fun. I'm always telling you to make some friends. Just don't cause too much trouble around town."

"Dad!"

Mr. Sullivan chuckled over the phone. "Love you, kiddo. See you when you get home."

"Love you, too."

Charlie shoved his phone into his pocket and spun around.

"You ready?" he asked.

Nash nodded.

"Your folks won't mind?"

"Nah. They're pretty cool with things."

"Right. Well, let's get this over with."

They stood there awkward, staring at each other. "What first?" asked Charlie.

Nash rolled his eyes. "Weren't you the one who had the grand plan?"

"I don't usually do things like this."

"And you think I do? What, that I just go around looking for troublemaking?"

"That's not what I meant, I just . . . okay, first thing we should do is get help."

Nash sighed. "Sorry. If we need help getting up to Hunter's Key, I think I know a guy. Fish McCollum."

Charlie rolled the name around his head before his eyes grew wide. "Fish? Isn't he a little . . . you know?" He twirled his finger near his temple.

"Pot calling the kettle black?"

"I'm not crazy." Charlie frowned, considering this, wondering if he was becoming like Fish.

"Neither is he. No one knows the woods of Hunter's Point like Fish."

Charlie shrugged. "Okay. I was thinking about asking the Vadiknov twins for help."

"And you were concerned about Fish being crazy! Those two *try* to look crazy, and they've made it clear they want to do it alone."

"They seem to know what's going on. Look, if we're facing some kind of insane serial nutjob, we could use any help we can get."

"True."

Charlie and Nash shrugged at each other and started jogging, following the twins' trail. It wasn't long before they caught up with them, but what they saw stopped them dead in their tracks.

In the distance, the Vadiknovs' books were lying helter-skelter on the ground as Lisa held on to the robes of a creature thrashing and flailing and scratching. It was hideous — a grayish-green devil, with long, skinny limbs and bulbous eyes — and dressed in elaborate robes.

"What is that thing?" Charlie asked, hoarse.

Nash shook his head as the thing hissed and bared its needlelike teeth, amazed and horrified at what he was seeing.

As his sister tried to strengthen her grip on the monster's robes, Liev tried, and failed, to pick it up. It slapped at Liev's hand and lashed out to bite Lisa. In the dusk of evening, its big black eyes flashed like an angry demon against the streetlamp's glow.

"Get it! Would you hurry up already?" Lisa shouted. It had just missed sinking its razor-sharp teeth into her arm.

"I'm trying! If you would . . . kindly . . . hold him still?"

Liev was aggravated too. His hands were swelling, and an angry shade of red from being slapped so much.

At last, the monster's slaps prevailed. Liev could no longer feel his hands and the devil escaped his clutch. With a resounding *THWAP!* its violence landed an effective blow against Lisa, and she lost her grip as well.

The runty monster fell backward, flailing, and scrambled to gain its footing before disappearing into some foliage, scattering remnants of snow into the air.

The twins, disappointed, rubbed their hands and watched the

bushes wistfully.

As Liev and Lisa stooped to gather their books, Charlie snapped out of the shock of what he'd just witnessed and nudged Nash out of his own stupor. They both jogged on shaky legs to where the twins stood.

The goth-chic pair saw them coming and straightened up like nothing had happened, ignoring the remainder of their books still scattered across the wet sidewalk. Liev gave his whitest smile.

"What on earth was that?" Charlie called out.

"What was what?" pretended Lisa.

"Oh come on! We saw it. Don't act like you don't know what I'm talking about."

"I'm sure I haven't any idea what you're talking about," Liev said. "And I doubt Lisa does, either."

The twins gathered their books, turned and began to walk along the sidewalk at a casual pace.

Desperate, Charlie called out to them. "It has to do with Hunter's Key, doesn't it?"

They stopped, shared a look, and turned around.

"What do you know about Hunter's Key?" Lisa called back, a hint of doubt in her voice.

"We know that it has to do with the missing people," Nash said. "We're going up there tonight, and thought you might be able to help us."

"You're going to Hunter's Key?" Liev asked surprised. He didn't believe Nash. "How's that? There's a gate, you know. A really big one. With no way around it."

"It's locked with an impossible silver chain," added his sister.

"I know someone who can get us onto the grounds," said Nash.

"Are you in or not?"

The twins looked at each other, silent communication apparent in their eyes.

Liev turned back to them with a faint smile. "All right. We're in."

The twins headed home to drop off their books while Charlie and Nash fetched Fish and Dink. Everyone was to meet at eight o'clock on Midday Street. On the way, Charlie voiced his concern about getting past the gate, while Nash tried to reassure him.

"Fish'll get us in, don't worry."

"Just in case he can't, it would be nice to have a backup plan."

"Right, but the twins said the gate had a heavy silver chain on it. I don't know about you, but I don't have a chainsaw handy. Or are you thinking about knocking?"

Charlie did have an idea, but he didn't want to say it. Nash would hate it, and understandably so.

"Chains usually have padlocks," he thought out loud.

"Usually."

"So I'm thinking if we had a key to unlock the padlock..."

"And you'd find the key, where?"

"Well, the property belongs to the mayor."

"Mmhm. And the mayor's going to hand over his castle-mansion key ring because...?"

This is where Charlie's idea got difficult.

"Not the mayor. His daughter. Darcy. She'll give us the key. Or, I think she might."

Nash stopped walking and gave Charlie an evil eye. For a moment, Charlie thought Nash might strangle him, but instead he burst into a laughing fit.

"Darcy Witherington! That's a good one." Then after a short pause, "Wait, you're serious aren't you?"

"Well, yeah."

"Are you crazy?"

Charlie flinched. "She stood up for us today."

"Don't tell me you bought that. She probably took a dare from one of her friends. Either that or she was trying to make herself look good, sticking up for the losers."

"I'm not so sure, and I'm not a loser."

"Well I am sure about Darcy. I doubt she would give us a spare umbrella in the rain."

The sky rumbled in the distance, as if Nash's mention of rain had excited it.

Charlie noted they would pass Darcy's house on the way back from Fish's place. It was clear that Nash was against the idea of inviting Darcy to their group, but Charlie was not ready to give up. He'd seen the guilt on her face and, given her family's connection to the Key, he felt like she could be a big help.

Still, Charlie kept it to himself. It was no use arguing with Nash.

By the time Fish's house was in sight, Charlie had become grateful that Hunter's Grove was a small town. They had been walking most of the afternoon, and there was a lot of walking still to do as the night continued.

Fish McCollum's place was small, unassuming. It was old and beat up—worn and well-used in its time. A steeped roof gave it a tall look, and the porch fashioned a rustic wood railing. A clothesline hung out of place to the right of the house, with a fish and a pair of scissors dangling from it. As they walked up the steps, Charlie's attention was drawn to the rusted horseshoe hanging over the door. Its two ends pointed upward.

Nash knocked loud on the splintered wood door. They could hear what sounded like a pair of lead-filled, sized 12 boots marching to the door. A man with a distant look in his eyes stepped onto the porch. He smiled and with a thick hand, clapped Nash on the back.

"Hey Nash! How you doing today? Or, tonight, I suppose at this point." The man looked at Charlie and smiled again. "Hey. . . there?" realizing he didn't know who Charlie was.

"Dink, meet Charlie Sullivan. Charlie, Wardley Dink."

Charlie shook the man's hand, wincing at the strong grasp and rough flesh, and said, "Nice to meet you."

"Yep, yep," agreed Dink. A second later he added, "Same to you. You two wanna come in?"

"Well," said Nash, "we actually have to get going kinda fast. I stopped by to ask if you and Fish could help us out with something."

Dink looked back into the house, cupping his hands in a circle around his mouth. "FISH! NASH STORMSTEPPER'S HERE! SAYS HE NEEDS YOUR HELP WITH SOMETHUN!"

At least he gets to the point, Charlie thought.

Moments later, a smaller man in a gray shirt, with a rabbit foot necklace and a thick flannel jacket adorning his frame, barreled down a rickety flight of stairs. A curious frown marked his otherwise friendly face as he approached the door.

"Did you have to announce it to the world, then?"

Before Dink could answer, Fish had welcomed Nash, been introduced to Charlie, and asked what all the fuss was about.

Nash explained the situation in brief, not mentioning the creature they had seen with the twins, and asked if Fish could help them get onto the Key's grounds. He reinforced his request by saying that it was urgent.

Charlie felt a wave of disappointment as he watched Fish's face become intense and apprehensive. He felt that Fish wanted nothing to do with Hunter's Key.

He was surprised when Fish agreed to help.

"Sure thing. We can get you to the gate."

Nash raised his eyebrows at Charlie as if to say, *Told you so.*

"Come to think of it, there is a section of the gate within a good view of the Key," Fish continued. "The ends of the gate reach into the woods a bit. We can take you there, but I wouldn't recommend trying to sneak past the gate without proper authority."

It was Charlie's turn to raise his eyebrows at Nash. "Proper authority? What does that mean?"

"Proper authority. A key, an invitation, the mayor himself."

"Why would. . . ?"

"Cool," said Nash, interrupting. He gave Charlie a look that said he would explain later. "So we're meeting some friends on Midday Street. Can you be there by eight?"

"Sure thing. That should give us enough time to prepare."

Before they left, Charlie saw Fish reach up and take the horseshoe down and hand it to Dink before the two odd men disappeared into the house.

"What was that about?" he whispered, once off the porch. "Do you know what 'proper authority' means?"

"Look, Fish is a superstitious man. We know the truth, but some people believe Hunter's Key is haunted, and that whoever goes up there uninvited will get . . . I don't know, hurt."

"And after seeing that monster the twins were wrestling with, you're not a little worried about superstition?"

"What do you suggest?"

"That we get some proper authority."

"You're not—"

"I am. With all the weird things happening, I'm not taking any chances. We need Darcy's help."

Lisa and Liev Vadiknov dropped off all their books, except the tome about Hunter's Key, and let their parents know they would be out for a while.

"Okay," Mrs. Vadiknov said as they walked back out the door, "Be careful, yes? *Spokoinoi nochi*, my darlings!"

"Do you think we can trust them?" asked Lisa.

"Who, Nash and Charlie? I think we can," answered Liev. "Unless they're really good actors, they had never seen a domovoi before."

Liev was referring to the Chief of Assistants. It was the closest thing to describing the little monster in their encyclopedic knowledge of Russian folklore.

"But," he continued, "if they are good actors, then it means they're probably not human and we've got an interesting night ahead of us."

Lisa frowned at her brother's odd sense of humor.

"What I wonder is who they'll be bringing with them?" Liev mused, rubbing his ivory chin.

"So how did your family get the name 'Stormstepper?'" Charlie asked, trying to break the silence, and Nash's anger.

"I'm the only Stormstepper in my family."

Charlie raised his eyebrows. "Really?"

"Yes."

"So, you're not going to tell me why?"

"Would you stop trying to be buddy-buddy? We're not. We're working together out of necessity."

"As teammates, then."

Nash belted out a heavy sigh. "Fine! It's like a local tradition. According to my family's legends, everyone's born with a name connected to some supernatural ability. The tribe's wise man was supposed to give us our names, knowing what ability we'd have. People still do it today. For tradition."

"Ability? What do you mean?"

"I don't know. We're supposed to have these powers I guess. But I'd be rich if I knew what my so-called ability was."

"Storm-stepping?" suggested Charlie with a grin.

Nash returned a dull scowl.

They walked up on the Witherington's house. Not that they would've missed it; it was a mansion after all. It didn't stand out much against the other houses in the "rich" neighborhood, having the same color and architecture as the other houses, only bigger. Charlie wondered again why the Witheringtons didn't reside in Hunter's Key, the mayoral mansion.

Was Mayor Witherington in on the disappearances?

The two teens climbed up the impressive marble steps, walked up to the impressive white door, and then knocked on it, with a not so impressive knock.

To their surprise, Darcy answered the door. They expected a butler or housemaid or something. She looked confused for a moment, and then returned to looking stubborn and prideful.

"Yes?" she asked, standing as tall as she could.

"Um, well. . .," Charlie stammered. He had not planned this far ahead.

Darcy cocked an eyebrow.

"Why did you come up the stairs against Donnie Wickles today?" Nash blurted out.

"Oh," she said, her shoulders dropping in a slight wilt. ". . . I'm glad you shut Donnie up. He deserved getting his butt handed to him."

"Are you apologizing?" asked Nash, astounded.

"No! I mean, yes. I'm sorry. There!" she added, as if to say *There, I've said it, are you happy now?*

Charlie looked at Nash, then at Darcy, waiting to see if they were finished.

"Right. What we really came for," he said, "is to ask a favor."

Darcy snorted. Not in a pig-like way, like most people do. It was a stately snort, if that is possible.

"A favor?"

"Yes. And it's important. It could affect the entire town."

"Really," said Darcy, crossing her arms. "Do tell."

Like Nash had with Fish McCollum, Charlie gave Darcy a brief and well-edited version of their theory about the missing persons and Hunter's Key. While he talked, she shifted from crossed arms and uninterested, to the classic hands-on–hips stance, to a more casual lean against the door, intrigued.

"Okay," she inserted after a moment's deliberation.

"Okay, what?" Charlie and Nash asked in unison.

"Okay, I'll give you the key. But on one condition: I go with you."

Nash had trouble not groaning, so it was good that Charlie had Darcy's attention.

"You sure about that? We'll be going through some pretty thick woods. And possibly facing a kidnapper."

"I'm not an idiot! I know what we'll be doing. I'll live in Hunter's Key someday, after all. Might as well go and see what the property looks like for once. Stay here."

Leaving them to stand in the open doorway to admire the magnitude of her entryway, Darcy raced through the hall and up the cherry wood, spiral staircase into her father's study, where he sat by the fire with his newspaper and a cup of evening tea.

Mr. Witherington lowered the newspaper, which he was merely pretending to read, and blew away the steam that attempted to twist its way to his nostrils. He smiled as Darcy entered, and sipped his tea, admiring the well-balanced, chamomile and lemon-infused flavors.

"Daddy," she said, in her most natural appeal to his heartstrings, "where are the keys to Hunter's Key?"

Eyes wide, and with a slight bobble of his double chin, Mr. Witherington spewed his tea all over his paper.

"Darling," he coughed while dabbing at his night coat and newspaper with a silk handkerchief, "whatever would you need *those* for?"

"I'd like to see it. I mean, I'll live there one day after I'm elected mayor. So I'd like to go ahead and see what it's like."

His shaking hands did not escape Darcy's notice. "Okay, that's quite all right. Remind me in a few weeks or so, and I'll take you up there myself. There's a dear. Now, run along and finish your homework."

He smiled at her and resumed pretending to read his soggy front page, gripping it tight so as to lessen the tremble in his hands.

"But Daddy," Darcy said firm, "I want the keys to the grounds. I'd like to visit tomorrow, perhaps."

"Darcy, dear, we shouldn't talk about such things as Hunter's Key. Not in such company."

Darcy looked around the room confused. "What company? There's only you and me."

"Yes, darling."

Darcy realized her father was skirting her request, and rather pitifully so. He wasn't good at lying, but neither was he a confrontational man.

Darcy narrowed her eyes with an indignant grunt, and marched out of the room.

The mayor wilted in his seat. That was too close for his comfort. He patted his coat pocket, empty. He rose and opened his top desk drawer to find the long, thin box tucked inside. He picked it up, holding it close, and felt the sting of sadness in his chest.

Meanwhile, Darcy barged into her bedroom, threw on a pair of jeans, a thick coat, and designer boots. They were the only pair of boots she had, and would have to do.

She returned to where she left Charlie and Nash standing and stepped outside, giving the door a soft pull behind her.

"It appears we will have to go around the gate," she said with a sour note, as if it were their fault.

"It's fine," Nash said. "Fish will get us through."

They began down the steps when Nash noticed Darcy's attire, and that she was following them.

"What're you doing?" he asked, though he feared he knew the answer.

"I'm coming with, of course."

"You don't have the key, do you?"

"Oh no, if you're going, then I'm going. And don't think about trying to ditch me. If I don't go up there with you, my father will hear about it."

Nash turned on Charlie. "This is why we should have left her out of it."

"What about your hair?" Charlie asked Darcy, trying to avoid a nuclear meltdown, but only making things worse. He pointed at her boots. "Or those boots? It's going to get messy trampling through those woods."

Darcy scowled at him and, with a *hmpf!*, marched past.

She realized she didn't know where she was going and turned to face them.

"Well?"

"Well, what?"

"Well, are you coming or not? Lead on!"

Chapter 6

It was ten after eight when Charlie, Nash and, to Nash's dismay, Darcy arrived at Midday Street. Darcy had long since put her hood up on the pretense that she was cold, but really she was hoping nobody recognized her strolling through town with present company.

Hmm, she thought when she saw the Vadiknov twins standing on the corner of Midday and Certifus. The one in black, Lisa, was sitting cross-legged on the ground reading a large book.

Wonder what they're doing here...

Then she noticed the town crazies, Fish McCollum and Wardley Dink, standing with the twins. Darcy became nervous when she realized they were headed straight for them.

"Wait!" she cried. She dragged Charlie and Nash into an alley by their jackets. "We're not going to see *them* are we?"

Charlie could see she was mortified.

"The twins? Yeah, why?"

"Well...it's just...You didn't say they would be here. And those two weirdos are here too."

"Hey!" Nash objected. "Fish and Dink are good friends of mine."

"Figures."

Nash balled his hands into fists, his anger boiling. He tapped his foot to keep from an outburst.

"I mean, they're all so strange. I don't want to be seen with them,"

Darcy added, ashamed at herself.

Charlie rolled his eyes. "Oh please, it's not like they're going to put a curse on you or anything!"

"And we'll be in the woods anyway," Nash said with a scowl. "So it's not like your friends will see you with any of us losers."

Inflamed with ire, Nash walked out of the alleyway and continued to where Fish, Dink, and the twins waited. Darcy watched Charlie follow. After a moment of chewing a nail and fussing to herself, she went, too, clinging to the shadows.

"Ahoy!" cried Dink to the newcomers.

The twins looked at each other and rolled their eyes. So much for silence.

"Hey, Dink." Nash pulled to a stop and gestured to Darcy. "We brought her."

He glared at Charlie.

"Everyone," said Charlie, taking the hint, "this is Darcy. Darcy, this is Lisa and Liev Vadiknov, Fish McCollum, and Wardley Dink."

Darcy nodded a curt greeting to the group and turned her back to them, seeming to examine the architecture across the street. Fish eyed Darcy, and muttered something to Dink. The two nodded.

Lisa's eyes narrowed. "Why is she here?"

Darcy squinted back. "Hunter's Key belongs to the mayor. If you're going to be stomping all over my property, I'm going too."

Lisa began to argue, but Fish cut her off, turning to Charlie and Nash.

"Right, so how close to the Key are you wanting to get?" he asked, rubbing his rabbit foot between thumb and forefinger.

"As close as we can," said Charlie.

He was nervous. Part of him hoped Fish and Dink would not be able to get them in, and he'd have an excuse to go home. And yet, the daydreamer in him was stamping like an anxious horse, ready to venture into the dark, sinister woods of Hunter's Point. It felt as if the Key was calling to him, pulling him closer.

"Follow me," said Fish.

Fish set off at a brisk pace, and soon they reached a wall of trees that ran along Certifus Street. One by one — or by two, in the twins' case — they disappeared into the thick of the trees.

Charlie watched as they were swallowed by the darkness. He paused, sucking in a long breath, like one would when jumping into the deep end of a pool, before diving into the suffocating timbers.

Darcy was last to enter. She was frightened of the woods, but that wasn't why she hesitated. She was more concerned about disappearing into the darkness with a motley crew of weirdos, loners, and goths. As far as she was concerned, they were psychos, lamebrains, and freaks. It didn't seem like a strong case for success.

It bothered her even more that she was now alone on a dark street, and that she might get left behind. Darcy took one last look over her shoulder, and jumped in after them.

The five teenagers were disoriented at first. The twins collided with Nash as soon as they breached the treeline, and Charlie jumped out of his skin when he saw a face staring at him in the darkness. He realized it was Fish standing with a flashlight shining on himself so that the others could see him. He waited on the lot of them to regroup before they moved on. Darcy rushed up behind them, slapping at scratchy twigs and branches. She squealed when she bumped into Liev. He waggled his eyebrows and half-grinned. Lisa rolled her eyes and pushed past them.

The two guides were used to ventures like this, and watched as the group tripped and stammered over each other. Fish and Dink found it comical. *And they think we're the simpletons,* Fish thought to himself. *Hmph.*

"All right," Fish said with a sense of urgency, "you need to understand it's important we stay together. You'll get lost if you wander here. I don't need anyone disappearing on my watch. Understand?"

They nodded in agreement, or fear, shivering at the words he'd used.

Lost.

Disappeared.

Missing.

Gone.

It wasn't something they wanted to think about in the cold, dark copse of trees, though that's exactly what had been on their minds all day.

They trudged through the night for what seemed like ages. At times the ground rose to a steep incline. Charlie pulled himself forward by grasping at the trees. Behind him, Darcy hemmed and hawed, clawing at the ground. No doubt her nails were filthy and caked with dirt. Charlie was amused at the thought. The twins managed to maintain their cool and collected behavior, somehow marching up without holding on to anything. Lisa hugged her book close. Darcy watched Lisa even closer. *There's no way she can walk up this hill like that!* Darcy thought. *She must be using her witchy powers.*

As Liev trotted past Darcy he whispered, "Hey there, fancy boots."

"Creep!" Darcy retorted.

Nash, who had gone hiking with Fish and Dink from time to time, navigated through the trees with some expertise and grace.

Of course, Fish and Dink were the real experts. Charlie was

surprised to see that Dink, who was so loud and clumsy before, moved with stealth and finesse, following Fish, who weaved in and out of sight like, well, a fish underwater.

As Charlie ducked under a low and heavy branch, the twins approached him.

"We were wondering. . ." Lisa whispered in a hush.

"How much do the others know?" finished Liev. He brushed dirt off his white jeans. "About Hunter's Key, we mean."

"Not much," said Charlie, tripping over a root. "We didn't tell any of them about that thing you were wrestling with —"

"Domovoi," interrupted Lisa.

"Domo, what?"

"That 'thing' is called a domovoi."

"Oh. Right. We didn't tell them about the. . . domovoi. But everyone agrees that something is up with Hunter's Key."

There was a moment where all that was heard was the crunch, crunch, crackle, crunch of their footsteps, before Lisa asked, "Why is Witherington here, though?"

"It's a long story."

"Sh!"

The group stopped and looked up. Dink had a finger pressed to his lips. He beckoned them to hurry to him.

Charlie, Nash, Lisa, Liev, and Darcy all hurried to catch up to Fish and Dink. They reached the top, where the ground leveled out again. Through the trees ahead, Charlie saw lights high in the towers of Hunter's Key. They looked bigger this close. He pointed a nervous finger.

Darcy scowled. "Who's up there?" she asked.

"Whatever you're looking for," urged Fish, "get on with finding it, will you? Don't want to be in these woods too long, with what crawls 'round here at night."

Crawls . . . at night? The blood in their veins froze, as if it needed any help in the chilled night air. Though they weren't aware, something, indeed, was watching from the trees — waiting, searching.

Charlie nodded at Fish and walked forward, Nash close behind, trying their best to move in silence.

"What are we looking for?" Darcy asked.

Liev smiled with mischief. "Anything that looks like blood, bones, clothing scraps, or maybe fur. Skulls hanging from trees. The usual."

Lisa punched her brother in the arm, but didn't offer any more appealing suggestions.

Charlie felt an ache press into the back of his eyes. "A book," he blurted out, though not sure why.

Nash frowned at Charlie, who was rubbing his eyes with vengeance. *A book?*

"We need to find a decent sized hole in the gate," said Nash. "It's old, there's got to be one somewhere."

The others nodded at his practical assessment. They fanned out like a search party, before realizing what they were doing. Charlie, still rubbing one eye, shifted to the middle of the group and provided a point of reference that everyone else could see and follow. It was strange that they should work together so natural, this unlikely mix of individuals hailing from such varying walks of life and experiences.

With Fish and Dink now walking in silence behind them, they walked to the edge of the tree line near Hunter's Key and stared upward, regarding it with reverence. They found themselves entranced by the foreboding height of the Towers. They also noticed how awkward the closest tower stood on the very edge of the house. More apparent to them was the sinister, disapproving way it glared down at them.

To their left, a black car rumbled toward them. Everyone shrunk back, tingling with fright.

Headlights illuminated their hiding place as it swung around the driveway, turning to circle an enormous, inactive fountain, but the driver didn't seem to notice them. At least, not that they knew.

This is the stranger, thought Charlie. *This is it.*

Terror—and the buzz of excitement—scampered up and down his spine, assaulting his back and limbs with waves of tension and shivers. His head felt like it was splitting in two.

The others were sharing Charlie's sentiments, minus the headache. The twins watched with excitement, attempting to discern what monstrosity lay beneath the stranger's human skin. Nash was less excited, and felt more provoked with each moment. If Mrs. McBranson had been hurt, he was simply ready to break down some doors and start a fight.

Beside them, Darcy fixed a frown at the car on her father's property. On what would soon be her property.

Something caught Charlie's attention, distracting him from the car. It was a sense, at first, a pang from his headache that made him look away. But then it was a glow, something stuck in a bush with small motes of light flowing to and from. Charlie moved toward it.

As the car came to a stop near the garages, much too close to the watchers hidden in the trees, Lisa and Liev leaned forward with anticipation. They wondered if the suspected monster was a *prico-lici*, or a *strigoi*, or even some other creature from their childhood stories, like the terrible *nalapsi*. Their imaginations were getting the best of them.

Many yards away, the dark stranger exited the car and walked to the garage, pulling it open. He was frustrated tonight, unsuccessful in his search.

From the woods, he heard a twig snap, followed by more crunching.

Like the night before, the stranger rallied to attention. He walked toward the trees and heard the scatter of someone trying to hide further into the woods. It wasn't hard for the stranger to see them—not with his glowing red, right eye. The urge to laugh bubbled up from his stomach, but he resisted.

The stranger could see one or two of their frightened faces, clear as daylight. Teenagers, probably bored and looking for adventure at the spooky house on a hill. Little did they know. As long as they stayed on that side of the gate, he didn't care.

He looked beyond the group and their two woodsmen guides, pretending to scan the trees before shrugging his shoulders and returning to the four-car garage. He drove the black car in and closed the door.

Among the thicket, the group let out a collective breath of relief. Each of them turned to glare at Charlie, since he'd been the one to step on the twig and fall on his butt, horrified.

In his own defense, Charlie held up an ornate, leather book.

"I found something," he said, rubbing madly between his eye and temple. "A book."

The twins came forward, forgiving him for the moment, holding an obvious interest in the old book. It looked priceless, and menacing; a dark mahogany color, inlaid with intricate lines of blood-red ink. The lines formed a complex, almost tribal pattern. *Otherworldly and dangerous*, were the words that came to them. Charlie studied it, wondering where the pinpricks of light had gone, and why his head still thrummed.

Everyone stared at Charlie — even Fish and Dink. *A book*, he told them earlier. And a book he had found.

"All right," said Nash, spooked. "So we know he's up here. And we have a book. I say we call it a night. We can report it to the police or something from this point."

"Actually," said Lisa, "everyone should come over to our place. We need to talk."

Liev nodded in agreement. "And we'd like to see that book."

Charlie was freaked out, wanting to run home and never have anything to do with Hunter's Key, or the book, again. But he was in too deep. If Charlie backed down now, it would haunt every nightmare and daydream for the rest of his life.

"I'm in," said Charlie.

He looked around at Nash, Darcy, Fish and Dink.

Darcy crossed her arms. She was already way out of her comfort zone, but this was too much to walk away from, especially with a stranger living in the mayoral mansion.

"Fine," she said.

"All right," said Nash.

"You guys go on ahead without us," said Fish. "We've got some business to tend to. But we'll make sure you find your way out of here," he added, rubbing the rabbit foot dangling from his neck.

As the group retreated into the woods, the Chief of Assistants looked down on them from a nearby tree.

His heart felt crushed. They found his master's diary! The one fledgling even seemed drawn to it.

The little monster scurried down the tree, careful to remain hidden. He hopped from foot to foot as they started to leave, thinking of how to get the diary back. Wringing his hands and gnashing his teeth with nervous energy, the creature rammed his head into a tree, leaving a dent in the bark.

His master beckoned him. He wanted to follow the humans, but he could not disobey the call.

The diary was so close, and yet, now, far away from his reach.

The Chief of Assistants wept bitterly as he skittered behind Hunter's Key, returning to his master.

Meanwhile, the dark stranger stood in the shadows, watching with his red eye as the five teens and their guides left the property. He crossed his arms and decided not to give chase. They might cause trouble with the town officials, but he doubted it. He was good at reading people.

If anything, they would return to satisfy their curiosity, at which time he would deal with them.

Chapter 7

The Vadiknov's home was well-organized, with minimal adornments and a traditional touch of elegance, until the library.

The library was crowded with books, almost too crowded. Big books, small books. Pile after pile, because there were no more shelves to contain them. Books with polished and modern covers, and books that were ancient and falling apart at the spine. Books that looked like they belonged in some European museum, and books that were only pages long. This personal collection gave Mrs. Nutterwicke and the school library a decent run for the money.

A white door and a black door, leading to the twins' respective bedrooms, stood on opposing walls. Both doors shut tight, with an air of supernatural protection around them.

Mr. and Mrs. Vadiknov were already tucked in for the evening, but Lisa closed the library door anyway. Liev invited everyone to sit and make themselves comfortable.

Several chairs and two tables dotted the library floor. Five chairs were dragged in a rough circle to the far end of the room, near the fireplace. Its warmth helped soothe some of the tension from the evening's events. Only Darcy remained rigid and uncomfortable.

Lisa held her hands out to Charlie. He scanned the book's cover and handed it to her.

Everyone could see it better in the light, which was not necessarily a good thing. Now they could see the inlaid red lines on its cover made a horrible pattern. It depicted the face of a frightening, horned wolf. The runic face of the beast sent a chill through the room.

Lisa examined the book and tried to open it, but found it secured against her will. There was a clasp on the book—a tiny metal dragon with ruby eyes. Its diminutive claws hugged the front and back covers, keeping the book closed and locked. But strangely, there was no keyhole. Lisa continued to struggle with the fastening until Liev, grinning, gestured for the book.

She grumbled, and handed it to him.

Charlie felt a sharp pain stab the space behind his eyes. Nash gave him a concerned look, but Charlie waved it off.

Liev squinted to read something on the back of the small dragon.

"Look at this," he said.

Lisa leaned over. "What is it? Is that Latin?"

"Yeah."

"What's it say?"

"It says *EXSECRIFER*. I don't recognize that."

"Hang on," said Lisa, retrieving a Latin dictionary.

"It's a cute little dragon," Liev mused, receiving strange looks from Charlie, Nash, and Darcy.

"Exsecrifer. It means *curse bearer*," said Lisa.

"That doesn't sound good," said Charlie.

Darcy rolled her eyes. "Please. Obviously, someone created this thing as a joke and it got lost in the woods."

"Don't say that!" Liev pretended to scold. "You'll hurt Exsecrifer's feelings!"

He stroked the dragon's spine like it was a pet, and that activated it. Ruby eyes glowed as the tiny dragon came to life. Its metal body moved with the sound of grating gears as thousands of microscopic metal scales scraped together.

The group recoiled. Liev stood up, careful not to drop the book.

The dragon shook its small body as if waking from an ancient sleep. It relinquished its grasp of the book's cover and crawled onto the front of the book, peering up at Liev. Then, baring a mouthful of miniature, needle-like fangs, it sunk a bite into Liev's left thumb. He yelped and dropped the book, trying to shake the serpent from his hand.

Releasing its clamp on Liev's thumb, the dragon fell to the diary and curled into a circle and flattened itself into a round depression on the book's spine. Its glowing eyes faded, and as quickly as the dragon had come to life, it became nothing more than another of the book's decorative pieces.

"Are you okay?" asked Lisa, rushing to her brother's side. He seemed shaken, and blood seeped through his clenched fingers, but he laughed it off.

"You know, that hurt, but who else can say they've been bitten by a dragon?"

Lisa growled at her brother's nonchalant attitude when Darcy interrupted. Crouching behind a chair, Darcy sounded both angry and scared.

"Okay guys, you got me. Very funny. Drag the popular girl through the woods, spook her out, and then play a stupid prank on her."

"What are you whining about now?" asked Nash in a heightened tone. Only Darcy could make this about herself.

In answer, she pointed an unsteady finger at the book.

"Don't expect me to believe that was real," she asserted.

Liev held his thumb up. Everyone could see the bite marks — dozens of small, jagged, blood-marked holes outlined by torn skin. The wound wasn't fake.

"Darcy," said Liev, "if we wanted to play a trick on you, I wouldn't volunteer getting my hand cut open. I'd volunteer Lisa."

Lisa jabbed another punch into her brother's arm and told him to go clean up. He returned a few minutes later with a bandaged thumb and fresh face.

Everyone sat down again around the strange book, staring at it like it was a criminal.

Liev leaned forward and, with a skeptical pause, picked it up. He held it and fiddled with it for a few seconds, determining that it was safe. When nothing came to life on the book, he handed it to his sister.

Lisa took it with caution. Without the dragon clasp sealing it, she flipped the book open.

She began rattling off in Russian. Some of the words must have been of a colorful nature, because Liev's eyes grew wide and he tried to calm her. She showed him the pages and his face fell. Lisa laid the book flat in her lap so the others could see; it was in a language none of them recognized.

"That can't be it," said Charlie. "There has to be something else here."

At the sound of Charlie's voice, the page lit up. The letters on the page began to glow, like ink made from fire. Everyone drew close in awe, and when the glowing stopped, the writing was in English.

"That's not possible," Darcy whispered.

Sharing a glance with each person, Lisa leaned back in her chair and began to flip through the pages. Everyone in the room sat on the edge of their seat, anxious. Lisa scowled as she flipped back and forth, restless and animated.

After several minutes of scouring the pages for answers to questions she wasn't sure to ask, she passed the book to Liev, holding open a page toward the back.

"It's a *varcolac*," she said.

"What's a varcolac?" asked Nash, perplexed.

"It's what's causing the disappearances. It's a . . . just think of it as a vampire, only different. Worse."

Darcy snorted. "A vampire? You must be joking. Or crazy!"

"Yes," said Nash. "It's all a joke. Can you leave now?"

"She didn't see the creature earlier," Charlie pointed out.

"It's called a domovoi," said Liev.

"What?"

"It was a . . . never mind."

Lisa glared at Darcy, closing the book and pointing at the dragon curled up on the spine.

"You saw this thing come to life. You saw what it did!"

"Look," said Darcy, "maybe weird things have happened tonight. Maybe that dragon statue moved around or something—I don't know. And someone's definitely up in Hunter's Key when they shouldn't be. But a vampire? Really?"

"I saw something today that made me believe," said Charlie, trying to reassure her.

"I saw it, too," Nash offered.

Liev looked her in the eyes. "We both did," he said, gesturing at himself and Lisa.

The twins glanced at each other. In their encounter with the domovoi, the little monster wasn't the only thing they had discovered, but the twins weren't ready to reveal everything yet.

Darcy stared at them like they had turned into vampires them-selves. She stood up, then sat back down again, wrestling with believing in their crazy theories. Still, it had been a strange night, and she believed more than she wanted to.

Seeing that Darcy had suspended her disbelief for the moment, Lisa turned to her brother.

"Read!"

Liev looked down at the page stained with time itself, and began to read aloud.

"The hunters' bindings are beginning to . . ."

He stopped, frowned, and read several sentences ahead. He dove deep into what was written:

> *The hunters' bindings are beginning to wane. Whatever magic the cursed mortals used upon me I am beginning to understand. Some of the Lesser have found holes in the gateway and are able to cross over. I myself cannot cross, nor can any of the Greater, but I will find a way soon.*

Liev stopped again. He noted that, in the diary, several distinct entries were written back-to-back.

Lisa nodded to him. He looked down and kept reading, turning a page as he continued:

> *I've started to send the Lesser out again, both to scout and to collect. The Ritual is not ready for a sacrifice yet, but I'm running out of slaves to feed on. I, prince of the royal line, have been forced to save the last two of the ancient warriors, as well as those new humans*

the Lesser have captured. I restrain my feeding to simple bloodletting. A slow, agonizing starvation threatens the fragile hold I have left on this castle.

I take comfort in knowing the barrier between the worlds is failing; that I'll soon feed on them freely.

And then, once I've sated my revenge on them, I'll complete the Ritual.

Lisa stopped him, turned a few pages ahead and pointed to another group of entries to read.

"I think this one's about Mrs. McBranson," she said, her own words making her ill. "And Bobby Muldor, after that."

The others shifted with discomfort in their seats at her tone, Nash in particular. Liev waited a moment before reading aloud the next two entries.

My damnable Lesser fools brought me a weak, fragile human. Its blood was dry and wholly unsatisfying, the flesh like flaking paper. I could not finish it. I need more if my strength is to return. Younger humans.

My strength returns. The last human's blood was fresh and moist. Young. But I still hunger. That must be dealt with before I can begin the Ritual.

No matter. The time is close. I'm sending my most trusted servant to gather the last needed item for the Ritual. Until he returns, this will be my final entry. May I finish the Ritual and bring fear and glory back to my family's line.

"It ends there," said Liev.

Charlie's hands went limp and numb, and he became ice-cold, despite the warmth of the fire beside him. His mind wanted to believe this was a sick person's joke. But he couldn't believe it to be a prank, as that would be denying the truth that was evident. Looking at the others, he realized they could no longer disregard the truth either—not even Darcy.

He thought about his recurring nightmares, about the Key, and about this so-called varcolac. *Could it all be connected?* he wondered.

Charlie discovered Lisa was staring at him. Her wide, dark eyes set him on edge, though he also found kindness and comfort in them. He broke his gaze and turned away.

Lisa's own thoughts were about his instructions to search for a book while on Hunter's Point earlier.

"You've found a varcolac's diary," she said.

"Yup," agreed Liev. "We're all doomed."

"Unless of course we kill the varcolac," she said, her thoughts slipping out for everyone to hear.

Liev grimaced. "That would be quite difficult."

"How do we kill it?" asked Nash.

The twins looked at each other.

"You can't," answered Liev.

Lisa turned a sour face toward her brother. "That's not true. You *can* kill it."

"Oh sure," agreed Liev, "if you can get close enough without it biting your head off."

"Well, I'm not saying it's easy, just that it's not impossible."

"That's arguable; look at Vlad Tepes. Nobody knows if he really ever kicked the bucket or not."

"We're not talking about a maybe-possible vampire from history. We're talking about a real, living varcolac."

Nash threw his hands up in frustration. "Look! I know you guys are excited, but just tell us how we get rid of the thing, okay?"

The twins considered Nash's request.

"It'll be hard," Liev said. "Give us until tomorrow. We'll find out."

"Good," said Charlie. "And then we have to go up there and kill it. Right?"

Everyone nodded, except Darcy.

"We should," said Nash. "We can't let this go on."

"Tomorrow night then. We'll meet again at Midday Street," Liev said. He looked at Nash. "Do you think you could get us back up there, or should you get Fish again?"

"I think I can on my own. Fish is a bit superstitious as it is. If he knew some sort of monster was up there, he may try to stop us."

Darcy chose to speak up at the notion. "You're all crazy! This is insane!"

She grabbed her coat and started for the door.

Charlie stood up. "Wait! Are you with us or not?"

She stopped. She knew she had to be. Deep down, it all made terrible sense. And though that terrified her, it didn't change the fact that she had to go along.

"Yes," she said, regretting her own words. "Just don't tell anyone."

"Don't worry," said Lisa, sarcasm tempting her voice. "Now that you're crazy too, we'll make sure no one else knows you're crazy with us."

Chapter 8

The Chief of Assistants hobbled forward. His master's eyes flashed crimson lightning, fingernails clicking slow and impatient against the armrest of the cold marble throne. The colossal hearth behind the throne cast a shadow the length of the Hall, and the Chief of Assistants groveled within its darkness.

"Where is it?"

The Chief of Assistants bowed his head until his knees bent and his face touched the floor. His floppy ears fell flat against the frigid flagstones. "M-m-my lord. Fledglings, th-they stole your diary."

A false smile flickered across the varcolac's sallow lips. "Human children. How did you let the humans touch you?"

"I d-d-don't know, my prince," the Chief of Assistants searched for a way out of his own failure. "They are different from other mortals. Strong, these fledglings are. Some have powers. Up to no good, my lord. Found them sneaking around in the woods. No good at all, gracious one."

The Dark Prince nodded. "We must be wary of them. And yet, their blood could be what I seek."

The varcolac stood and prowled toward the trembling figure. Depressing a morbid fang into his own wrist, the Dark Prince drew blood. Dipping a talon into the blood pooling into his palm, he smeared letters upon the Chief of Assistant's bare head, forming an ancient word: *VISVS*.

"You are my eyes, now. Go and follow them."

The Chief of Assistants nodded with relief, ready to be gone from his master's presence. Stumbling as he went, he shuffled to exit the great double doors.

"Heed my warning!" the varcolac called.

The quivering monster skidded to a stop and bowed before the Dark Prince once more, his ears fanned wide to show he was listening. The varcolac's face was shrouded in the darkness, but wrath shone fierce in his eyes.

"Losing my diary was no small failure. If you disappoint me again, you shall regret it. This much I assure you."

"Y-y-yes, m-my lord."

"What is wrong with you today? Darcy!"

Darcy peered over her shoulder before facing her friends' interrogation. They stared at her with questions in their eyes.

"Hm?"

"You seem off," said Caitlin. "Like you're not here. Is it a boy?" she whispered.

"What? No, I just . . ."

Darcy saw the twins pass by. Lisa looked her dead in the eye, waving in spite.

"Were those the Vadiknovs?" asked one of her friends. "What did she want?"

"Well how should I know?" grumbled Darcy, keeping an eye out to avoid Charlie or Nash.

"Are you under a curse?" asked another friend. "O . . . M . . . G . . . we could be infected too! Please tell me we're safe."

"Shut it! There's no curse. Stop being lame."

"Well, they are witches, everybody knows that. I heard those two have the head of a genie in a crystal ball in their house. It helps them to spy on people. I wonder if they've ever watched me."

Darcy rolled her eyes and let out a sigh of exasperation, then recalled the events of last night. *I guess anything's possible at this point,* she thought.

Caitlin popped a large, pink bubble, breaking through Darcy's far-off gaze. "You know, I dropped by your house last night. Where were you?"

"Out. I . . . I'll see you guys later, I've got to get to class."

Her friends watched as Darcy jogged through the hallway, clutching her books tight in her arms, looking over her shoulder as if somebody, or something, was following her.

Nash sat restless in Miss Felton's class, fidgeting, and changing his position in the desk every few seconds. His classmates noticed, and decided to have some fun at his expense. Paper balls and pencil erasers began flying his way whenever the teacher wasn't looking.

Miss Felton noticed Nash's increasing impatience, though she was oblivious to the flying objects being launched at him. She decided to talk to Nash after class and try to learn what was bothering him.

That was until she sent him to the principal.

Johnny Brown had advanced from throwing tiny paper balls at Nash to shooting spit balls. Miss Felton missed this, of course, but happened to turn around in time to witness Nash jump from his desk and hurl a pencil at Johnny.

Johnny was sent to the nurse's office with a scratched lip. Nash was sent to Mr. Adams' office, and stormed his way to an immediate detention.

The twins were not the fidgeting types, but they were antsy in their own way. Lisa passed the time by reading up on the history of Hunter's Key, while Liev pretended to sleep through class with his eyes open. He blinked from time to time to reply to Lisa's mutterings and musings about the legends of the Key.

Mr. Switzler soon caught their inattention and was by their side. He snatched the book away from Lisa.

"What is this, young lady? No outside reading, thank you. And no talking in class, either. You two find different seats."

"What?" cried Liev.

The rest of the class looked up from their books. The Vadiknov twins, separated?

Mr. Switzler narrowed his eyes. "You heard me, Vadiknov. Move."

Liev glowered at his teacher, but felt a calming hand on his arm. He turned to see Lisa shaking her head.

Reluctantly, the twins moved to opposite sides of the class.

As for Charlie, he would've been certain to visit the principal's office for his inability to focus on his assignments, had he not been so fortunate that Mrs. Pinkerly was out sick today. Another, more vivid, nightmare haunted his thoughts, clashing with his ideas about what might be in his immediate future.

He was only too thankful, then, that Mrs. Pinkerly was absent, and that Mr. Snout was substituting. Mr. Snout did not, due to well-considered personal policy, pay attention to students. He only had eyes for the chalkboard. After twenty-nine years of professional substituting experience, he learned that paying attention to students only placed one in unpleasant situations.

The fact that Charlie was imprisoned in a school desk for an entire day following the prior evening's trek through a sinister forest, tripping over an ancient diary—that so happened to host a miniature living dragon—and discovering that monsters really do exist, made certain that he was not having a day better than any other. As soon as the bell rang, Charlie raced through the hallway.

And so it was that Charlie Sullivan, the Vadiknov twins, and Darcy Witherington all flew out of the main school doors and, desperate to avoid each other, took the long routes to their respective homes.

An hour later, as the sun toiled in the west, an angry Nash Stormstepper was released from detention. Donnie Wickles, who had hung around after school like he always did, noticed him stomping out of the library and past the school parking lot. Donnie raised an eyebrow and followed Nash at a safe distance.

The fledglings didn't stay together. The Chief of Assistants was disturbed and confused by this. Worse, none of them carried the diary.

He looked from the siblings, to the boy, to the girl with her head hung low. Which one would the master want him to follow? Where was the fifth fledgling?

Ramming his head on the roof of the school, the Chief of Assistants decided to follow the boy. The one with the magic forming in his eyes. He had found the diary. Perhaps he had been the one to keep it.

Quickly, the Chief of Assistants moved from his perch and began to follow Charlie.

Chapter 9

"H ey Dad!" Charlie called out as he closed the front door.

"Hello?" Mr. Sullivan called from his study.

Charlie ducked into the kitchen, grabbed an apple, and skipped a quick pace to his room. He almost tripped and bumped into Mr. Sullivan when he reached the landing of the second floor.

"Hey kiddo. Going somewhere fast?"

His mouth full of apple, Charlie nodded. "Me and some friends are going to a, uh, movie. Told them I'd meet 'em after school."

He shuffled into his room and dropped his backpack on the floor, looking for his pocket flashlight.

"Oh?" said Mr. Sullivan from the landing. "What movie?"

Charlie hesitated. He didn't want to lie to his dad, but what could he say? That he was going to kill some type of vampire-ish monster, who, by the way, had been the cause of all the missing people?

"*Vampire Reign*," he offered with a tinge of guilt staining his voice.

Then he grimaced. It was the first thing that came to mind, given yesterday's events, but he wasn't sure if his dad would be too happy about him seeing a gory horror flick.

That, and he was lying.

"Really? Tell me how it turns out, will you? I was thinking of taking your mom to the movies this weekend. Thought she might like it."

Charlie smiled to himself. He doubted his mom would enjoy *Vampire Reign* at all.

"Sure thing!" he called. He found his flashlight and escaped down the stairs, through the front door, and calling behind him, "Love ya! See ya!"

Mr. Sullivan smiled and sipped his coffee before diving back into his writing. *They grow up so fast these days*, he thought.

Darcy was surprised to see she was the first to show up for the scheduled meet. She wore what she thought to be a drab hoodie and plain jeans, making sure no passerby would recognize her. After hovering around one corner, she glanced around, feeling foolish and wondered if the others would show.

She jumped when Lisa's voice cracked the silence behind her.

"Punctual, aren't we? I thought you'd have locked yourself in your room."

Darcy quickly composed herself. "And what is that supposed to mean?"

"Only that I don't really see what's in it for you. Are you just trying to get the juicy gossip, or do you have the hots for one of these guys?"

"Easy," Liev whispered to his sister. He knew Lisa hadn't been in the best of moods today.

Charlie arrived, running. He bent in half and grabbed his knees, trying to catch his breath. When he stood up straight again, he was rubbing his eyes. Judging by his severe bloodshot look, the others assumed he had a sleepless night.

"Well," said Lisa, her lip curling, "there's your boyfriend. Or wait, is it the other one?"

"Hey guys," said Charlie, paying no attention to the conversation between the girls. "What's up?"

Darcy *hmphed* and turned to look at the trees as Lisa spun in the opposite direction. Charlie and Liev shared a shrug and an awkward look before Charlie spoke up.

"So, how do we kill it?"

"Well," Liev began, matter-of-fact. "Lisa and I did some checking. The most trusted method would be to find the varcolac, drive a nail into its heart, behead it, cut it into pieces, then burn it and scatter the ashes."

"Oh," said Charlie, rubbing his neck. "I see."

A few minutes later, Nash arrived in his customary fury. After a session with the library's dreadful brown wall, he was late, and that upset him. The gossip reached him as he left detention that Nash Stormstepper was love-struck over a certain girl, and that upset him even more. He stubbed his toe and tripped on his way here, and that upset him most.

"Hey," said Charlie, like a good friend would.

Nash glared at him until Charlie shrunk away.

"Everyone ready?" Liev asked, looking around.

It was bad timing. Darcy was texting with Caitlin when she cried out in despair.

"Oh, no!"

Everyone questioned her in unison, "What?"

"I just realized my phone battery is dead!"

Nash fumed. "Your *phone battery*? We're about to go kill a

vampire—"

"Varcolac," interjected Liev.

"—and you're worried about a phone?"

"Figures," said Lisa, rolling her eyes.

"No one asked you!" Darcy bit back.

"Really? That reminds me of something," said Lisa, tapping her chin in mock thought. "Like, how nobody asked you to come along!"

"Oh yes, somebody did! I believe it was Charlie and Nash who showed up at my house last night, asking for my help. Remember, Charlie?"

Charlie shrugged and stammered. "I, uh, when you say . . ." He never thought it beneficial for a person's health to get involved in an argument between rival females.

Flustered, Darcy turned to Nash. "Right?"

Nash looked as if he would burst into flames any moment. He raised his finger and opened his mouth, but Darcy cut him off.

"See?" she said, taking their stammering and hesitation as affirmation. "They remember, you elitist bookworm!"

"Hey!" cried Liev, defending his sister.

Lisa, capable of defending herself, stood nose to nose with Darcy.

"Elitist bookworm? I suppose a pompous, rich brat like you wouldn't understand the value of knowledge!"

Nash—his temper now measurable in degrees Fahrenheit— jumped between them.

"Stop yelling! You blockheads are going to attract attention."

The two girls, and Liev, all took offense at being called blockheads and turned their attention on Nash. A cacophony of bickering teenagers rose into the night.

Charlie inched forward, hesitant. "Guys, really, calm down." He laid a hand on Nash's shoulder.

Nash reared back. "Don't tell me to calm down!" he yelled, raising his boot and smashing it as hard as he could into the ground.

Blue, purple, and white sparks flew from beneath Nash's winter
boot, scorching the sidewalk and causing the others to jump, taking
cover. The lightshow continued as a bolt of electricity erupted
from Nash's boot, flashing like lightning. The air crackled around
them as the bolt arced to the nearest street lamp with the force of
a speeding train. The metallic light ruptured sideways, flickering out.

Scattered on the ground in a broken circle, the five teens
exchanged looks of disbelief. Charlie pushed himself up and walked
to the street lamp.

"The metal is melted." He stared at Nash. "How did you . . . ?"

Nash looked as stunned as everyone else.

"I don't know!" Then his face stretched into a grin and he dou-
bled over with laughter.

Charlie started chuckling, nervous at first, but with ease after
seeing Nash punch-drunk. Lisa raised an eyebrow at her brother,
who returned a knowing look. Nash's strange phenomenon came
as a smaller surprise to them.

When Darcy laughed, it was from sheer terror. She wasn't afraid
of Nash, but of the voice deep inside that whispered, *See? I told you.*

Lisa let them laugh out the nervous stress. A man on a bicycle
passed by, observing in confusion. Nash pointed at the man, and
they laughed harder. When the delirium subsided, Lisa raised her
hand to speak.

"I think we know," she said. "We know what that was."

Nash sobered up and listened in earnest, wiping his eyes with
his palms. Darcy sat down on the street curb, staring at the ground

like it would fall from beneath her.

"The book about Hunter's Key," the Vadiknov sister continued. "It talked about the beginnings of Hunter's Grove. Haven't you ever wondered how this town started out? How it got its name?"

They all stared at her, dumb as the end of a hammer.

"It was named for the people who built Hunter's Key, and the town after that. They believed there was a large doorway into another world somewhere on Hunter's Point. They were known as monster hunters, and lived their lives dedicated to keeping monsters out of our world. Those people were said to have certain abilities. Supernatural gifts. But each person, and their power, was unique."

Liev took over for his sister. "We have a gift," he said. "We can't get a handle on it, but we discovered it when we were trying to catch that domovoi yesterday. We caught it with some sort of *laser beam*." He grinned at the memory of it.

Lisa glared at her brother. "It's not a laser beam. It was more like a thin sheet of pliable energy. But we don't know how to control it, and the monster got away."

"So my gift is shooting lightning bolts?" asked Nash.

"It would seem," Liev said.

Nash stood up and walked to the alley across the street. The group followed.

"Do I have a power?" Charlie asked.

"Do I?" echoed Darcy.

"We don't know," Lisa said. "The book didn't exactly say how to tell."

"Well," said Darcy. "Guess you can't learn everything from books, can you?"

She and Lisa engaged in another glaring contest.

Ignoring them, Nash flung his arms out at the brick wall at the end of the alley like some wigged-out rockstar. He pointed and punched the air, trying to fire off another lightning bolt, but to no avail. He tried again, and again, and began to feel foolish.

There was no way he had imagined it — the others had seen it too, after all. Still, perhaps it was simply a freak of nature, like ball lighting or midsummer snow.

Charlie watched Nash's shoulders slump. He remembered their uncomfortable conversation the day before, about Nash's name. "Stomp!" he said, thinking aloud.

Nash frowned. He stomped once, and again, feeling like an idiot. He stomped a third time, feeling a surge of heat prickle up his neck with embarrassment.

And that was when another bolt struck, crashing into the far wall, leaving a black scar in the red brick.

Nash gave an excited *whoop!* Charlie and Darcy celebrated with him. The twins, however, charged forward having heard a small shriek in the alleyway, coming from behind the dumpster. Lisa and Liev returned a moment later, holding a struggling, grayish-green figure hovering in the air between them.

"See?" Liev said, grinning from ear to ear. "Laser beams."

"They're not laser beams," Lisa corrected, exasperated.

A strand of flickering light that was somehow black and white at the same time was wrapped like a rope around the Dark Prince's highest ranking servant — the Chief of Assistants. It blinked out completely at one point, and the twins had to hold with both hands what they called a domovoi.

They also saw the freshly blood-painted word across his forehead: *VISVS*.

Nash and Charlie stared at the creature. Darcy stared, too, starting to accept this new reality she found herself in.

"No, no, no!" the small devil cried. "You will let me go! The master will destroy you fledglings! Let go!"

"Your master?" Charlie said. The group shrunk back into the alley, avoiding the remaining daylight. "Your master is the varcolac, isn't he?"

Nash stepped forward, taking care not to step too heavy. "How about you tell us where we can find your master, and we might play nice?"

The Chief of Assistants bit his lip, drawing a drop of slimy-black blood, and shook his head in panic.

To speak would be to die. He would have bit the black and white ones' hands, were there not so many of the fledglings. And were it not that the angry one had discovered his gift. His master was right. One of these humans probably had the required blood for the Ritual.

Stay, he heard his master call. *I see through your eyes.*

The servant wilted in defeat. He could not disobey the master's direct command.

The girl's blood is the blood I need, the Dark Prince continued. *Stay and get it for me.*

The little monster trembled, eyes fixating on Darcy. Despite being afraid, she stood tall and proud, ready to take charge. The Chief of Assistants understood. His gaze flickered among the others, before settling on Charlie's bloodshot eyes.

In his mind, the little devil felt the varcolac take notice of the boy. *That's the one. This child has the Sight.*

The Chief of Assistants gasped in awe.

100

Meanwhile, Charlie and Nash argued about the ethics of torturing a monster.

"It's not right," said Charlie.

"It isn't human, and neither is its master. We need to get into the Key. This creep knows how."

"But it isn't right."

"I know a way," said Darcy.

Everyone turned to stare at her. She held up a rusted key; the old kind, with an elaborate head, a thick body, and stubby teeth at the end.

"Is that the gate key?" asked Charlie.

"No, I don't know where my dad keeps the key to the gate. But this unlocks an old tunnel that leads to the Key. I used to play in it when I was a kid."

"I read about that," Lisa said, nodding as if she had already thought about it. "A tunnel dug by hunters, hundreds of years ago."

"Where's the tunnel?" Nash asked Darcy.

"It's under Tavern's Quick-N-Go." Suddenly, she felt in her element. "Follow me."

"Wait," said Lisa. "If Darcy's tunnel really leads to the Key, there can't be any turning back."

Nash nodded. "She's right."

"We've come this far," said Charlie. "But what comes next is going to be difficult, and dangerous. If anyone wants to go home, now's the time."

They fidgeted and looked at each other, but not one of them made a move to leave. Charlie smiled and stuck his hand out, palm down. Nash was the first to step forward, putting his hand on top of Charlie's. Next were the twins with one pale, white hand

and one hand with accentuating onyx fingernails—the Chief of Assistants still held between their other hands—followed by the perfectly manicured, yet hesitant, hand of Darcy.

The frigid evening air warmed by a few degrees; slight, but powerful. Everyone, including the suspended monster in their midst, could sense a palpable shift of energy and confidence.

Hunter's Grove had its monster hunters once more.

Chapter 10

"Hi Tavern!"

"Hey there, Darcy." Tavern raised his eyebrows as he noticed her company, four of the more diverse and eccentric students of Hunter's Grove.

The stronger looking one — Nash Stormstepper, if Tavern remembered — was carrying an odd-shaped bundle wrapped in his own hoodie. Tavern thought he was imagining, but the bundle seemed to twitch and kick.

"You want me to pull a few tables together for you and your friends?"

"No. Thanks." She tried to look in charge, ignoring as best she could the people in the restaurant staring at her. She hoped word didn't get around town that the mayor's daughter had started hanging out with freaks and loners. She knew it would, though. It was Hunter's Grove, after all.

The bundle squirmed again, and Nash gave it a tight squeeze. Inside, the Chief of Assistants fell still in compliance.

Darcy leaned forward and whispered so no one in the building could hear. "Actually, we came for a different reason. Do you remember that old brick passage? The one I used to play in when I was a kid?"

"The one under the storeroom? Sure. Why?"

"Think we could take a look?"

Tavern scanned the group again. Darcy was not the trouble-making type, but then Darcy's posse were usually smacking bubblegum and overworking their thumbs on smartphones across social networks.

"You know your father thinks the tunnel is dangerous."

"Please, Tavern? It's really important," pouted Darcy.

"Okay." Tavern took one last, suspicious look before lifting the wooden panel on the serving counter and waved for them to follow. He called to the nearest waitress.

"Mary, I'm going to run to the back for a sec. Take over for me, will you?"

Tavern was apprehensive about letting them into the tunnel. After all, Mayor Witherington had forbid his daughter from going into that tunnel two years ago. The door that kept the evil in check was locked, he knew, and the mayor had the only key. *What harm could come from a group of teens having a little old-school fun?* he thought.

Charlie, Nash, and the twins gawked as they walked through the kitchen. They'd never seen this part of Tavern's store and restaurant. It was bigger than they had imagined, with the restaurant itself being so small.

As they reached a large metal door, Tavern produced a thick key on a heavy key ring and unlocked it.

"I'll leave the door unlocked, then, so you can get out. Let me know when you're done with whatever it is you're doing, so I can lock it up."

He pushed the metal door open to reveal a freezer full of the perishable food that Tavern stored for the restaurant side of Tavern's Quick-N-Go.

"It's that way," he told Darcy, pointing past racks of frozen meat, cheese and dairy items, and boxes of assorted veggies. "You remember, don't you?"

Darcy nodded and smiled. "Thanks, Tavern!"

She led the group into the room. They wrapped themselves tighter in their coats and jackets until she found the open hole in the storeroom floor. Tavern had left the space open. During winter, it produced a frigid draft that kept his perishables colder. Less dependency on the freezer unit meant lower utility bills. In the summer, he kept it covered with a metal trap door.

Had he known what lay on the other side of the tunnel—had he really known—he might have paid extra for the utilities, sealed the trap door, and layered it with crucifixes, salt, iron, garlic, and all manner of protective wards.

Tavern watched them climb down the ladder, one by one, until they disappeared from view. He closed the door to the storeroom and returned to serving his dinner guests, trying his best to ignore the worry tugging at his gut.

The varcolac knew the moment when the five had entered the tunnel. The strong boy released his servant and pushed the Lesser creature forward. These fledglings came with intention to destroy whatever evil they might find. Their goal was to pierce his heart and rend his body, then scatter his ashes in the earth.

He chuckled.

The Dark Prince didn't fear them. He hailed from one of the oldest family lines—a direct, noble descendent of the Ancients.

Fear was not an emotion he was acquainted with.

He knew, however, these humans could pose a threat to accomplishing his purpose, as their forefathers had, two centuries earlier.

The varcolac was too close to make that mistake again. He could not allow them to come any closer.

He reached for his red quill and began to write.

"Are we there yet?" Liev asked, slipping on a frozen puddle and leaning head first into the dank brick wall. He wiped tunnel grime from his face onto his bleach-white jeans, repulsed.

Darcy held a hand up to him. "Sh! I'm trying to remember."

Dead ends branched to the right and left, leaving the tunnel to progress in a straight line. One passage presented a door. That passage, if it was the same one Lisa had spoken of, would be the way to Hunter's Key.

Darcy stole a glance at Lisa. The twin was reading the varcolac's diary with her pocket light. Charlie had given Darcy his own light so she could see where she was going.

She remembered playing down here as a little girl with friends, but hadn't seen those friends in a long time. At some point in her life, she became picky about her friends. Darcy regretted that now.

I remember playing hide and seek down here. Someone would count, and the rest of us would choose different passages to hide in. Then the seeker would try and guess which passage we chose. I remember hiding one day. . . I found a big door. . . I remember marking the tunnel so I could find it again. What did I mark it with?

It was a key, she remembered. Darcy drew a key on one of the walls, to remind her of a door. A key, for Hunter's Key. She almost laughed about it now.

"Look for a key," she said.

"You're joking, right?" asked Nash.

Darcy ignored him, examining the tunnel walls carefully. She drew it in crayon, and wondered if it would have faded after all these years.

Her thoughts were cut short as Lisa gasped. Everyone stopped to see what was wrong. The pages of the diary were blown by an intangible, hellish wind, until the turning stopped dead on a single page.

"What is it?" asked Liev, stepping forward to look at the diary. The twins stood with their heads craned downward.

"It's him," said Lisa. "He's writing in the diary!"

"What do you mean?" Nash said as the little monster he was holding began to whimper and quiver. "That's impossible, we have—"

He stopped in midsentence. Charlie and Darcy hurried to look.

On an otherwise blank, ancient and yellowed page, words were appearing. Letters formed, written with fire, searing the page in bright, orange-red luminescence.

A simple, yet chilling, message:

> *Greetings, children.*
> *I know what you hope to accomplish. Your forefathers, the hunters,*
> *also tried to destroy me. Fully trained and skilled warriors . . . it*
> *was a delight to dispose of them! A game, really.*
> *Do you expect to succeed where they failed?*
> *Come, then, if you dare.*

The writing ended, leaving the five teens shivering in the dark.

"What should we do?" asked Darcy.

They looked at each other. Brave words escaped them in that moment.

Except for Nash. "We should keep going," he said. "We've come this far knowing what we were up against. Why stop now?"

Darcy's voice was low and harsh. "He said it was a game with the hunters! What does that mean about us? We have no idea what we're doing!"

"But we have to," said Charlie, calm.

All eyes turned to him.

"We have these . . . abilities. Don't we? We're the only ones who can stop him. We can't let him keep taking people whenever he wants to. I can't. I wouldn't be able to live with myself knowing what I know now."

They considered his words, which didn't do much for their confidence still.

"He's right," agreed Darcy. "I don't like it, but he is."

Liev offered his own brand of humor. "Guess that sucks for us, doesn't it?" He waited for the others to get the punch line. Nothing. "Get it? Sucks? He's like, a vampire."

Their groans broke the tension. Charlie took the first step, and the others followed, slower than before.

After about ten minutes of walking, Darcy stooped forward and began scratching at a wall. The others couldn't see it at first, but she could. She knew what she was looking for. On the wall was a faded, dirty scribbling of a key. Moisture had washed over a portion of it, but Darcy still recognized her old drawing.

"This is the way!" she said.

She began to run, and the others followed. The tunnel twisted once, and then again before straightening. The group kept a rapid pace until they came to a towering door. It was carved from the rock and was faced with thin bars of cast iron.

"That's it!" Darcy cried. She jammed her elaborate key into the lock and turned it. The door didn't budge.

"Great," said Lisa. "Now how do we get it open?"

"Move!" said Nash. "Let me try."

He passed the Chief of Assistants to the twins and squared himself. Then he picked his foot up and stomped as hard as he could.

Nothing happened.

He stomped again, this time a crackling bolt rushed forth and crashed into the door. The door held fast, with only a scorch mark to show for the effort.

Darcy leaned against it and pushed, hoping that Nash had, at least, jiggled the lock.

"Hey, help me push, will you?"

Liev, Charlie, and Nash—Lisa was left holding the monster-servant—put their shoulders to the door. All four pushed with everything they had, but it still wouldn't budge.

"Maybe we should try the woods again," said Lisa from behind them.

The others stopped pushing and leaned against the wall to catch their breath.

"I mean, we tried, right? It'll take longer now, but we could still go in through the trees and look for a hole in the gate."

"No," said Darcy, stubbornness kicking in. "We're right here. If we could just. . . ."

She started shoving again.

"Nash, see if you can aim at the lock and zap it. I'll push. Maybe together we can get the lock to let go a little more."

"I might hit you, though."

"Try it!" whispered Lisa.

Liev laughed. Darcy scowled.

She shook her head and backed up before attempting to ram the door. "Just try—" She screamed, but the sound was cut off as she fell into the door. Literally, fell *through* the door. She disappeared into the stone, except her legs, which were still sticking out at the bottom of the wall. The rest of Darcy had melted into the door.

Fearful for what they just witnessed, the others backed away with caution.

Darcy—or, at least, Darcy's legs—shifted into a kneeling position. As she stood to her feet, the rest of her body appeared again, moving through the door as easily as moving through air. She turned around, a concerned expression on her face.

Charlie, Nash, and the Vadiknovs watched as Darcy placed an experimental hand on the door and pushed. She pushed harder. Then she stopped and gently placed both hands against it and walked straight through the stone and cast iron.

"I guess that means Darcy's gifted," Lisa said, sour.

Darcy's face re-appeared on their side of the door. She projected a fiendish grin, which freaked everyone out.

"Hey guys, I think I have an idea!"

She disappeared again and, a moment later, they could hear mechanisms inside the door grating back and forth. Darcy phased back through the closed door and waved for them to come over.

"Help me!"

They did, hopeful, but still creeped out. The door creaked on its old, crusted hinges and swung open, grating against the earthen floor.

Darcy put her hands on her hips, appearing pleased with herself, and led the way into a strange room that looked more like a square cave. Stretching the width of the room in its center was an old metal elevator. A western, abandoned mine shaft came to mind. Above it, the rock was carved out in an endless vertical tunnel, the top of which was cloaked in darkness.

"Coooool," said Charlie and Nash at the same time.

"How do we work it?" Lisa asked, examining the aged machinery that consumed half the space in the room. Liev stayed close to her as they secured the Chief of Assistants between them.

Nash was looking toward the opposite side of the shaft, where an old-fashioned generator had been installed as a power source.

"There's a lever over here!" Nash tried to pull it, but it was jammed. "Someone want to help me out?"

Charlie pulled on the lever with him. It took all their strength, but the lever scraped into the "ON" position. A puff and a sputter and a crackle of electricity, and the generator shuddered. It fell silent, except for a slight hiss.

Lisa looked over the jumble of machinery. "Great job, guys."

Nash crossed his arms over his chest. Then he had an idea. Uncrossing his arms and facing the lift's generator, Nash stomped. An electric stream shot from his foot to the generator, and the contraption clambered to life again.

Charlie clapped Nash on the back. "Nice work. Come on, everyone!" He was first to jump in the lift.

Lisa looked apprehensive. How much juice could one stomp

give?

"How do we know this thing's not going to sputter out when we're halfway up, and drop us?"

Liev grinned. "Like a freefall ride at the fair? Wouldn't that be fun?"

She huffed and got in, dragging Liev and their hostage with her.

When they were all in, Nash pulled down the metal screen. Charlie pushed the crude green button shaped like an up-arrow.

The elevator jerked upward, then down, then flew up several feet before sputtering and evening out to a steady, and slow, pace toward their unknown destination. Frightening as it was, everyone had plastered themselves to the floor. This made the ride worse, as the floor was layered with dust and grime over planks that were rotting through.

"See?" Nash said as the large metal box was swallowed by the vertical tunnel. The room they had entered was no longer visible below. Rough-cut walls of the stone shaft were all they could see. "It works!"

Lisa rolled her eyes. "How comforting."

The stranger had been writing. His study was dark, silent. Calm.

So the faint crash that caught his ear was jarring. His hand hovered over the small, thin mirror that laid face down on his desk. It was an artifact he had found in the old mansion, and one he had determined would come in handy.

With reverence, he placed the mirror in its protective box. He doubted the mirror would be needed for whatever had caused the crash. It sounded too clumsy. Human, probably.

He shook his head. It was just as well. He'd been expecting the company.

He reached for his modified, runic shotgun, though, just in case.

The stranger walked toward the library in the Head Wing. If they were arriving in that old elevator, he would have plenty of time.

Chapter 11

Traveling in a cramped, dust-ridden, and rickety lift that grated against stone walls as it poked upward did nothing to sooth already frayed nerves.

"Get off!"

"Quit pushing!"

"AAAAH!"

THUMP, THUD, THUNK.

Charlie, Nash, and Darcy fell out of the elevator as soon as Nash lifted the metal screen.

"Remind me not to do that again," growled Darcy, rubbing her elbow.

Lisa wedged in a bit of sarcasm. "Just remember, I suggested we take the wooded route, but you insisted on your elevator. So stop your whining."

Charlie looked up, sliding his legs beneath him. "Where are we?"

"Dunno," said Darcy, ignoring Lisa's sentiment.

Lisa moved forward, only to trip on Nash. She managed to maintain her balance, bracing against Liev and the Chief of Assistants. The monster squeaked and huffed, being stretched and scrunched between the twins.

"I can't see a thing."

"I noticed," muttered Nash.

She pulled out her book light, shining it into the darkness, but there was nothing for them to see.

"Everyone spread out, look for a door or something," said Charlie.

"Hey!" Liev exclaimed, after a short, blind search. His hand rounded over what felt like a doorknob. "I think I found a way out."

In that moment, the door flung wide, pulling Liev forward.

"Out!" said the silhouette of a man standing in the doorframe. "Everyone out, slow and easy, in single file!"

It was the stranger.

He was unlike anything any of them had expected. The man looked rabid. His white hair defiant, framing a time-worn countenance. Crystal-blue eyes pierced their souls from deep-set and craggy facial features. He was wiry and short and older than their parents, but the half-crazed look in his eyes told them he could take them all on. At the same time. With his hands behind his back.

They did exactly as he said.

They'd come expecting to fight, but the stranger had caught them by surprise. His strange-looking weapon didn't help their confidence.

The stock sat against his shoulder, sights trained on the floor at their feet. It wasn't ordinary by any stretch, but a custom-crafted weapon with strange, rune-like symbols carved into the wood. The barrel was sawed off, and there was duct tape on the stock. There was something gritty and graceful about it—supernatural, almost.

Nash would have shared one of his newfound bolts of electricity with the stranger, but Liev was in the direct path of his aim. Darcy wondered if she could slip through and catch the man off guard. She weighed her risk and decided not to try anything rash.

The five teens slumped as they walked, defeated. They had been in Hunter's Key no more than five minutes, and already failure had found them.

Lisa and Liev walked out last, still holding the Chief of Assistants. The dark stranger looked between them and saw the monster, the black-white energy still flickering on and off around his little frame. The wily man gawked for a second, and then lowered his weapon.

"You!" he growled.

The Chief of Assistants hissed in response, not bothering to struggle against his bonds.

"Glad to see you've found your way back, scab. Looks like you had some help this time."

After a short walk, they were lined up against the wall, next to an old sofa.

With nobody between him and the stranger, Nash was waiting for the right opportunity to stomp his foot. He wasn't sure how accurate his aim was, and he had yet to master the ability. If he stomped and nothing happened, it would likely be the last chance he got.

In the midst of the ruckus, Charlie's head began to pound again. Blood felt as if it were going to drum through his head until it reached his ears. It was his nose, however, that began to bleed.

His eyes felt as if they were being pierced with a thousand shards.

Charlie pulled and swatted at his eyes, gasping and cringing, then threw his hands out in front of him like he was shielding himself from an attack, all the while reaching to grab hold of something.

He fell to the floor, shivering in cold sweats. His eyes flickered, closed tight one second and open wide the next—bloodshot. Charlie recoiled as if he was being assailed by flashing bursts of light. Continuing to swat at things that weren't there, he whimpered about a throne room and something that sounded like, *"not again."*

117

Nash and Darcy jumped to Charlie's side, concerned, but the stranger raised his weapon toward them.

"Back, both of you, leave him be! There's nothing you can do for him now."

They glared at him, but obeyed.

"Now then," the man said. He lowered his shotgun with the barrel-end on the ground and leaned on it like a cane. "Would you mind telling me what you're doing in my house?"

Chapter 12

Your house?" Darcy spat, diplomacy escaping her. "This is my house."

The stranger raised an eyebrow and smiled, amused. "Is that so?"

"It is! I'm Darcy Witherington, the mayor's only child. Hunter's Key is rightfully mine."

"Does that matter right now?" interrupted Nash. "Something's wrong with Charlie. We need to help him!"

"I told you, there's nothing you can do for the boy," said the gruff man.

He honed his gaze in on the domovoi, noticing for the first time the bloody word, *VISVS*, smeared on his forehead.

"Well, well, we have ourselves a spy."

The Chief of Assistants drew his head into a hunch between his shoulders and growled as the dark stranger took off his jacket and tossed it to the twins.

"Wrap this around his head. Make sure he can't see anything."

After they wrapped his head, he flicked the Lesser monster's head and demanded, "You, scab, be useful and tell them what's wrong with the boy."

"The fledgling," the monster hissed. "His gift is surfacing."

"What gift?" Nash asked. Whatever was happening to Charlie, it hardly looked like a gift.

"The gift of Sight. Horrible thing, it is. A dangerous gift to live with, especially for a *human*." The Chief of Assistants chuckled and licked his lips.

"That's enough for now," the dark stranger growled. He turned to Nash. "Happy, kid? Now let him be and let's move on, shall we?"

Nash scowled in reply. He and the others had stumbled into their gifts by happenchance. Why was Charlie suffering for his?

Hunter's Key's lone resident looked the disheveled group over with a critical eye.

"It's time you bunch are educated. You've trespassed on the Key's grounds, and yet you're all still alive and in good health. No doubt you had some sort of authority coming here. A key to that elevator, perhaps?"

"That's right," said Darcy, hands on her hips. "My father's key. Just like this is my father's house."

"Right. I'm already weary of your waggling tongue. Here's your first lesson of the evening."

The man stretched out his hand and pinched his thumb and forefinger together. In that moment, Darcy's mouth closed and she was no longer able to open it.

"Mff mmm hchchcmmm!" she attempted, but to no avail. "Mmmf? Mmckmck . . . *Mmckmckmck!*"

The others were speechless, but not due to their captor's strange magic. Rather, they cowered in fear and wonder. What kind of man was this that could hush Darcy Witherington?

"Now, I can hear myself think," said the stranger. "Hunter's Key was built with protective wards molded into its construction and around the surrounding property. You should never come here without my permission or another form of proper authority.

Otherwise, the Key will incapacitate you."

"Incapacitate, how?" asked Lisa.

The man ignored her.

"But since you're here — and alive — it's time you know the truth. I've been waiting for you. My name is Loch, and I am the keeper of this fortress. The rest you'll learn over hot cocoa. You all need it, by the looks of you. Follow me. And if any of you have any special abilities that might compromise my personal well-being, I'd appreciate you refrain from using it until you're wiser to your circumstances."

Loch turned his vision to Nash. The iris of his right eye flashed red for a twinkling, too fast for any of the teens to notice. He saw beyond the physical realm and recognized the boy's gift to be combat-oriented.

This is good, he thought. *A natural fighter would serve the group well in the days to come.*

Loch turned and opened a door. Nash hoisted Charlie up from the floor and gestured for Darcy, still numb with shock, to help him. She slipped her head under Charlie's other arm and together they guided him forward.

Most frightening were Charlie's eyes. Everyone noticed earlier that his eyes were inflamed and irritated, but now they were unnaturally wide. Only his pupils remained unchanged — tiny dots in a sea of crimson.

The five followed Loch, who waited for them at the door. Even in their uncomfortable situation they were awestruck by Hunter's Key. Loch had led them to the Library, which was massive, overwhelming..

It was built to be a circular atrium, with open visibility from the ground floor to the ceiling. Five balconies were stacked to overflowing with books, books, and more books. It was enough to make the twins forget they were escorting a monster.

No sight they saw after that was less grand. Loch led them from the Library through a hallway lined with stained-glass windows, and lit by cast-iron torches.

Every door was fashioned from oak, with unpolished brass adornments setting striking contrast to the natural character of the wood. Marble stairways were lined with silver or gold railings throughout, and each room in the Key depicted hand-carved walls crafted with depictions of monsters and historical accounts of battles waged throughout the ages.

As they walked, Nash glanced at Charlie, cringing at the ghastly sight of his friend's eyes.

"Charlie?" he whispered. "Can you hear me?"

To his horror, Charlie's head made a slow pivot on his neck, and with his eyes widening even further, he slipped into the deepest places of Nash's mind. He didn't speak, he just stared, his pupils penetrating everything hidden in Nash's soul. Nash began to sweat, and his breath labored in short gasps. Nothing he had encountered was as disturbing or haunting as Charlie's eyes.

Nash looked away, and remained silent from that point on.

The Dark Prince realized something was wrong.

The old hunter had blinded his servant, but the varcolac was cunning. As long as the twin fledglings held his servant, he could extend his power to see through them.

But then he felt someone invade his own mind. The boy. The boy was looking through the varcolac's eyes—not by practiced magic, but by the gift of Sight.

Panicked, the prince covered his face. A grave scowl darkened his face and in a rage he threw his marble throne across the room, shattering the royal chair and the pillar it collided with.

The ancient prince took a breath to calm himself — stirring the dust in his lungs—and spoke the words that would protect him from being spied upon by the boy's developing gift of Sight.

The young humans had discovered their gifts, and now their leader had emerged from among them. The varcolac cursed in the dim light. He could not allow this to go any further.

"Well, it wasn't the grand tour," Loch said, shutting the door behind the twins as they entered an expansive kitchen. "We'll get to that later. For now you need to know the mess you've gotten yourselves into."

He looked at Nash, who set Charlie on an available barstool. Charlie slumped, but managed not to fall off the seat.

"You, boy," said Loch. "Go look in those cabinets over there. I assume you know how to make hot chocolate?"

Nash glowered as he pulled a giant jar of cocoa powder from the top shelf. "I have a name, you know."

"Oh, you do? It hadn't occurred to me. What's your name, then?"

"Nash."

"Parents only give you one name, eh?"

"Stormstepper."

"Ah yes, well, it matches the attitude. Who's the boy with the eyes?"

"Charlie. Sullivan."

Loch nodded. The five would need a leader, and Charlie, having the rarest gift of all, would emerge as that leader. His gift of Sight would guard and guide them through lightless days and lonely nights. He would require extra training, focused counsel.

"And you two." He waved at the twins. "Who are you supposed to be, Paper and Ink?"

"Lisa Vadiknov," said Lisa.

"Liev Vadiknov," said her brother.

"Twins. Joy. All right, to get started—oh wait, and you are?" he began, looking at Darcy. "Oh, that's right. You can't speak. Never mind."

Darcy crossed her arms, struck a defiant pose, and scoured a look that communicated every word she was unable to speak at the moment.

"To begin with, you five ninnies trespassed the residence of an elder monster hunter. That would be me, in case you were still confused. I've been here for a couple years now, looking for a specific beast. I see you caught a Lesser monster yourselves," gesturing to the domovoi.

"I'm guessing you've managed to figure out this has something to do with the missing persons from the last couple of years. Am I correct?"

"We have," said Liev.

"Good. Now, the monster I'm after is a tricky one. There's a portal behind the Key, but I can't get through. I'm not certain what has taken up residence on the other side of that portal, but I know for sure that it's a Greater. If I'm correct—and pray I'm dead wrong—then this little tomte is one of the beast's many servants."

"Tomte?" Lisa asked questioningly.

"Yes, miss. That'd be the thing you and your albino brother are holding between you."

"No, this is a domovoi."

Loch arched his wild, gray eyebrows.

"You know, I'm impressed you know that. It *is* a domovoi, if you speak Russian. But if you're a Scot, you'll know it as an uruisg. If you're a Swede, perhaps you'll call it a tomte. Remember, just like humans, monsters appear in every region of our world. Different folk call 'em different names. Capiche?"

Beneath his makeshift blindfold, the Chief of Assistants raised a proud chin, unimpressed with any human's comprehension for what he was. *What do these crude humans know of my beauty and regal line?* he murmured in his mind.

"Now I've told you what I'm doing here, it's your turn. What were you hoping to achieve by breaking into my house?"

"We were coming to kill the varcolac," said Lisa.

Loch paled. "Varcolac! What varcolac?"

Instead of telling him, Lisa rolled her eyes and removed the diary from beneath her jacket and pushed it across the countertop, centered in Loch's view. The tiny Exsecrifer dragon was still curled on the spine.

Loch picked the book up, hands trembling.

He knew the varcolac she spoke of. When he arrived in Hunter's Grove, Loch knew the possibilities. But there had been a glimmer of hope the Dark Prince would never return. That he'd been starved out.

Loch poured through the weathered pages of the diary, while Nash served steaming hot cocoa in silver goblets studded with gemstones he found in the cupboard. He made a cup for Charlie too, and sat next to him after he served everyone else.

"I'm not sure he'll need that," said Liev, solemn.

"I can hear you," Charlie said in a strained whisper.

Everyone jumped at the sound of his hollow, distant voice — except for Loch, who was too immersed in the varcolac's diary to hear anything else in the room.

"Thank you, Nash," said Charlie, though his cup remained untouched. He stared, unblinking, at the stone-tiled floor.

Loch continued reading, the pages crackling with each turn. Nash was restless, so he found soap and a rag and washed the pot he used to heat the cocoa.

Charlie blinked. No one saw it, but the whites of his eyes began to reappear. His breathing quickened; not quite a regular rhythm, but less comatose.

The Chief of Assistants squirmed. The twins had let go of him, but he was sitting snug between them. He rubbed his slinky arms, which stung from their black-white bonds. The courtly servant sniffed at their hot cocoa, his senses dancing. He liked what he smelled.

Raising a long finger, he produced a small, polite cough.

"Eh, dearest young human," his thin voice beckoned Nash.

"Name's Nash."

"Yes, silly me, yes...*Nash*...ah, what, please reveal, is that lovely liquid? Be any remaining for you to share with a humble servant?"

Loch snapped the diary shut. He marched over and ripped the jacket from over the Chief of Assistant's head. The monster's pupils constricted in the sudden light. Loch grabbed the wet rag that Nash had been using and tried to wipe the bloody word from the monster's forehead, but it didn't work. The dishrag hissed and steamed, as if it had been placed on a burning stovetop.

Loch threw the rag in the sink and raised the Chief of Assistants by his scrawny shoulders, shaking him.

"You! Scab! What's your name?"

The creature growled, shaking his head in frenzy. Names were not to be revealed to humans, especially hunters. They could be used against a monster in many different ways.

"You'll tell me if you know what's good for you! Or should I get some salt? I know I have some in one of these blasted cabinets. Boy—Nash—do me a favor and look on that shelf over there, will you? There should be—"

"No! *No! Dräng!* My name...is Dräng," he panted. Loch waved Nash off the search for salt.

"*Dräng, eh?* You're the one I've seen lurking about the grounds, aren't you? And there are more of you, aren't there? Don't lie!"

The Chief of Assistants hesitated before offering a shameful nod.

"Tell me, Dräng, your master wrote this diary, yes?" He waved the diary in the Lesser monster's face. "What's your part in all of this?"

Loch knew what he was doing. For one, having Dräng's name would force the little beast to give an honest answer. Also, Dräng's kin were mischievous creatures, but not inherently evil. Accusing him of kidnapping and murder would summon a guilt trip, which the tomte would be quick to show.

Still, there was a grimace on Dräng's face as he spoke.

"I am the master's Chief of Assistants! I am loyal! I keep records,

I run errands, and I-I-I am only his assistant. I simply mark the targets! It's the Collectors who take them to the master. Not me!"

Just as Loch had suspected, guilt overwhelmed Dräng. This Lesser, he thought, could prove to be useful. After reading the diary, Loch knew these five young hunters-to-be would need all the help they could get. And if the tomte was indeed the chief servant to the Dark Prince, his knowledge of the Otherworld would be invaluable.

Loch decided to try a new approach.

"Tell me, Dräng." He poured on the sympathy. "Do you like what you do?"

The Chief of Assistants stared at the man in horror. He knew the master was listening. He wanted to tell the truth, that he hated marking the humans for such a fate, but what would the master do to him if he admitted it to the humans? His treachery would be a death sentence, and the master was known for his inventive death sentences.

Loch pressed. "Well?"

Dräng sputtered, then clamped his mouth shut. His jaw bandied up and down, up and down, soundless. Then he wrapped his arms around his head, cringing in fear.

"N-*n-n-no*. I don't like any of it."

Instantly, the terrified little monster heard — no, *felt* — the master's burning anger.

"Well that's good to hear. Maybe you can help us, yes?"

The stubby devil did not answer. He was staring, defeated, at the floor. He pondered how much longer he would live, and if his death would be quick.

Darcy stood up abruptly, knocking her seat over without accident. Grumbling through sealed lips, she pointed an urgent finger, spilling her cocoa.

Everyone saw what she was pointing at. The varcolac's diary was spewing rays of light between its covers. Loch reached over and flipped it open to the illuminated page. New words were being inscribed, their fiery glow lighting up the kitchen:

> *Be warned, hunter. If you continue prying into my private affairs,*
> *my hell hounds will be at your doorstep.*
> *Stay away.*

Chapter 13

Loch stood motionless, staring at the page.

The Chief of Assistants chose that moment to flee. Using a magic common to his kind, Dräng summoned a glow that spread over the twins' chairs. The chairs zipped several feet away from him in opposite directions, his captors now imprisoned in their seats.

He bolted from his seat, ducking Loch's grasp as he ran. Dräng stomped the hunter's toes and blasted him with a flash of light from his palm, sending Loch reeling backward and stunned.

He paused in front of Darcy, pretending to look for the door, all the while knowing precisely what he wanted to accomplish.

Darcy tackled the frantic monster, and Dräng fell effortless under her weight. Careful not to swallow the blood, he bit deep into her arm.

In shock, Darcy phased, and the trickster passed through her arms, his feet slapping hard against the kitchen tiles as he ran. Shards of lightning flew above his head and he was thankful the Stormstepper boy had yet to master his gift.

Dräng was at the door, his escape assured, when to his alarm, his feet were lifted from the floor. He ran until he couldn't breathe, feet swimming in the air, unable to move forward or backward. He looked down to his feet in dismay at his lack of progress, and let his impish legs go limp.

Nash helped Lisa, Liev, and Darcy off the floor before turning to see the old hunter standing, his fist outstretched gripping the air. He sight was fixated on Dräng. It was clear that Loch had employed a supernatural binding, levitating the monster in the air.

"I'll be back," said Loch. "Stay here, all of you. The Key can be dangerous for those who get lost in her halls. I'm going to secure this one where he's safe. Safe from his master, and safe from me!"

He left them stunned at what they had witnessed and, one by one, measured their steps back to their seats. Darcy tried speaking, found she could not, and buried her head in her arms.

"Hey guys," said Charlie, his voice weak. His eyes were still tinged with red, but they could see he was returning to normal. "What happened?"

Nash shook his head. "Man, you really gave us a scare."

Except for Darcy, they took turns telling Charlie everything that had happened since entering Hunter's Key. It was as much for Charlie's sake as it was for theirs. He took a sip of his cocoa—which was no longer hot—before being bombarded with their questions.

"What happened to you?"

"Do you know what happened to your eyes?"

"Could you hear us or see us?"

Charlie shivered, staring at his knees. His irises were still shrouded in red.

"I'm not sure what happened. I mean, I guess I've got a gift after all. I just started seeing things all of a sudden. It's like I could see through someone else's eyes. Then, I realized I was looking at myself, from your eyes," he gave a nod to Nash.

Nash flushed pale, spooked.

Charlie continued. "I think it was because you were closest to me. I saw what you saw."

Charlie shivered again, remembering what else he'd seen. A vision of a fierce battle raged in his mind, and a death—the same as his nightmares. He was too afraid tell them. Maybe another time.

"You looked like you were in pain," said Nash.

"You can't imagine," said Charlie. "It felt like my eyes were trying to squeeze out of my head and multiply. At one point I was seeing what all of you saw, all at the same time. It hurt, like there were too many people sharing my head."

His friends listened and tried to show their concern. None of their gifts had been painful to acquire. Truth be told, they were afraid, but they all felt that something was different, special, with Charlie.

Darcy pushed an experimental finger through the kitchen counter, still amazed with her own ability, and making sure it was still there.

"And there was something else," Charlie said, sitting up straight.

His irises had relaxed to a reddish brown, and his pupils were restoring to their usual size.

"It wasn't inside the Key. I think I was seeing what the varcolac was seeing. He was sitting in this great big hall, with a quill in his hand. And then everything got jumbled. He stood up and it was like all of the light had gone out. I think he knew. I caught a few glimpses after that but they were blurry, like he was trying to keep me out."

"That's freaky," said Nash from his place by the sink. "But kind of cool, too."

Lisa sat forward. "The domovoi, Dräng, he said it was called the Sight."

"He was right," bellowed Loch from the doorway.

That they were startled was an understatement.

133

"It is the Sight. Quite a remarkable gift, and not one that's common." He stared at Charlie, distant and lost in thought, making Charlie more than uncomfortable.

Loch was sure now. Charlie was the one. The Sight was not simply a gift. It was a calling, of sorts. It certainly was not something one sought out on purpose. Many hunters considered it a curse. Either way, it was a powerful gift, only found in hunters with great potential.

He would have to teach the boy everything. He would have to teach them all.

Loch broke from his thoughts. "It's half past ten. You should go home and get some rest.

"Go home and rest?" snorted Lisa. "After all we've seen? I, for one, still have questions."

"Fair enough, but no doubt you've all had a big day, so go home and get your bearings. I'll expect you all back here tomorrow. There is much to do, and not much time left to do it. So, tomorrow?"

None of them agreed or disagreed, but he knew their answer.

"Come to Frederickson Street tomorrow afternoon at five o'clock sharp. You all have some learning to do. I'll show you the way out and you can be on your way."

When they reached the steps beyond the castle's front doors, he pointed them to the section of woods where they had hid the night before.

"There's a small hole in the gate covered by a bush. It isn't far from where you were attempting to hide last night. You know your way down from there, don't you?"

They all looked at the woods, embarrassed.

"Frederickson Street, tomorrow. Five o'clock!"

They turned to go.

"Oh," Loch added, feigning forgetfulness. "And Darcy?"

Darcy turned and leveled a sour look at Loch.

"You can speak now."

He slammed the massive doors before she could say anything.

Chapter 14

Charlie had worn sunglasses during school, with a note from the nurse's office saying he'd suffered a bump on the head, making him "sensitive to light." Mrs. Pinkerly was unhinged that she had no say in the matter, given the official nature of the note. With his eyes shaded, she couldn't tell when he wasn't looking at the board, or the floor, or her mismatched socks for that matter. It also meant that Charlie was allowed to leave class five minutes before the bell so that he could escape the chaos of the hallways between classes. At last, Charlie had the upper hand in Mrs. Pinkerly's class.

He considered getting "a bump on the head" more often.

At exactly five minutes before the final bell, Charlie dashed to the classroom door and flashed a hearty "See ya!" to Mrs. Pinkerly. She bristled with anger, knowing she was powerless to stop him.

Charlie made a rapid exit from the school campus and, after a pitstop home, jogged across Certifus Street until he was under the gnarled trees of Frederickson. Under cover of the trees, he removed his sunglasses and found the black car waiting, silent and mysterious. He hesitated, remembering the times he'd seen this car drive up to the Key, speculating about the driver. Finding the door unlocked, he climbed into the front passenger seat.

"It's about time," Loch muttered from the driver's seat. He kept his eyes on the rearview mirror, watching for the others.

Nash crossed the street and approached the vehicle, with Lisa and Liev on his heels. Lisa had the book about the history of Hunter's Key back in her possession, Charlie noticed, as they piled into the back seat.

"How's the hand?" asked Charlie, pointing to Liev's bandaged thumb.

"It's fine," said Liev. "Lisa thinks it's infected, but she's paranoid."

Lisa huffed at her brother, scooting him aside so she could fit in the backseat.

That left Darcy. Charlie was concerned she wouldn't show, but just as the concern entered his mind, she trotted around the corner with her arms crossed and chin held high. It was clear she was still less than happy about being muted the night before.

Showing off her newfound ability, Darcy slid into the back passenger seat of the car without opening the door.

"Hey!" cried Lisa, as Darcy slipped through her as well. Lisa pushed her brother further, squishing both Liev and Nash into the other door, and shifted to make space for Darcy.

"Don't. Do. That!" Lisa demanded, unnerved that Darcy phased through her.

For once Darcy said nothing, and just smiled.

"All in?" asked Loch. "Good. Now hold on."

They held the door straps, the backs of the seats, each other, and anything else they could use as an anchor as the car rocketed over the rough terrain.

Not far from where the car had been parked, Donnie Wickles hid behind a tree. He had been curious while watching Charlie Sullivan and his new acquaintances the past two days. He could tell something was going on, and he wanted to know what.

His curiosity measured off the charts when he observed the five teenagers getting into a black car at the edge of the woods leading to Hunter's Point.

When he saw Darcy jump into the backseat—without opening the door—Donnie tripped backward and fell to his butt in shock. He rubbed his eyes, unable to believe what he saw. He sat, trembling in fear, as the car raced up the hill toward Hunter's Key.

After a few moments, Donnie stood up. Still trembling, pieces of his own past began to make sense as he thought about his uncle, Hunter's Key, and all the people who had gone missing. Suddenly he regretted everything he'd said over the years about the missing people in Hunter's Grove.

To witness Darcy Witherington slipping through the back door like that, perhaps Donnie's uncle had not been crazy after all. And if Donnie's uncle hadn't been crazy—if his tales about monsters and superhuman powers were true—how could Donnie get his hands on a power of his own?

Donnie Wickles made a decision.

"I think I prefer walking," Liev commented from the back seat.

The car came to an abrupt stop. The passengers flew forward, only to be choked back by their seatbelts.

Loch got out of the car and walked to the gate while the group looked on. It was as foreboding in the daylight as it was under the gaze of the moon.

Loch unlocked the padlock and proceeded through the lengthy process of getting through the gate.

"You do that every time?" asked Charlie as Loch buckled himself in.

"Of course. Why wouldn't I?"

"Just looks tedious."

"That gate, when locked, could keep out a werewolf and any manner of supernatural beast, and not just because of the silver chain used to lock it. The original hunters of this area put protective wards all over that gate as well as the Key. Though, some of those wards have grown weak over the years. I do what I can to keep them alive."

The car drove past the trees and entered the courtyard, revealing the Gothic grandeur of Hunter's Key. It looked less sinister by day, but still overwhelming. Little did they know the Key had become more accepting of their presence, since Loch had invited them.

"That reminds me," Loch continued. "Have any of you wondered why it's called Hunter's *Key*?"

"No. Why?" asked Nash.

"Right. Take a good look at the place."

They did. Whatever Loch was getting at, though, it was lost on them.

"Cool gargoyles," said Liev, looking at the stone grotesques sitting atop the three towers.

"Don't look at them," said Loch.

"Why not?"

"Nash," said Loch, clearly ignoring the question. "Do me a favor and open that garage. See the chain? Just pull it."

Nash did, and Loch pulled the car in behind him. Once inside, Loch took the responsibility of closing it.

The garage looked like a renovated stable. It was filled with old saddles and buckets hanging along the walls, along with modern mechanical tools.

"Follow me," Loch waved.

He led them through a door at the far back wall of the garage. "This," he continued, "is the Teeth Wing Hallway. We're on the bottom floor —"

"Teeth Wing?" Liev asked with a smile.

"Yes, also known as the East Wing, but we'll call it the Teeth Wing. As I was saying —"

Liev couldn't help himself.

"*Thennn*, what do we call the West Wing?"

"The Head Wing! Stop interrupting me!"

Charlie noticed a spear propped against a door jamb. He could have sworn it whispered his name.

"What's that?" he asked, reaching for it.

"That old thing? It was a good weapon at one time. But that was a long time ago," Loch said, shifting his conversation back to the layout of the Key. "Directly above us is the Teeth Wing Tower. But you don't need to see the towers today."

A chorus of sad moaning halted Loch. He stopped and looked at them.

"What?" he said in disbelief. "You want to walk up twelve flights of stairs?"

"Twelve?" asked Charlie. "Is that all?"

Loch huffed, "Fine. Follow me." He muttered something about babysitting schoolchildren.

Revealing a hidden stairwell in the back corner of the hall-way — up, up, up they went. Passing three different landings, they came to a sloped trapdoor.

Beyond the trapdoor was the roof of Hunter's Key, higher up than Charlie had realized.

The roof was a long battlement, with palisade walls as high as their knees on either side. The five teens looked down the walkway, to where the three towers of the Key stretched to the sky. Loch raised his voice to regain their attention as they were frozen in wonder and delight. Most people spent a lifetime in admiration of the Key, only ever seeing it from the perspective of the town below.

"Are you going to dally there all day?" he yelled, standing on the uneven steps of the tower.

Loch waited for one of them to look down and point out the shape of the Key, but no one ever did. He couldn't blame them. The stairs of the Teeth Wing Tower were crooked, uneven, and high in altitude. No one wanted to look down, period.

They reached another trap door that opened onto a circular balcony. The view was breathtaking. They could see the mountains surrounding Hunter's Grove, with the little town nestled below. Behind the Key was a garden that had long run wild, with a small white bridge connecting to a restless, glistening lake.

A single stone archway led into the tower's only room. To every-one's dismay, there were some chairs, oil lamps, and a desk with writing utensils, but not much more. The only interesting things were dusty crossbows hanging on the wall, and strange white stones with leather straps scattered across the desk. The stones were circular and smooth with holes in the middle, like tiny doughnuts.

"There, are you happy now?" asked Loch.

Darcy frowned. "This is it?"

"I'm not sure what you were expecting, but yes. This is a watch-tower, you see. Watchtower guards are supposed to watch, not play videogames or stare at a TV. If it's something interesting you want, why don't you all pick up those oculi."

"What's an oculi?" asked Nash.

"Those stones with the leather headbands. They are what the watchtower guards would use. No, not you," he said, holding Charlie back as the others rushed to grab the archaic devices. "You need to learn to use your gift."

Charlie frowned, but stood next to Loch. He felt left out, but more than that, he was scared of his gift. The Sight was painful and terrifying, and altogether disorienting.

"Walk out to the balcony, and be careful not to drop those oculi with your butterfingers!"

They group kept a wary distance from the edge of the stone path while Loch instructed them on how to strap the oculi to their heads. "Now, look down," he said.

Several excited gasps bounced through the air, as Nash, Darcy, Lisa and Liev pointed at all the new things they could see, making comments about their discoveries.

"What do I do?" Charlie asked.

"Look down, boy, but don't just look down with your eyes. Imagine *magic*."

Confused, Charlie frowned. He stepped to the edge and tried to imagine.

At first, all he saw was the roof, which only made him dizzy.

Charlie gripped the balcony, afraid he would fall.

"Don't look at what's there, boy. Look at what's unseen. Look at the magic flowing around the Key."

Charlie sighed. How could he see what was unseen?

That thought did it. An explosion of colors began to spread out for what seemed like eternity, and Charlie could see a glimmering sheen envelop everything he could see. He didn't know how, but Charlie understood the colors. Protective wards surrounded the Key, heavy and poised to attack anything that dared to breach the mansion's threshold uninvited.

There were other colors, still dangerous, yet less hostile. They flowed freely, without constraint. Behind the Key, Charlie noticed the white bridge again, his attention attracted to a dim, black light hanging in the air.

It was encased in a pink luster, a shimmering ball of energy. Looking closer, the energy was disintegrating, fraying almost.

He could hear the excitement from the others and looked to where they were pointing. It was easy for him to see the sheen over the roof of the Teeth Wing. He pushed with his mind, looking deeper. It was a powerful magic, he realized. If he used his Sight, he could see through the layer like a window into the Key.

The oculi must have allowed watchtower guards to see inside the Teeth Wing, and Charlie soon realized why. He saw that the bottom floor was home to hundreds of holding cells, probably designed for monsters in centuries past. The Chief of Assistants, Dräng, sat in one cell with what looked like a pail of milk. All the other cells were empty and dirty from years of neglect.

"Charlie!" Nash blurted with excitement. "Charlie, where's your oculi? Here, take mine, you've got to see this!"

"Thanks, I'm good. I can see it."

"Really? How can you—oh—"

Nash broke off when he saw the hollow and unnerving cloud of red in Charlie's eyes again.

"What you're looking at," said Loch, "is a magic screen the builders of Hunter's Key established over the roof. These stone oculi were hand-crafted and spelled to work with that screen. With this installed, the watchers on this battlement could see inside the Key and keep guard over *everything*. Of course, any watcher who happened to have the Sight, like Charlie here, wouldn't have needed a stone."

Everyone except Nash turned to stare at Charlie. They saw his eyes, and decided to stop staring.

"You can probably see this area also served as sleeping quarters and a storage attic. I haven't had time to go through it all, but you can bet there are valuable artifacts there."

The team shared a conspiratorial grin as they pondered what artifacts they could get their hands on to play with.

Charlie found Dräng's tiny figure again and noticed a hole in the monster's cell floor. Then he noticed that there was a hole in every cell floor.

Lights pulsed in the opening of each hole.

Curious, Charlie pushed further with his mind and saw past the Key, deep into the earth, where the strange lights came from. There were hundreds of them, glowing streams of color, coursing in every direction. He looked to where the lines seemed to come together. It took a moment for his Sight to adjust, but Charlie saw that the lines intersected under the white bridge—under the disintegrating ball of energy.

"Loch, what are those lines running under the ground?"

Loch hesitated. "What lines, Charlie?"

"There are bright lines under the ground. It looks like the holding cells were built over them. And they all come together at—"

"Hold on." Loch stared at the boy in amazement. Most with the gift of Sight wouldn't have been able to see so much so soon, without proper teaching.

"I'll tell you, Charlie. But not now. All in good time, m'boy."

Nash was looking everywhere with his oculi. "What lines are you two talking about?"

"Right, so now that you've seen the Teeth Wing, we should move to the Main Body." Loch flung open the trap door and ushered them through, and onto their long and winding trek down dreaded flights of stairs, across chilly battlements, and through strange rooms.

If the group concluded one thing, it was that much of Hunter's Key seemed like an unfinished jigsaw puzzle. The architecture was mismatched, drawing from equal parts Gothic cathedrals, Roman palaces, and early European manor-houses. It was crooked and disproportionate, as if the place had been built in a rush.

Standing in a dusty attic, Loch pointed out three looming stairwells to their right.

"This is the Main Attic," Loch said. "Think of it as the crossroads of Hunter's Key, where you can go left, right, up, or down. From this room you can get to the battlements along both wings of the Key. Those three stairwells lead up to the Towers from this room, and the middle one also leads down into the main foyer. Seeing as you were there last night, and I'm not letting you into the Towers yet, we'll be moving onto the Head Wing now."

Again, a chorus of groans swept through the group. They wanted to see the insides of the Towers, which were always spooky at night, viewing from the town below. Loch ignored their groaning this time.

The Head Wing's battlement walk was nearly identical to the walk along the Teeth Wing. The difference here was that there was no tower, rather a humongous castle turret instead. It was both shorter and wider than most of the Key's architectural features, like a Roman Coliseum had been attached to the end of the structure.

Loch reached the door leading inside the massive turret and opened it, smiling with pride.

"This," he said, "is the Library."

Loch scooted next to the Vadiknovs.

"I see you two like this room. Besides the eternity of books here, there's something else the Head Wing is home to."

He crossed to a certain book shelf and pulled on a bookend that had the head of a human, a lion's body, and wings — a sphinx. The circular shelf slid to the left, revealing a hidden staircase adorned with lush, red carpeting.

"What lies beyond used to be the war room. I've converted it to use as my study. You'll be spending a lot of time in the war room from now on."

He disappeared behind the wall, climbing the staircase. The group scampered up the steps a quick moment behind.

Chapter 15

The old war room was every bit as big and circular as the Library, but with lower ceilings. Two tables, each long enough to accommodate ten hefty chairs, were pushed to the edge of the room. Loch whisked around an imposing, timbered desk—like an overgrown child with bad manners—and plopped his feet on a chair he had positioned behind the desk for the sole purpose of plopping his feet. Near him were a black journal, an oil lamp, and a gold fountain pen. With discretion, he shoved a thin black box into the top desk drawer and locked it with the war room's master skeleton key.

He waved to the seats around the tables. "Grab yourselves a seat and gather 'round!"

The clamoring of wooden chairs being dragged and scooted across the stone floor was pandemonium. *How could five teenagers make so much noise while simply taking a seat?* Loch thought to himself. He closed his eyes until there was silence, and then opened his eyes and began to speak. "As you might have noticed—"

Creak, CRASH!

Liev lay sprawled on the ground, muttering angry words in his parents' tongue. His chair, with its two rotted legs, crumbled underneath the moment he sat down.

Everyone, including Lisa, let loose a chorus of laughter. Brushing splinters from his white jeans, Liev chose another chair for himself and dragged it next to his sister—somehow making more noise than before.

"Are you finished?" Loch asked.

Liev answered with a bright, sarcastic smile.

"As you might have noticed," Loch attempted again, "Hunter's Key was not built using conventional methods. At first glance, there is no apparent rhyme or reason to it."

"You've got that right," Darcy muttered.

She had been surprised to find the Key in such a state of crooked disrepair. It bothered her and removed some of the mystique about the place.

Loch pulled a large, folded parchment out of a desk drawer and let if fall open on the table before them. Four ornate keys, each the same, were skillfully drafted across the vellum. Each key was drawn resembling a circular head at the top, and a long neck that led into two teeth jutting from the bottom end, with a strange protrusion stretching past the neck. The drawings looked familiar.

Loch smiled as, one by one, he watched comprehension dawn on their faces. The group realized the drawings were not of keys, but of the Key—Hunter's Key!

They were maps. Four different maps for each of the main floors of the mansion. The Library was the Key's round head, with the long hallways and Main Body making up the neck, and the horse stables—now garages—being the "teeth" of the Key.

Nash slapped his forehead.

"That's right," said Loch. "Hunter's Key was built in the shape of a key. Novel, isn't it? There's purpose behind the idea. You see, before Hunter's Grove was founded, this area was the location of a gateway to the Otherworld, the world of monsters. Underneath this very hill are hundreds of ley lines. You, smarty pants," he barked, pointing at Lisa. "I'm guessing you know about ley lines?"

Lisa nodded.

"Tell your friends what they are. Go on, then."

She squared her shoulders, grinning.

"Ley lines are lines of magic that run throughout the earth. Certain creatures can travel through ley lines, but more importantly, many people believe that when these lines intersect, big things happen."

Darcy shook her head. "Big things, *like?*"

"Like gateways," Loch interjected.

Charlie recalled the glowing lines he had seen beneath the Key, intersecting under the white bridge. "Those are the lines I saw."

Loch nodded.

"What lines?" asked Nash.

"Up on the tower," explained Loch, "none of you could see it with the oculi, but Charlie—with the Sight—saw the ley lines."

"Hundreds of them," said Charlie, excited. "A lot of them ran under the Key, where the holding cells were. And all of them met under a white bridge behind the mansion."

"Right," said Loch, taking over. "The builders of the Key built the holding cells above a large grouping of ley lines. There are openings in the floor of each cell. The idea was each cell would be built over a magic current that would suck up monsters traveling across the ley lines. For the most part, it worked. In fact, that little scab you brought with you is residing in one of them now.

"As Charlie noticed, many of these lines converge at a single spot, the small bridge behind the mansion. That's the gateway to the Otherworld. Two hundred years ago, the founders of Hunter's

Grove were trying to stop a monstrous tyrant from passing through. The Dark Prince, the same varcolac whose diary you found, was responsible for the deaths of many good people. After many battles, the hunters were able to push the varcolac and his horde back through the gateway. They held them there long enough to build the Key, a magical construction all to itself. Hunter's Key is what keeps the bridge closed—locked, if you will. But the old magic is waning.

"I was hoping the Dark Prince was still locked away, but this," he said, pulling out the diary, "this book, and the missing persons over the last two years, proves the varcolac's servants are getting through. He'll be trying to get through, too, but I can't let that happen. He's a cruel creature, coming from an old line of varcolaci. The Dark Prince believes he should rule over everything. Even worse, he's mentioned something about 'the Ancients.' If he's talking about what I think he is, he *cannot* be allowed to wake them. They are old gods from a forgotten time that bring the end to everything as we know it. And that's exactly what they'll have in mind if they ever open their monstrous eyes again. The varcolac can't get through the portal yet, but his Lesser servants can."

"What are the Lesser servants?" asked Darcy. "And the Greater? I keep hearing about them."

"The Greater and Lesser are two classes of monsters. If you're a monster, you are one or the other. The designation dictates your social rank, your range of power, and other things. That scabby tomte is a Lesser. The Varcolac Prince? He's a Greater. Lessers are servants and underlings of Greaters. Usually."

"But the Greater can't get through the portal, when the Lesser can?" Charlie asked.

"I believe so. The construction of the Key and its protections are complex, but as far as I can tell the Greater are too big and bulky with their powerful magic and gifts to get through the gateway as long as it's locked. The Key's protective wards are weakening, but are still intact enough to keep Greaters from passing through. On the other hand, some of the Lesser, who are a bit more slippery and who have less bulk, are small enough to slip through the failing wards. The holes in those protective wards are growing larger each day, though. Understand so far?"

A collective, "Yes," was murmured.

"Good. Since you volunteered to kill the village vampire, and were unsuccessful in your first attempt, I'm going to train you how to do it."

An uneasy shift rippled through the gang.

"What do you mean?" asked Lisa.

Loch sighed. It was time for them to know the truth.

"For some reason I, like the varcolac, can't pass through the gateway. I don't understand it. The Key shouldn't block me, but when I try to pass through to the Otherworld, I can't. Perhaps the varcolac is blocking me. Either that or the Key's magic is so old and broken that it's locked the portal both ways. So . . . you're going to do it."

"What?" cried Darcy. "Don't we have any say in the matter?"

"Miss, I believe you have a say in every matter, whether it's yours to say or not."

"So what," asked Lisa, "you're just going to send us over to our doom to try and kill a super-vampire?"

"Didn't you try to do just that last night, of your own accord?" Loch inquired, raising an eyebrow.

"Well, yeah, but—"

"But *what?*"

Lisa closed her mouth.

Charlie stood, commanding their attention.

"We made the decision last night. We decided we couldn't let people keep disappearing, not when we had the power to stop it. Now we find out the varcolac is more powerful than we thought, and that he's about to break through some gateway. Hunter's Grove will be destroyed. We still have a job to do. The only thing that's changed, is that it's more urgent than ever."

Loch watched him with an inner smile. The boy would make an excellent leader—if he lived long enough.

"But that's the problem," said Lisa, serious. "We didn't know the varcolac was that much of a threat. If Loch could subdue us so easily last night, then what will the varcolac be able to do? No offense," she added to Loch.

"None taken," Loch said. "But let me remind you, girl, that the tides of history have often been turned by a select few. With a little hope, an oppressor can be overthrown. I can teach you how to do that—how to fight. But you have to make the choice. Will you run away, cowards? Or will you do what you know in your hearts is right?"

A heavy pause thickened the air between them.

"Well," said Liev. "When you put it that way . . ."

"We'll do it," said Charlie.

Loch nodded.

"I thought you might say that."

Chapter 16

The Chief of Assistants had to use human means of trickery, since none of his magic seemed to work in the cell. After hours of grinding the chain of his shackles against the floor with his ghastly strength, it cracked and broke. With swift movements, Dräng bent a piece of metal into a jagged rod-shape. He shuffled to the cell door and jammed the makeshift blade in the lock, shattering it. The cell door swung open on its hinges.

His master had stopped watching him some time ago, but the Lesser monster was afraid the Prince might try to look through his eyes at any moment. He knew he had to hurry if he was going to be successful.

He took a deep breath, his small heart fluttering. His next move would either be his best thieving yet, or lead to his death.

Looking both ways in the deserted hall of cells, he leapt into a sprint through the prisons of Hunter's Key.

Loch observed each of them display and utilize their gifts. He'd seen or heard about most of their abilities, and was able to coach them in practical and effective uses. The only gift he was unfamiliar with was Nash's storm-stepping—a powerful fighting ability. His primary objective in training was their survival. What they were about to face would be no easy task, even for the most seasoned team of monster hunters, and he had precious little time to work with them.

"You two, Black and White," he called out to the twins. "Your gift is certainly unique, but it's wild. Concentrate on the energy. Make the stream flow solid. And don't be afraid to use it as a weapon. It's more than a binding. Learn to use it separately, as well as together."

The Vadiknovs grunted, intrigued but exhausted.

"Why do we have gifts?" asked Nash after blasting another round of targets with sharp, concentrated bolts of lightning.

"That's a good question," replied Loch. "Many scholarly hunters have asked why humans and monsters are endowed with one or more gifts —"

"No, I mean, why do *we* have gifts? Why did we discover ours, but others never do."

Loch smiled, leaning back in his chair. "An even better question."

"Wait," said Liev. "You're not going to tell us that greatness falls on some people, are you? Because I already knew I was awesome."

"I'm going to ignore that," said Loch. "Every human being has a gift. Some people discover it when they stub their toe on a piece of furniture. Some when they meet the monster hiding under their bed. But most people have forgotten about the boogeyman, or trolls living under the bridge. They've given up on magic and, if we're honest, they've given up on their dreams. It's hard to be extraordinary, Nash, because it involves change. It's easier not to change. So most people never discover their gift, or their purpose in this life. Does that answer your question?"

Nash nodded. "I think so."

Deep thoughts, regrets, and the weariness of the burden he carried creased his forehead. The others felt the weight of Loch's words, and were adrift in a wave of dreams, aspirations, and fears. Focused on the task at hand, Loch brought everyone's attention back to their training.

Charlie wasn't doing well. Fighting wasn't natural to him like it was for Nash. He wasn't confident like Darcy, or scrappy like the twins. Their gifts were more useful in combat, he felt. He was Charlie Sullivan, daydreamer and school loner, with a gift that let him see things. What was he supposed to do with that when a monster charged him?

Darcy broke through Charlie's weak block and struck his shoulder. He winced at the sting.

"Darcy," called Loch. "You and Lisa take a turn."

Darcy nodded, more than happy to pick a fight with Lisa. The two girls sparred, perhaps rougher than they should have.

Loch approached Charlie. "What's wrong, boy?"

Charlie wiped the sweat from his eyes and shrugged. "What do you mean?"

"You seem to be having trouble. What's holding you back?"

"I don't know. I'm not used to it, I guess."

"You're not ready to fight, and yet last night you came here to kill a varcolac?"

Charlie's shoulders slumped. Loch was right. What good was he to them?

The old hunter smiled with a knowing look. "They look up to you, you know."

Charlie stood a little taller. "What?"

"Your friends look to you for direction. I'll bet it was you that brought them together. Am I right?"

"We did what we had to do," said Charlie.

Loch raised an eyebrow. "You're telling me those four put aside their differences and decided to get along by themselves?"

"Well, I guess I suggested . . ." He stopped midsentence, thinking it over.

"And they listened. Whether they realize it or not, they follow your lead. When they walk through that gateway, they'll look to you for direction. You'll be the one that keeps them together. And for that, you have to be strong. Stronger than you've ever dared to be."

Charlie nodded. He was both invigorated and terrified.

Loch patted him on the back. "Now get over there, and show me what you're made of."

The team trained hard for hours. Purpose, and a hint of desperation, saturated the air. Though it was physically draining, they began anticipating and sensing each other's attacks, slipping into each other's defenses. Countering and retreating, parrying and blocking. They began to move as a cohesive unit, and began to respond to one another as though they had been together for years. Loch admitted to himself that he'd never seen anything quite like it, and in such a short span of time.

Hope swelled in his chest.

He also knew from personal experience that being in the Otherworld would strengthen their abilities, natural and otherwise. It would heighten their senses and sharpen their movements. Their gifts would become more potent, and they would be able to think more quickly on their feet. Soon, he thought, they could start weapons training.

Then, he heard an alarm go off. Loch stiffened. The alarm was something he had installed recently, an old, loud thing that he set up with a trip wire in the dungeon cells.

Dräng had escaped.

"That's good for today," Loch said, zipping between them like a tornado, gathering small tools from his desk. "Go home and work on what I've taught you. I have some, er, unexpected business to attend to. And Nash, try not to zap your parents, yes? Make your own way out, and close the passage if you would. Don't touch anything, and no exploring, or I will personally hunt you down."

Just like that, he was gone.

They stood, staring at each other, unsure of what to think.

The group finished up their exercises and made their way to the front door of the Key. Despite the task ahead, spirits were high. In the past three days, they had transformed from small town middle school students to monster hunters-in-training, preparing for the fight of their lives.

The only one of the group not buzzing with nervous excitement was Darcy. Loch had answered a lot of her questions about the supernatural forces they were dealing with. She had even gained insight about why her mother—

Darcy stopped herself mid-thought, wiping tears away so the others would not see.

Loch had not answered every question, nor could he. She knew who could, though.

"Hey guys," said Darcy, stopping them before entering the tree line. "What do you think about stopping in at Tavern's before we turn in for the night?"

Charlie, Nash, Lisa and Liev were shocked. Was Darcy offering to hang out?

"Sure," Liev grinned. "But only if you're buying."

"Oh, I'm not thinking dinner," she retorted. "I'm thinking answers."

Their interest soared.

"What have you got in mind?" asked Charlie.

The Chief of Assistants was long gone by the time Loch reached the edge of the trees. He could see the trail of magic the creature had left in his flight. After running in circles, Loch realized the trail looped back on itself and rounded numerous trees. The little tomte had tricked him.

He cursed.

The Chief of Assistants had escaped.

Some miles away Dräng slowed to a stop. He had used magic to leave a false trail for the hunter, but his magic was weak. These trees were oppressive, uninviting to his kind. It was hard not being able to rely on the full measure of his magic. Fleeing without a trace exhausted the little imp.

It was understandable, then, that when he stopped for a moment his ragged chest heaved with great effort to breathe.

Safe from the hunter, Dräng removed the vial of blood hidden in his tattered robes. It was the girl's blood, the one his master pointed

160

out to him. He had bitten her the night before and was careful to drain the results of his bite into the vial. He also uncovered his master's diary, which he stole while baiting the hunter out of the house.

He felt the master's eyes watching him.

Dräng felt a pang of regret for what he was about to do, but it was the one way he could survive. Otherwise, the Dark Prince would certainly exterminate him.

The Chief of Assistants opened the vial and poured its contents onto the diary's cover. Darcy's blood soaked into the intricate red lines inked into the cover. Wherever the blood flowed, the lines turned a sickly green color, until the entire cover was transformed into an intricate web of emerald.

The monster's face on the cover glowed brighter, alive, ready to complete the Ritual.

In his mind, the Lesser servant heard his master's approval.

Well done, my little liar. Now bring me the book. Soon, the Ancients will rule both worlds, and they will reward you for your part in their release.

The Chief of Assistants felt the Dark Prince withdraw from his mind. He smiled. He would be spared after all.

But Dräng remembered what the Ancients were like, and the true character of his master. *Do I really want to help release them into our worlds?*

Torn and confused, he raised his head to look through the trees at the town of Hunter' Grove. He knew he had to make a decision.

. . . Now.

Mr. Witherington sat at the bar, enjoying a drink and lively conversation with Tavern.

The mayor and Tavern were shocked when a motley group of five teenagers, led by the mayor's daughter, barged into the restaurant.

"Sorry folks," Darcy called out, picking up an empty root beer bottle from a table, "Tavern's is closed for the night."

"Darcy, dear?" asked Mr. Witherington, "Whatever is the ma—"

"I said Tavern's is closed, people! Out!"

By the time the place had cleared, Mayor Witherington and Tavern were too shocked to be angry, and too angry to speak.

"Let's play a game, Daddy dear," Darcy quipped, in her element now. She placed the bottle on the counter with a purposeful *CLUNK,* pointing the narrow opening of the bottle at Mr. Witherington. "Truth, or Dare?" She paused long enough for the question to sink in. "Oh look, it's your turn. I'll take . . . *the truth.*"

Chapter 17

Mr. Witherington cracked a nervous smile, and patted his pockets with a desperate fidget. "The truth? Darcy, I'm not sure I know what——"

"Don't! Don't even start! You knew, didn't you? About Hunter's Key."

Charlie decided to let Darcy do the talking. The others had resolved to do the same.

Stunned, Mr. Witherington looked from Charlie to the Vadiknov twins, and from the twins to Nash. "Darcy, I really don't think we should——"

"Stop it! Just say what it is. How much do you know?"

The rotund man spread his hands outward and forced a chuckle. "I don't know anything."

Darcy took a step back. Even the most stubborn spirit feels the pain of a loved-one lying to you.

She had given him the chance. Now they had passed the point of no return. She picked up the bottle.

"Watch, Daddy." Slow and deliberate, with her free hand, Darcy phased her fingers through the bottle. "Look what I can do."

Tavern gawked in amazement, but Mr. Witherington jumped as if stung by a hornet.

She let the bottle slip through the back of her hand and fall to the floor, shattering in every direction. Charlie and the others were unsure whether this was an accident, or for dramatic effect.

"And I know the truth about the missing people. You let it happen, didn't you?"

Tavern saw the pained expression of William Witherington, and realized the terrible blow his daughter had dealt. "Darcy, your father—"

"And how much did you know, Tavern?"

Before Tavern could respond, Mr. Witherington said something that not even Darcy had expected.

"You remind me so much of your mother. . ."

Darcy stared at him as if he had just turned into a purple pumpkin. Tears welled up in her eyes and her face began to swell. She tried to keep everything inside, under control. They never talked about her mother, especially not in public. Not since her disappearance—the first to go missing when the disappearances started.

Never listed as a kidnapping, it was reported as a car accident. Her red Volkswagen was reduced to charred fragments, barely recognizable from the wreckage, but there was no body. Elizabeth Witherington, Darcy's mother, had simply vanished.

Mr. Witherington buried his face in his hands.

Tavern took over, asking, "Do you remember when people first began to go missing, Darcy?"

"Two years ago," came the automatic reply.

"Our town marked Mrs. Witherington's death as the beginning of our most miserable season as a community. However, the first person actually believed to be kidnapped was Mr. Tonson, the local locksmith. The last anybody had seen of him was in his shop, just before closing time on the night he disappeared."

Two years, Darcy's thoughts were fitting like puzzle pieces revealing a much larger picture. *Two years...*

"What are you saying?" she urged, feeling like her lungs could not expand anymore. "Daddy? What is he saying?"

"She never told me everything," Mr. Witherington said, blubbering into his hands. "I knew some things, but she always had her secrets...said it was for the good of the town...that she was protecting it. I know, I know!"

He wobbled out of his chair, taking hold of Darcy's shoulders.

"Your mother, my Elizabeth...You *know*, Darcy. Think! You know about the Key, and the old man. He came here two years ago. Not long after her death. Don't you remember?"

"The disappearances stopped," said Tavern. "Seven people gone — eight, counting your mother. It stopped after the stranger arrived. Until these last few weeks, at least."

But Darcy was no longer listening to Tavern. She was staring at the shriveled shell that her father had become. Tears coursed down her cheeks as she coughed out some of the grief she'd been holding in.

"You're saying she was a monster hunter, aren't you?"

The others finally understood, having watched the whole scene unfold in a mess of confusion. William Witherington nodded his head in regret against the bar.

Darcy straightened her spine. "Well, so am I."

Her voice cracked, feeling like a rusty nail was caught sideways in her throat. Yet, it felt good to admit it. The news was out, without any doubt or denial. Darcy openly aligned herself with the strange mix of individuals standing behind her, with the dark stranger residing in Hunter's Key, and with a history and lineage of monster hunters centuries before her. Most tangible, she realized a connection — a deep, resonant connection — with her mother. Darcy felt her mother's presence, powerful and watchful, swell in the air around her. She gasped as hope pulled at her heart.

Mr. Witherington's head snapped toward her. His sad expression turned to fear. "What did you say?"

"I'm a hunter now. Like Mom. And I'm going fix this." She turned and looked at the others. "We're going to fix this. We've found the source, and we're going to stop it."

Mr. Witherington shoved both hands into his coat pockets, searching for the necklace box. On this rarest of occasion, he'd left it at home locked away in his desk. He needed something to hold onto, something solid. But it wasn't there.

"Darcy," Tavern pleaded, "you're just kids. What can you do against such things as monsters? Tell us how. Tell us what you've found, and we'll handle it."

"We're not just kids! And you had your chance. If you wanted to help, you could have gone up to the Key and seen Loch about it, but you didn't. Now it's our turn."

She stomped to the door, and paused.

"I'm going home now. Tomorrow," she looked at her new friends, "we are going to end this. Maybe I won't make it back." Her voice grew small, afraid. "But at least I'll know I did the right thing."

The front door to Tavern's Quick-N-Go slammed. Charlie opened it one more time, allowing a gust of frigid air to set its chill against the two already frozen men left standing at the counter. Four teens slipped out realizing they very much needed to go home to be with their families. Darcy had lit the fuse. The full weight of their decisions pressed down on them. Tomorrow they would enter the Otherworld.

Tonight they would share what could possibly be the last night with those they held most dear.

Charlie prepared three cups of hot chocolate, carrying two upstairs, knocking on the door to his father's study. He entered and set one of the mugs on the desk, where his father was fleshing out his next novel.

Mr. Sullivan was an author of thrillers, and he always let Charlie read chapters of his books as he completed them.

"Thanks," said Mr. Sullivan, rubbing his bleary eyes and taking a sip. He stood from his swivel high-back chair and stretched his stiff muscles.

"It's a cold night," Charlie said, crossing to the window. Flakes of snow had turned from a lazy drift to plummeting like fallen angels. "Figured you'd like a cup."

Mr. Sullivan stood next to his son. By the way they both stood with mug in hand, one might mistake them for the same person, except for the obvious difference in height.

"It is a cold night. Seems like we're in for one of the coldest winters we've had in a long time."

"I don't know," said Charlie. He shared a smile. "I'm hoping it'll get a little warmer before the end of the year."

"You are, huh? I guess we'll see."

The room fell silent, save for the crackling of the fire.

"How's the book coming?"

"It's coming along really well," said Mr. Sullivan. He rubbed his neck at the thought of writing again. "I'm almost to the part where . . . well, you'll just have to wait to read it."

He smiled at his son. This was a friendly game they would play. Mr. Sullivan would let Charlie read to the edge of a cliff hanger, then tease him about having to wait until the next chapter was finished.

Charlie smiled back until his father looked away, then he hid his face; it had become a mask of pain as Charlie realized he may never get to read the next chapter.

Mr. Sullivan stretched again and set his mug on the desk, staring at his chair. "You know, I think I'm done for the night. Let's do something fun."

Charlie wiped his eyes before turning around. "What about a game of Scrabble?"

His father grimaced. "How about something like Yahtzee instead? I need a break from anything to do with words. Go set up a board game that doesn't involve words, I'll get your mother."

At the Vadiknov house, two teenagers were petting their cat, Selena. Mr. Vadiknov was skim-reading one of his old encyclopedias, while Mrs. Vadiknov solved a crossword puzzle in her rocking chair. At dinner, Liev spun stories of old, enchanting the whole family, although he would add his own humorous twists.

After dinner, the twins sat in the living room with their parents, which was not their custom, pampering their cat and reminiscing about past vacations and their fondest memories.

At exactly ten o'clock, the twins stood and, to the surprise of Mr. and Mrs. Vadiknov, gave their parents long hugs and told them how much they loved them, and that they were lucky to have them as parents.

The revelation at Tavern's had caused Nash to wonder about what his own parents knew. He knew they believed old folk legends. Had they known, in some way, about the varcolac, too?

Following their evening meal, Nash offered to do the dishes while his parents sat at their hand-carved, oak table, sharing small glasses of autumn wine.

"Do you believe in ghosts?"

Chinook Lightholder and Nina Plantspell looked at each other, astonished. Chinook glanced at his son, who was standing at the sink, his back facing his parents.

"Of course, son. Why do you ask?"

"What if I said I believe it was something. . .like a ghost. . .that was abducting the people in Hunter's Grove? Like Mrs. McBranson."

Chinook, broad shouldered and tall, sat back in his chair and placed his hands on his knees. "That would be a serious thing to say."

Nash stopped scrubbing in anticipation. "But do you think it's possible?"

"Of course," Nina replied softly, turning in her chair. "But why do you ask?"

He placed the last plate on the rack to dry and turned the water off, spinning on his heels to face them. "I know what it is. It's a monster, evil and hungry." Nash was quick to back up his vague theory with, "I'm not crazy. I've seen evidence. I know I'm always getting into trouble, and I know that disappoints you, and—"

Chinook held up a gentle hand. "We're not disappointed in you, son. You always do what you think is right, no matter what. It can be hard for a parent to see their son punished for doing something good, but if anything, I'm proud of you. And we do not think you're crazy," he added with his trademark warm smile. "Or at least, I don't. Your mother, though, you know how she can be—"

Nina kicked Chinook's shin under the table, and for a moment they remained there with smiles that warmed the entire house. Nash hoped he would be able to come back home.

"Have you ever seen anything in Hunter's Grove? Anything unnatural, I mean?"

Nash's father, illuminated by the orange glow of the fireplace, hesitated before nodding. "I believe strange things have happened here. And there is a sense of darkness lingering in places. But promise me you won't let this bog you down, son. Unless you have the way—and the duty—to stop something evil, you should always make the best of what you have."

Nash smiled in reply.

"I promise, dad. I'm going to try and get some sleep. I love you guys."

"We . . . we love you too, son."

Nash walked out of the room, stopping just short of the hallway. He thought about the legends of his people, about their names—it had certainly come true, in his case. What about his parents?

He poked his head around the corner. "Dad?"

"Yes?"

"Have you ever tried to hold light?"

Chinook's forehead wrinkled. "What do you mean?"

"Just. . . imagine that you're holding a ball of light. You should try it sometime."

He left the room and his parents heard the close of Nash's bedroom door a few seconds later. Chinook Lightholder looked at his wife, puzzled.

"Hold light?" Nina asked.

Chinook focused his thoughts on the picture his son had placed in his mind.

Nina gasped at the sight of her husband's hand. "Chinook! *Look at your hand.*"

He did, and in his hand, a burning, white ball of light had formed and hovered in his palm. The entire room was resplendent with vivid, living light.

Nash could hear the mutter of excitement and shuffling against the floorboards. He grinned, closed his eyes, and slept deeper than he had in years.

Chapter 18

Mr. Witherington unlocked his front door and entered the house. It was warm, but quiet and hollow, like the day his Elizabeth died. He patted his empty pocket and felt as if he was losing her all over again. Only this time it was his daughter, the singular love of his life now.

He forced himself up the stairs and into his study. Darcy sat by the fire, facing away from the door. Still, William Witherington could see that it was Elizabeth's framed picture she was crying over.

"Darcy," he pleaded. She whipped around to face him. He shuffled through the doorway. "Don't do this. I have already lost one precious person in my life."

Darcy wiped a rebellious tear from her cheek. "You're not the only person in this house. I lost her, too! And what about the others who have gone missing? What about their families? If you won't do something about it, I will."

"Why would you do this to me? Why would you go and fight this foul beast when you might not come back?"

She flung the picture frame across the room. Its four corners spiraled through the air, toppling over each other like the edges of a square wheel. Mr. Witherington ducked out of the way in time. It flew past him and hit the wall, shattering. Broken glass splintered across his desk, and the cherished photo of Elizabeth Witherington floated down amidst the shards.

He looked at her. She looked at him. Darcy was just as stunned as he was, but she shook it off and marched for the door.

"I'm going," she said as she huffed past her father. "I dare you to try and stop me."

Mr. Witherington looked at his desk.

"DARE!" he shouted, beyond emotion.

Darcy stopped.

"What?"

"Truth or Dare, Darcy. You started this game tonight. I dare you to stay."

"I can't. This is something I have to do."

He hung his head, defeated. Darcy's father opened a desk drawer and stared at the long, thin box laying there. He picked it up and ran his thumb lengthwise against the box, as if to say goodbye.

Before she could leave the room, and before he could lose his nerve, William Witherington held the box out to his daughter.

"I won't try to stop you. Just . . . take this with you."

Darcy leveled a questioning look, but took the box and lifted the lid. Inside was a necklace. She had seen it before — played with it while sitting on her mother's lap when she was a small girl. Elizabeth would sing her a song then — a lullaby — but Darcy had long forgotten the words.

Darcy picked up the thin, serpentine silver chain. A pendant fell, hanging at the bottom. It was crafted from a dark metal, ornately carved into eight concave, circular sides. The middle of the octagon was hollow, and on each of the eight points was a small gemstone, each a different color: Purple, brown, orange, red, black, green, yellow, and blue.

The entire thing fit in Darcy's palm, similar in size to an eyeglass.

"It was Eliz—your mother's," Mr. Witherington explained. "I don't know what it does exactly, but she always carried it with her. It had something to do with her—you know, all of *that*. She always talked about giving it to you, when you grew up. And, well, I guess you've grown up enough to have it now."

Darcy looked from the necklace to her father. He may have retreated into a shell of the man he once was, but she still loved him. And she realized he loved her, too. It was why he was so fearful.

She rushed into him with an unreserved hug.

Several moments passed before they released one another. He let Darcy pull away first, and watched her slide the necklace over her head.

"Be careful, wherever it is you're going. And come back."

"I will, Daddy. I will."

He was in the great hall with stone pillars. His friends stood beside him. All of them.

They had made it! No one had died or was injured! He cheered. They'd done it.

Then came that familiar laugh. It echoed everywhere within the Great Hall.

Suddenly, he was on a battlefield surrounded by creatures all around. Monsters from the very worst of nightmares. A blood-red castle loomed in front of him. He looked back and saw that one of his friends was being pulled away.

Dying a thrice death.

The Dark Prince was there, filling the space of his dream.

"Are you prepared for the sacrifice?" asked the varcolac, piercing his soul,

speaking through the dream. "Are your friends prepared to give their lives?"
The Dark Prince laughed triumphant.

Charlie's bed sheets grabbed at him like a hundred angry ghosts as he lunged forward, covered in cold sweat. His head ached and his throat felt like he had been drinking broken glass. A sound sent shivers up his spine . . .

He realized the sound was coming from him. He was screaming. Still.

Charlie clamped his mouth and threw himself back into the pillows, wiping his eyes. It was the same dream he had each night, only worse, more vivid. Somebody was being pulled away, taken — but Charlie still couldn't see who.

The door flew open as Mr. Sullivan launched into the room, bone-tired and rattled. The sound of Charlie screaming penetrated every corner of the house. "What's wrong? What happened?"

"Nothing," Charlie sniffed. "Another nightmare. Sorry, Dad."

Not wholly awake, Mr. Sullivan scanned the room looking to throttle the Sandman himself for putting nightmares in his son's head. Little did he know it was someone — some*thing*— much worse that was invading Charlie's sleep.

"You want to talk about it?"

Charlie shook his head. "Not tonight. I need to try and sleep."

Mr. Sullivan nodded, patted his son on the shoulder, and shuffled back to his room.

Poor kid, he thought, *so much going on with extra schoolwork, new friends, and the recent detention. So much pressure on kids these days.*

He frowned, hoping Charlie hadn't been getting into trouble with these new friends. He would talk to him about it tomorrow, after school.

The last thing Mr. Sullivan thought about when his head hit the pillow was how inflamed Charlie's eyes looked. He was fast asleep before the thought could fully form.

Loch cursed as the erkling stepped through the gateway. Its filthy boots landed heavy thuds on the meager, white bridge as the monster trudged toward the elder hunter.

Still, he thanked whatever powers may be that it wasn't the Dark Prince crossing over. Loch stowed the mirror box in his coat pocket and raised his shotgun, his right eye glowing red in the night air.

"Get back!" he demanded.

The erkling slathered a vile grin, its teeth crooked and sharp. It raised its royal sword and stepped off the bridge, inhaling its first free breath in over two centuries.

BOOM!

Nearby birds scattered, twittering and frightened by the gunfire. The shot knocked the erkling backward onto the bridge, but it merely stunned the powerful Greater monster.

Loch's heart sank. They were out of time. Now Greaters were able to get through. It was only a matter of time.

The erkling stood and drew its sword, snarling at its bloodied chest and torn uniform. It launched at Loch with a strike to the hunter's throat. Loch stepped aside, the erkling's rusty blade missing for the kill, but ripping into his shoulder.

It had been some time since Loch had been involved in personal combat. He grunted in pain and struggled to keep his footing as a winged, stone figure fell from the sky. Its shadow swallowed both monster and hunter before splitting the earth between them.

Chapter 19

A purple sun burned through angry clouds, bathing Blood Castle in a sickly light. The Alpha wolf prowled the inner bank of the castle's black moat. He could hear the wodnik below, clawing through the filthy waters. The Otherworld bustled with the fitful energy of the Dark Prince, contempt and rage swelling in a macabre dance of evil intent.

The Sagemistress flew out of the mammoth stone doors of Blood Castle's gatehouse, throwing them aside like splinters. She waved an impatient gesture to the ogre manning the bridge.

That looming deformity pulled with giant arms, heaving gears into motion. The bridge lowered with a small dam sinking into the moat beneath it, temporarily stopping the flow of water so the witch could cross.

As the water ceased to flow, the wodnik poked his frog-like face out of the moat, curious. Seeing the Sagemistress crossing the bridge, he re-entered the water with a plop.

The wodnik pressed through the murky waters with his webbed claws and fish-like tail. With a splash he leaned the top half of his scaled body onto the mud-caked ground, creating a dirt puddle as he splashed about. The wolf lowered a questioning look over his muscled shoulder, and sniffed dispassionate at the wodnik.

"What news from the Prince, Sagemistress?" croaked the wodnik.

Her electric-blue eyes acknowledged him with disdain as she

stepped over his blackish puddle.

"They are coming," she said. The three restive monsters looked in the direction of the portal, past the Graveyard that stretched over a great portion of the Otherworld. It was far away, but not far enough.

The witch scowled. "The Prince wants us ready, of course. He wants them alive, but incapacitated. The fool! We should not take the chance."

"Sagemistress!" the wodnik urged. "Be wary of what it is you say! You never know if he is listening." With a nervous fidget he stroked his scraggly beard, which looked like algae dripping from his chin.

The wolf growled in agreement.

"I know better than you think, Grandfather Bilibin," the witch warned.

The Sagemistress turned without another word and launched into a graceful stride. Even with her long legs, the witch's speed was unnatural. She glided over the land, disappearing over Wyvern's Peak.

Sensing the anger of the witch, the wolf and the wodnik shared a glance; centuries of betrayal and hatred bubbling just below her leathery skin.

The ogre lifted the bridge, allowing the black waters to agitate and flow around the castle once more. The wodnik shook his head and splashed back into his watery domain.

Long ears stood erect on the Alpha's head, and his eyes flashed with bloodlust. The wolf stood on his imposing hind legs and began to pace the bank of the moat again. He sniffed the air, hackles rising. His instincts harbored no doubt, and the savage warrior let loose a feral howl.

War was coming to the Otherworld.

Darcy woke to the memory of a song. The words replayed over and over in her head.

> *Purple Monster, Yellow monster, Brown monster, three,*
> *Why are you jumping on my bed?*
> *Blue monster, Black monster, Purple monster, see?*
> *Now I am stomping on your heads.*

She frowned at the image in her mind. Was it something she had eaten? *I knew I would regret those tacos*, she thought.

Darcy slipped out of bed, and another verse—another rhyme altogether—came to mind:

> *Red monster, Red monster above your head,*
> *His friend, Blue monster, under your bed.*
> *Ugly faces is the game they play,*
> *So listen close to what I say.*
> *Scary from the closet, green eyes glowing bright.*
> *Soon, very soon, will come the morning Light.*
> *Never fear the Dark, or these faces here,*
> *For all the help you need is here, very near.*

The lyrics came with little tunes, each song flowing easy. She'd heard them before.

Closing her eyes to remember, Darcy recalled her mother singing these rhymes to her at bedtime, strange as they were. It had been so many years ago. Her mother would play with the necklace while singing, brushing the colored stones with her fingers.

The memories were blurred, but Darcy kept reciting them — over and over again — until she remembered. If for no other reason this was a memory of her mother that belonged to her.

Never fear the Dark, or these faces here . . .

Darcy gripped the necklace tight before standing and getting ready. She took her time, knowing this might be her last hot shower. She needed to hurry, even so, as she had every intention of having that last caramel-drizzled coffee before departing. It may be her final morning in this world, but she was going to have her coffee and caramel. No monster would deprive her of that joy. She chuckled at the thought.

Later that morning, Darcy was finishing her hair and makeup. It seemed silly to her now. She was going into a foreign land to hunt monsters and save the world — or at least Hunter's Grove — but if there was a chance she might not come back, she planned on going out with style.

Cute jeans, fashionably scuffed boots, a nice jacket, and minimal makeup — accentuate the eyes. "That'll do just fine. *MWAH!*" she praised herself in the mirror.

To make sure she wasn't crazy, Darcy placed a hand on her dresser and pushed gently, watching her hand disappear into the woodwork. She giggled.

Darcy grabbed her bag, moved quietly through the hallway, and placed a kissed hand on her father's bedroom door. Downstairs, she set the note for her father on the table.

It took a moment to find her nerve, but she was ready. Darcy took a deep breath and walked out the door.

Nash and the twins were waiting outside. They had agreed to meet at Darcy's before stopping by Tavern's for breakfast on their way to the Key.

"Fashion much?" Lisa yelled.

"Sh!" Darcy hushed, shuffling down from her porch. "You'll wake up my dad! Now what did you say?" she asked, close enough to talk without yelling.

"I was just wondering if you looked good enough yet to go monster hunting. What's with the goofy necklace? That is so not you," Lisa mocked with a valley-girl tone reminiscent of Darcy's entourage.

"Shut up! It belonged to my mom. My dad gave it to me last night. It's one of the only things I have from her. Oh, and if I'm going to face a big-bad-boogeyman, I'm going to look good doing it. You'll not catch me wearing a belt of wooden stakes and garlic."

"Sorry about the necklace. I didn't know. But wooden stakes might help. According to some legends —"

"Forget it," Darcy said, squashing Lisa's know-it-all rant. "Not going to happen."

"Glad to see everyone's chipper!" Charlie hailed, jogging to meet the others. "All joking aside, this is it guys. Take a deep breath and —"

"Rumbling. Stomach. Breakfast," croaked Nash. "Can we just head to Tavern's and talk on the way?"

"Sure," agreed Charlie, "let's go."

As they walked, Liev leaned over and whispered in Charlie's ear.

"Charlie, you look tired. Have a hard time sleeping last night?"

"It's nothing," Charlie reassured, eyes forward. He didn't want to talk about his dreams — or the death that haunted them.

The Chief of Assistants ran as fast as his clammy legs could carry him, panting, sweating. The perspiration froze on his earlobes and chin as the temperature continued to plummet.

He had been running most of the night. Hunter's Grove wasn't exactly an expansive area, but avoiding lights and humans kept him on edge. He was an enemy to the humans, as much for what he was as for the things he had done. Charlie Sullivan and his pesky friends had discovered him and revealed him to the hunter. This human world was crumbling in around him.

Though he had filled his master's diary with the necessary blood for the coming Ritual, Dräng knew he couldn't return to the Otherworld. The release of the Ancients would make his life even more miserable. Soon, his master would know of Dräng's further betrayal, and there would be no escaping his wrath. No human, or monster, would trust him now.

Dräng was caught between two worlds, without home, family, or friend. He was cold, scared, and hungry. The few squirrels he had caught did little to fill his appetite. Soon, a Collector would be sent to track him down and return him to Blood Castle to face his master. Starving would be better.

The little monster found himself running to the far side of Hunter's Grove, as far from the Key as he could. It was then that he had the idea.

There was one human in Hunter's Grove who might let Dräng explain himself. One who knew of the existence of monsters, and one who might help him set things straight. He had seen the human many times in the forest issuing loud, verbal warnings to "whoever or whatever was out there."

He prayed his diplomatic skills were still intact, and that they would be enough for this human.

Run, Dräng told himself. *Run faster. Seek this human out. He is your last hope for survival.*

A bell jingled when the door opened, ushering in five teenagers. All heads turned to stare. Many of those same heads had been there last night when Darcy interrupted their dinner, and those who weren't there had heard about the incident.

People went back to dining, turning a wary gaze from time to time. In one corner of the room, Donnie Wickles picked up a menu to hide his face.

"Hey Fish, Dink," Charlie greeted, noticing the two men on their way out.

"Hey . . . there," Fish said, awkward.

Dink offered a smile and waved, never making eye contact.

They stood there for a moment before Fish snapped to a quick step and took for the door.

"Well, see ya later. Dink and I are off for, um, some early winter huntin'."

Charlie nodded. "Stay warm."

"Will do," Dink said. "And you keep safe, ya hear?"

After they'd exited, Darcy frowned. "What was that about?"

"You do realize of whom you speak?" asked Liev, dripping with sarcasm.

Charlie noticed Fish and Dink's strange — or, stranger — behavior, but he chalked it up to, well, their strangeness.

His stomach grumbling like a bear out of hibernation, Nash hurried to the nearest open table, eyes drilling holes through the menu.

Tavern emerged from the back of the restaurant, and stopped when he saw the group, catching Darcy's eye. They both looked away. He sighed and grabbed his pencil and notepad.

"Morning," said Tavern, a touch apprehensive as he neared the table. "You all here for a nice, warm, quiet breakfast? Can I get you some drinks?"

"I'd like a hot cocoa," Charlie said, breaking the ice.

"Sure," said Nash. "Same thing."

Tavern took their orders and made his way to the kitchen. No one prodded Darcy as to what transpired after they departed last night, or how she had gotten the necklace.

The table was round, forcing them to look at each other, which was uncomfortable. They had snuck into dark forests together, trained to hunt monsters together, and they'd even faced Darcy's father together, but being friends was still a new concept.

Nash grunted, nodding his head toward a corner in the restaurant. A scowl was brewing across his face. The others turned to see what was making him upset.

Donnie Wickles sauntered toward them, hands shoved in his

pockets.

"Uh, hi. Can I sit?"

"No," said Nash.

"What do you want?" asked Darcy.

"I just want to talk. And to say I'm sorry. Can I sit?" he asked again.

They exchanged glances with each other before settling on Charlie, who blushed at having the other four staring at him. What did they expect him to do?

Then Charlie remembered Loch's words, about him being a leader.

"Sure," said Charlie.

Donnie grabbed a chair from the next table and spun it around. "I've noticed how you guys hang out a lot lately."

"I wouldn't say a lot," said Darcy. "Maybe just the past week or so."

"And I saw how you all went up to Hunter's Key in that big black car together."

They stiffened.

"So?" asked Lisa. She narrowed her eyes, trying intimidation.

"I don't want trouble," Donnie said, lifting his hands. "I just, you know . . . my uncle went missing when it all started happening. His name was Robert. Uncle Rob."

Charlie looked at the others and leaned forward. "Yeah, we know."

"I thought he was crazy. Uncle Rob was always talking about old ghost stories and monsters. I thought he just wandered off one day. It wasn't right talking down about him and the other people who've . . ."

He looked between Darcy and Nash.

"I'm sorry."

Darcy lifted her chin, feigning disinterest. In truth, she was trying not to cry.

"That's all you came here for?" she asked.

"No," said Donnie. "I know what you're trying to do. And I want to help."

"What are you talking about?" asked Liev, before Lisa nudged him.

"My uncle, before he was taken, he told me stories about monsters, and the people who dealt with monsters. He told me how some of those people had powers. Like I said, I saw you go up to Hunter's Key."

He pointed his gaze at Darcy, and then they understood. He had seen her slip into the car without opening the door. Donnie's intentions were becoming clear.

Four pairs of eyes cast their accusations at Darcy.

"I just want to help you guys. It sounds like fun, and maybe a way to fix what I've done wrong."

"Fun?" asked Charlie. He shuddered at the terrors haunting his dreams. "So you're not afraid to die."

Donnie faltered. "Well, n-no, of course not. I mean, we'd all do what was necessary, right?"

"And you're not afraid to fail?" Charlie continued. "You're not afraid that if you lose, all the people who are left behind would suffer, because you failed?"

Donnie looked at the five faces, their solemn expressions, sadness marking their eyes. They looked older, more mature than the classmates he knew a week ago.

"I don't know what you think you've seen us do, but you don't have the full picture. This isn't fun anymore, Donnie. You want to help? Go home. Stop pushing people around at school. Pray that we don't fail, and that maybe we'll come back alive."

Shocked, Donnie stood and took a step away from the table. *Were they really afraid of dying? Was it really that bad?* He wondered to himself.

"Yeah," he said. "Yeah, okay. I see how it is."

Donnie turned and, with a final look over his shoulder, walked out of the restaurant and headed to school.

Breakfast arrived at their table. A feast eaten in silence as they pondered Charlie's words.

Ghostly shapes drifted through the air and over the water, wailing in their peculiar way as they left the shore of Banshee's Stay to cross to the Otherworld's mainland.

On the opposite side of the Otherworld, a horde of cats skulked out of steamy Boggart's Marsh.

Near Blood Castle, pale rusalkas ran for the moat to join their Grandfather Bilibin — the wodnik — lurching on long legs with greenish hair flapping behind them. They dove in the water; a host of flaming green eyes peered out of the muck.

In the Graveyard, the Spirit Tree stretched and creaked, rustling in the absence of wind.

Howls filled with angst drifted from Wolf's Lair, pensive and bloodthirsty, spreading across the length and breadth of the Otherworld, inciting eager and disturbing chuckles from the fires of Demon's Gorge.

Inside his abode, the Dark Prince felt their anticipation build, and watched their excited movements across the dreadful land.

He sat back on his throne and waited.

He was ready.

Chapter 20

Loch was expecting them. His car idled on Frederickson Street, purring, impatient.

The drive to Hunter's Key was somber. They were nervous, and Loch's silence wasn't helping. No one spoke. In fact, only when they'd entered the war room did Loch turn to look at them. He opened his mouth to speak, a worried expression deepened on his face—until he spotted Darcy's necklace.

"What?" she pressed, seeing his brow furrow.

"I take it that necklace belonged to your mother."

"Yeah. She, um, she was a hunter."

"Oh, I know. The Key was her post. It's just . . . your mother had a very good reputation, but I never knew she had a Ward Amulet."

"What's a Ward Omelet?" asked Nash. His mind still ruminating about breakfast.

Lisa rolled her eyes. "*Amulet.*"

"Not just any amulet," said Loch. "There are precious few Ward Amulets in existence, each crafted with specific magical properties."

Darcy was infused with excitement. "So you can tell me how to use it?" she said.

Loch frowned. "No. I've never seen a Ward Amulet, Darcy, only read stories about them. I'm sorry, but that's a riddle you'll have to solve by yourself."

Noticing her dejected demeanor, Loch patted her on the shoulder.

"Loch," Charlie said, remembering how somber the old man had been on the way up, "is something wrong?"

"I'm afraid there is. Yesterday that little scab escaped, and he stole the varcolac's diary."

The room went cold as each took in the news. The diary, they knew, was instrumental to the varcolac. If Dräng had escaped with it, they had lost an advantage.

"What's worse," he continued, "something came through the gateway last night. It was a Greater, an erkling. I was lucky to see it before it saw me."

"You killed it?" asked Lisa, impressed. She and Liev were the only ones who knew what an erkling was, and how dangerous one could be.

"It was handled, but that's not the point. Point is the Greaters are starting to come through."

Charlie understood. "So you're saying we need to go soon."

Loch stood for a moment, mouth open, before he shut it and nodded. It felt wrong sending them into the Otherworld when there was so much left to teach them, but there was no other way.

"I'm ready," said Darcy. Each one of them had spent the last night saying their goodbyes.

Liev looked at his feet, serious. "I'm ready, too."

Lisa nodded once after her brother.

Nash patted Charlie on the back, who looked at Loch.

"It's okay," said Charlie. "We can do this."

Loch turned away for a second, pretending to look at the door to his security room. He was hiding his guilt for not being able to take care of this himself. This was his job, not theirs. And the chance of survival was slim, even for him.

He turned back to them. "Not yet, you're not. The Otherworld is dangerous. You'll need better ways to defend yourself. Follow me."

He led them to a far wall holding several racks of weapons.

"You've been busy," Liev remarked.

"I've been working on this since last night," said Loch. "Take your pick, but don't go wild! Too much will weigh you down."

Eagerly, they examined spears, swords, crossbows, clubs, and daggers. There were odd contraptions like a strange potato-gun, homemade grenades, and modified, unstable-looking firearms.

The weapons looked rustic, handcrafted. Each was crafted to fit a hunter's needs — constructed with monster slaying materials like silver, iron, and certain types of wood, with the occasional strip of duct tape. Odd weapons, for odd targets.

Loch noticed the way they fumbled with the weapons.

"I, uh, don't suppose any of you have had weapons training. Ever been to a shooting range? No? Fencing lessons, at least?"

They looked at him like he was wearing meatloaf.

Didn't kids play with dangerous things anymore? This lot looked afraid to attack butter with a branding iron.

Loch sighed and started pointing at various items.

"Each of you should take at least one dagger. They're small and lightweight. Still, I'd take a longer weapon like a sword or spear. For you girls, I'd suggest foils, which are lighter than swords."

Darcy raised an eyebrow. "Are you saying we're weak?"

Loch glared at her. He picked up one of the homemade grenades. "And each of you carry some of these. Just be careful, they can be dangerous."

"So glad you let us know," Lisa quipped.

"But not like you think," he said, ignoring her. "They aren't made for human warfare. These are filled with bits of iron, salt, silver, and garlic—generic monster hunting staples. Still, I wouldn't stand next to one after you pull the pin."

Nash and Liev raised their eyebrows with obvious interest.

"A jack-of-all-trades weapon, huh?" Liev remarked.

"Aye, you could say that. And this goes with it."

He picked up what looked like a grenade launcher with a bronze trumpet for a barrel. It seemed to have traveled from the 18th Century, complete with flintlock.

"I like it," Liev said with a mischievous grin.

"I thought you would," Loch said, grinning himself. He showed Liev how to load it, how to lock it, and gave him a few tips on aiming.

Nash felt left out—it was the only grenade launcher—but Loch had something special in mind for him. He heaved one of the strange potato guns into his grip. A thick, hose-like tube was attached to it, running to a bulky black vest that Loch strapped on.

"Nash, m'boy. Take a look at this baby. We call it the Salt Machine Ultrageous Grapeshot Gun. S.M.U.G.G. for short." He giggled to himself; indeed, he snorted.

The group of young hunters watched their mentor with concern.

"If anybody carries this into the Otherworld," he said to Nash, "it should be you."

Darcy wrinkled her nose. "S.M.U.G.G.? That sounds like something old people would come up with. Wait, did you come up with that?"

Loch glared back. "Funny. When you've fought monsters for decades, you'll appreciate a touch of madness, too."

Holding the S.M.U.G.G., Loch spun to face the other side of the room where he had stacked a pile of old chairs. From the vest he took a canister the size of a salt shaker, which contained deadly salt grapeshot, and loaded it into a chamber on top of the gun. He pressed a button on the front of the vest and the tube tightened, emitting the hiss of pressure building, and pulled the trigger.

THOOSH!

A muted explosion and loud crashes followed.

From the top down, the stack of chairs collapsed in a cloud of salt and splinters.

"See?" Loch yelled over S.M.U.G.G.'s racket. "Simple! Load, aim, fire! I just wish they'd make 'em smaller!"

"And quieter!" Liev added.

Loch punched the on/off button on the vest and the S.M.U.G.G. whirred down. He held it to Nash, who took it with pleasure, buckled on the vest, and began swinging the barrel around.

Lisa and Darcy each took a crossbow, requiring more accuracy than the other weapons, but not difficult to master. They listened as Loch shared insights and instructions.

Charlie examined the weapon racks, which held cultural items from all over the world, but only one thing caught his eye.

It was the spear he noticed on his first trip through the garage. It was thin, but made of sturdy wood. The head was a silver tip, and a ball of iron had been welded onto the bottom.

"All these amazing weapons," said Loch from behind him, "and you choose that thing?"

"It was yours, wasn't it?" asked Charlie.

"A long time ago, yes."

Charlie nodded. "Then it's good enough for me."

Loch felt his heart beat a proud beat. He patted Charlie on the shoulder and turned to the rest of the gang to keep from getting sentimental.

Loch was satisfied they had the weapons they needed. It wasn't enough — they weren't enough — but it would have to do.

"Good," he said, ignoring the doubt in his gut. "Everyone have a foil and a dagger? I'm hoping nothing gets that close to you, but anything can happen when dealing with beasts in the Otherworld. It's best you're ready for as much."

They exited the War Room and trekked through the Key until they came to a short hallway with a cast iron door. It opened up to the same garden they'd seen from the tower above. It was an expansive, sprawling passage. Now into winter, it was dry and brittle; colorless, and haunting. Beautiful in its own way.

Charlie saw it first, because he was looking for it. That small bridge, scuffed with peeling white paint.

Heavy rivets drove into the wood at the foot of the bridge, which was stained badly. The ground leading up to the bridge held deep, fresh marks in it — claw marks dug through the snow. A dragon-like gargoyle stood next to the bridge in a fierce battle position. Charlie didn't remember seeing this gargoyle from the tower the other day. Had Loch moved it there since? If so, how had he moved something so massive out here?

Something else commanded his immediate attention. It didn't take long for his eyes to transform into seas of red. Above the bridge, he saw what the others could not. The energy and magic sustaining the mist-like gateway were barely visible.

Their time was up, indeed.

The bridge crossed a slushy, half-frozen river, disappearing into trees on the other side. The air grew more frigid the closer they got.

"I'm afraid this is where you go on without me," Loch said.

Nobody realized he had stopped walking, and now stood several paces behind them with his hands behind his back. His weathered face framed a sad smile. "I wish you the best of luck, all of you, and that I could go with you. Or rather, that you didn't go at all —"

"It's okay," said Darcy. "We understand. None of us hold this against you. This is destiny."

There was a unanimous nodding of heads.

In the last two days, all of them had come to respect the elder curmudgeon. They knew, despite his put-on grumpy demeanor, he cared about them.

Loch scoured at the ground, then lurched forward. He remembered one, important, item he forgot to give them.

"Charlie, wait!"

"Yes?"

Loch pulled a small black box out of his jacket pocket. It was the same box he kept locked in his desk drawer. He beckoned Charlie to come close for a private conversation.

Loch passed the box to the boy. "Inside — don't open it! Inside is a mirror of sorts. A looking glass, if you will."

"A mirror?"

"Yes."

His voice grew quiet, and the others couldn't make out what was being said. Only when he stood taller than Charlie could they hear his last words, a bit of good news to their ears.

"With this, you'll have an advantage the first hunters didn't. But whatever you do — and this goes for those blockhead friends of yours as well — you must not look at the mirror yourself! The mirror is facing the bottom of the box, so you know. Do you understand what you have to do?"

Charlie nodded with grave understanding. He could well-enough imagine what would happen if he looked into the glass, and he didn't need any further dissuasion.

"Good. Now off you go. And Godspeed to you all!"

"What was that about? What did he give you?" asked Liev, forever intrigued with trinkets, gadgets, and mysterious items.

"A tool. But it's dangerous," warned Charlie. "Don't worry about it for now."

Loch watched as Charlie Sullivan, Nash Stormstepper, Darcy Witherington, and Lisa and Liev Vadiknov stepped onto the bridge, side by side. They exchanged glances before setting off across the bridge together, proud and with purpose.

Halfway across the bridge, the five monster hunters of Hunter's Grove . . .

. . . vanished.

Loch sighed and looked at the empty bridge. He waited, selfishly hoping they would reappear. They did not.

He looked at the gargoyle and nodded, releasing it from its current duty and commanding it to protect them — praying that it *could* protect them. The stone sentinel waited for Loch to look away, and then Loch heard the sound of stone skin brushing against itself.

When Loch turned around, all that remained was an old white bridge, covered with bloodstains. He pulled his winter coat tighter and trudged through the thin snow back into the protective embrace of Hunter's Key.

Chapter 21

The air pulsed like the deep throb of a laboring heartbeat as they passed through.

The pounding penetrated their skulls, blood rushing and pumping in their ears and temples, growing stronger the further they fell through the portal. And their skin — oh, their skin! It felt as if it had traveled separately in carry-on bags, and had been reattached to their bodies with helter-skelter pins and needles.

Nash thought his lungs were going to implode before he realized he needed to breathe. He gasped for breath, falling to his hands and knees on a black, splintered bridge. He was aware of something flying over him — like a large, heavy eagle — but was too preoccupied to look.

Lisa coughed up trapped air, while Liev held his head and winced, hoping the pounding would go away.

Charlie was writhing like a doll being thrashed in the teeth of a wild dog, seeing through too many sets of eyes at once. His nightmare raged at him, though this time it felt less like a dream. He could smell the reality of his visions, feel them crawling through his skin.

He curled into a ball and clenched his teeth, waiting for the pain to go away.

Darcy was unconscious on her back, half-phased through her crossbow and the ground beneath her. When she opened her eyes, she saw a lady sitting on a window seat surrounded by bright, warm lights, lulling a little girl to sleep. The girl held a strange necklace, while her mother sang a gentle song.

"Red monster, Red monster," her mother sang, "above your head."

As the little girl watched, dreary-eyed and at peace, her mother pressed her thumb twice against the red gemstone on the necklace.

"His friend, Blue monster, under your bed."

She pressed against the blue gemstone . . .

"Ugly faces is the game they play,
So listen close to what I say.
Scary from the closet, green eyes glowing bright."

The green stone . . .

"Soon, very soon, will come the morning Light."

Yellow . . .

"Never fear the Dark, or these faces here,"

Finally, the black stone . . .

"For all the help you need is here, very near."

Her mother smiled and caressed her face. She felt the love of a thousand years sweeping across her skin.

Darcy snapped to full consciousness, startling the others as she cried, "That's it! That's it!"

"Shhh!" Lisa was still rubbing her dry throat. With a raspy voice, she continued, "We don't know what's around us, or how close we are to any monsters."

Darcy ignored her and fumbled for her mother's necklace. She found it, stared at it, and pressed her thumbs against the red gem twice, then the blue stone, and then the green one. Thumbing the gemstones reminded her of texting, which made her laugh.

What were the last two lines?

"Soon, very soon, will come the morning Light."

She pressed yellow, and then . . .

"Never fear the Dark, or these faces here."

. . . black.

With a crackle, the hole of the necklace lit with a pale light. The light shot outward. Lisa, being closest, fell back with a yelp.

The light projected a beam reaching out several feet, ending in a flat, octagonal disc. She set the necklace on the ground and the disc of light stood to their waists, like a table. There were shapes in the light. Hills, peaks and valleys, flat land, bodies of water, and a massive tree—with words written over each area being illuminated.

Realization dawned on Darcy, and she gasped. The other's gathered around the scintillating display, even Charlie—his eyes were crimson fires, otherwise, he seemed recovered.

"It's a map," observed Nash.

"Obviously," said Lisa.

Liev nodded. "Convenient."

Darcy searched the map carefully, as did Charlie. It was meticulous in its detail and labeling, presumed to have been created by the first hunters to cross into this haunted land. In the center of the octagon was a triangular piece of land resembling an arrowhead, labeled: *OTHERWORLD.*

Several labeled islands broke off from the mainland; *Boggart's Marsh, Banshee's Stay*, and *Witch Island*. A prominent section in the middle of the Otherworld indicated *Graveyard*. Behind it was an area labeled *Spirit Tree*, along with other areas within the triangular section; *Manticore Den, Basilisk Pit*, and *Wyvern's Peak*. None of them brought any comfort to the group.

"We're here," said Darcy, touching a point labeled *The Bridge*. They were still on the bridge, where the gateway had, without concern, deposited them. This bridge was black, not white, and there was no sign of the Key behind them.

"Right," said Charlie, his black pupils swimming frantically in a sea of red as he scanned the map. "And we need to be here."

He pointed to the tip of the arrowhead, where it pictured a dismal fortress, and its not-so-welcoming black moat. *Blood Castle*.

Everyone groaned. It was the farthest point on the map from where they stood. Behind the castle was an area called *Demon's Gorge*, flush against the back wall of the fortress. That meant they could only enter from the front, where they would blatantly march into the faces of their enemies.

A large cave on the map rose in front of the castle. *Wolf's Lair*.

Liev shook his head. "We are so scr—"

Lisa elbowed him hard in the ribs.

"Which way do we go?" asked Nash, desperate. Charlie turned away from the map, searching the land with his dreadful eyes. He saw so many things. Glimmers of light rising from the earth, ley lines under the earth, and traces of magic that he didn't understand flooded his perception. He searched hard, but there was no glowing neon sign that said *"THIS WAY."* No billboard reading, *"BLOOD CASTLE, THREE STOPLIGHTS AHEAD ON THE RIGHT!*

STOP HERE FOR SLUSHIES!"

To the left was Boggart's Marsh, and beyond that was Manticore Pit next to Demon's Gorge.

To the right were Witch Island, Wyvern's Peak, and Banshee's Stay. Advancing further toward Blood Castle, Wolf's Lair opened its ghastly den to untold horrors.

"Left," said Darcy.

Charlie didn't like the shimmer in the air to their left. He didn't like the right, either, but he had a feeling left was a worse idea.

"I think we should go right," he said.

Darcy scrunched her nose. "Why right?"

"I don't know, but I think it's better if we go that way."

"I don't think so. I don't like the sound of Wolf's Lair. And besides, we'd have to climb Wyvern's Peak. Left would be easier."

Lisa looked at the map with her brother. They knew a lot about these monsters from the dusty tomes they'd read over the years, and neither direction looked hopeful.

Basilisk Pit was straight ahead, lying between them and the Graveyard.

"Darcy's right," said Lisa. "If we go left, we can march up the side pretty easy. Maybe we can cut between Boggart's Marsh and the Graveyard. We may steer clear from the worst of it before approaching Blood Castle."

The others agreed. Charlie tried to ignore the sinking feeling in his gut, giving them the benefit of the doubt. He held his spear close, eyes scanning, with dread encroaching at each step.

Darcy scooped her mother's necklace off the ground and the map winked out. The light in the hole swirled and drifted away like a mist. She looped the ward amulet around her neck, thanking her mother for the help with a hushed and uneasy exhale.

"For all the help you need is here, very near."

She took the crossbow off her back and loaded it with one of the iron-tipped shafts. Lisa did the same.

Liev let a maniacal grin slip across his face, loading his bronze grenade launcher and shifting it to his left hand, brandishing a foil in his right. Two grenade belts were strapped across his torso in an X, while two hung in another X at his hips and waist. He looked like a steampunk commando, and he loved every moment of it.

Nash heaved S.M.U.G.G. to his shoulder, loading several canisters of salt grapeshot into the chamber tube. He pressed the button on the front of his vest, and a slight hiss indicated the weapon had whirred to life.

Charlie marched behind Darcy, wielding his spear sideways in a two-handed grip. As Lisa suggested, they trailed near the left edge of the Otherworld's border, not far from the waters beyond the dirty banks.

The painful disorientation of traveling through the portal wore off as they continued through the frigid region. As the effects of first-time interworld travel faded, Nash noticed how good he felt.

"Anyone else feel that?" he asked, stretching his legs as he strode.

"Heck yeah!" said Liev.

He'd realized a few steps back that his senses were sharper than usual. He could see the miniscule fray in the right knee of his white jeans, and he could smell the minerals in the stones to his left being lapped by the murky water.

"What?" asked Darcy.

"You don't feel it?" Lisa asked, staring into the sharp detail of the black and gray clouds contrasting against the luminous purple sky. It was the most beautiful and terrible thing she had ever witnessed. Liev stooped and picked up a small pebble, flinging it at Darcy's back.

In an instant, Darcy whipped around—sensing a tiny gust of wind behind her—and plucked the pebble from the air without thinking.

"*That*," said Liev, emphatic.

Darcy looked at the pebble. "Oh."

"It's like we're meant to be here," said Lisa, spreading her arms. She spun around, dancing. "Like we have the greatest potential here. I wonder what our gifts are like in this environment."

"Yeah," said Nash, noticing how much lighter S.M.U.G.G. had become. It was like a feather in his grip.

"Which means we need to be careful," interjected Charlie.

It was the first time he had spoken in half an hour. He had noticed the change, too, as his Sight had become even more detailed, more frightening. He could see pale figures in the water, watching the five humans with fiery-green eyes. Charlie doubted the others could see the water spirits.

"We can't become complacent or too excited. We aren't the only ones here with heightened abilities. My guess is that whoever, or whatever is here, has had a lot more practice than us."

Charlie was right and almost too late as a creature appeared in that same moment. Before they could react, a horse-like beast, with the flesh of a dead fish, rammed through them from behind, knocking them forward like bowling pins. The monster turned to face them, pawing the ground with clawed hooves.

To their horror, the monster opened its ragged mouth and spoke, its voice a nauseating whine.

"You killed him. You killed my master."

"What are you talking about?" cried Charlie, terrified. "I didn't kill anybody!"

"This is for my master!" the wretched horse shrieked. It charged him, opening a mouth rowed with shark-like teeth.

"Charlie!" Lisa called. "This is an erkling's steed! Its master must be the one Loch killed."

"That's just great! What am I supposed to do with it?"

"Get the heck out of its way!"

Charlie tried, but it wasn't enough. The only thing he managed to do was make himself a sitting target for the beast. He clenched his eyes shut, reprimanding himself for dying so soon.

Again, there was a heavy whoosh over their heads, the same that Nash felt after crossing the bridge. *Something* flew above them.

Whatever it was, screeched, piercing their eardrums, and snatched the monster up like a dragon hunting livestock. Charlie felt the pounding of bloody hooves and the gust of wind, and then heard the angry cries of the steed retreating into the distance. He opened his eyes and sat up in time to see a gargoyle carrying his would-be killer away. It was the same dragon-like gargoyle that had been poised next to the white bridge at the Key. He was sure of it.

"What was that thing?" asked Darcy, hysterical.

"Which one?" said Charlie.

Darcy didn't have time to clarify before Nash yelled, "Oh, crap!"

"Don't say, 'oh, crap,'" Liev said, his white shirt now thoroughly soiled. "We just had an 'oh, crap' moment and we don't need another one yet."

Nash was pointing in front of them, left of where the gargoyle had flown.

"Oh," said Liev. "Crap."

They expected monsters, ready to fight. They had not, however, expected what stood before them.

A clowder of cats rounded a bend in the land that was connected to an island — Boggart's Marsh.

"Boggarts," whispered Lisa.

Charlie didn't see cats, like the others. He saw fogs of swirling spirits, disguising themselves as cats. His stomach knotted in fear and frustration.

"We should've taken the other way."

"We're in their world," snapped Darcy, defensive. "We were bound to run into a monster at some point."

The cats continued moving toward them, lurking in a way that told the group they'd been spotted. The Otherworld was aware of their presence.

"Lisa," asked Charlie, "how bad are boggarts?"

"Uh . . ." In the face of the enemy, Lisa froze.

"They're bad," said Liev, coming to his sister's rescue. "They're a nuisance most of the time, but they can be murderous. And a whole pack of boggarts? Let's just say —"

Charlie didn't need Liev to finish the sentence. "Let's go back the other way," he said.

The five turned to retreat, but from behind them flew a harpy, and it wasn't there to welcome them. A bird the size of a stallion, bearing the angry, wretched face of a woman, crested a hill to their left. Two massive creatures joined it; a large-nosed, gray giant, and a pitch-black, faceless humanoid. Faceless — save its three spellbinding eyes — the humanoid beast stood on the legs of a goat and threatened them with six clawed arms.

The boggarts, the harpy, and the two giants pressed the group in on three sides, leaving the only escape through the water beside them. They were trapped.

Terrified, the five hunters backed away from the encroaching monsters, pushing them dangerously close to the water.

"Don't step in the water," Charlie warned.

"It may be our only chance!" cried Darcy.

He grabbed her sleeve. "There are things in the water, Darcy! Things you can't see. Put one foot in and I guarantee it'll be worse than standing your ground here."

She had never felt fear so heavy, so real, as she did when he spoke those words to her. She was afraid to die, and she trembled with that realization. "What are we supposed to do?"

"Hold them off," he urged. "Hold them all off. Choose our monsters and fight!"

"I've got the boggarts," Liev said, sheathing his sword and raising his grenade launcher. He knew the salt and iron compacted within the grenades would level damage against them.

Nash pointed S.M.U.G.G. in the direction of the two massive hulks trudging over the molehill toward them. "Then I've got Tweedledee and Tweedledum."

Lisa and Darcy looked at each other and then at Charlie. "We'll take down the bird," Darcy offered, raising her crossbow.

Charlie grimaced. "No offense, but I don't want to battle that thing with a spear while you've got a crossbow pointed at my back. You two help Nash and Liev. The bird is mine."

As if it heard him, the harpy opened her beak and screeched a song meant to incapacitate whoever was within earshot. Charlie gritted his teeth and brought his spear up, ready.

Liev took aim at the approaching cats. He pulled the antiquated trigger, launching a black grenade, cracking the head of the nearest cat. The angry boggart left its cat skin, becoming a swirling mist a split-second before the grenade exploded.

Nash squeezed S.M.U.G.G.'s trigger and opened fire on the gray troll. Large holes ripped into the monster's thick arms, edges blistering as the troll swatted to shield himself. Lisa and Darcy let their arrows fly against the frightening giant striding next to the troll. To their surprise, one of the shafts hit a hoofed leg, crippling it. Darcy was quick to reload and stole a glance at Charlie.

The harpy was close enough for Charlie to strike. He thrust his spear forward, aiming for one of its eyes, but the large animal was quick—quicker than he expected for a giant bird—and dodged the attack.

Lank, greasy hair flew behind its massive head as the beast ducked forward to pluck something vital out of Charlie's head or torso. It was aiming to finish him.

To his surprise an arrow shaft broke through the creature's forehead with a FLUNK.

The harpy screeched and flew back in retreat, clawing at its own forehead.

"Still sure you don't want me to watch your back?" called Darcy.

Charlie nodded his thanks before turning to plunge his spear into the wounded harpy's exposed neck.

"Darcy! What are you doing?" cried Nash, bringing her back to the reality of her own battle. The six-armed beast had recovered and was running for them at an alarming pace. Nash was forced to negotiate his aim away from the troll and open fire on the other giant.

The angry troll — the bone of his left arm exposed, chest and face blistered — lifted his great wooden cudgel and heaved it forward, head-over-end toward its antagonists.

Nash and Lisa dove headfirst for cover, but Darcy hadn't noticed, having just shot another bolt into the six-armed monster.

"DARCY!"

Darcy looked up to see the cudgel flying straight at her, but it was too late. Crying out in fear, she turned and curled into a ball. There was a deafening boom as the wooden club crashed into Darcy, splintering around her and flying past in mangled pieces. Lisa and Nash stared, gape-mouthed, as did the angry troll.

Darcy opened her eyes and stood, realizing she was still alive. She looked at the shattered wood lying around her, and comprehended what had happened.

"That was . . . good," she said, shaken.

"How come she gets all the cool gifts?" asked Lisa.

"Gifts!" cried Nash, inspired. "We have *gifts!*"

He raised a foot and stomped harder than he'd ever stomped. In the human world, Nash could stomp out a single bolt of lightning. Here, in the Otherworld, his gift was amplified as a storm of electrical charges coursed through the darkness.

Raging, crackling bolts of pure energy danced with each other across the rise of the molehill, charring the nearer six-armed beast and flinging it backwards, electricity still sparking along its burnt flesh. The troll was grazed by the blast, but still flung backward, unconscious.

"Um, help?" Liev pleaded.

Lisa, Nash, and Darcy looked to where Liev stood amid

grenade-ridden patches of ground. Beyond him, a horde of strange and terrifying beasts approached.

Charlie plunged his spear into the harpy over and over until the monstrous bird gave its dying breath, shuddering from horrible head to scaly toe before tumbling into the water. As soon as it hit the water, six pale rusalkas jumped from the water, their pale-green eyes burning bright, and dragged the harpy down into the depths of the water.

Charlie looked away before he could see what happened next. He turned to see how his friends were doing and saw the army of monsters marching toward them. From now on, he decided to pay more attention to his gut feelings.

"Come on," he cried to the others, "this way!"

Without questioning him, Darcy, Nash, and the twins ran toward Charlie, turning back every few strides to be sure a battalion of monsters weren't biting at their heels.

The Otherworld's atmosphere let them run long distances without so much as breaking a sweat. They had survived their first real encounter with the Dark Prince's army of foul monsters.

Charlie knew they would have to face that army again, eventually. His dreams had revealed that much to him. For now, he tried not to think of what else disturbed his dreams.

The varcolac cursed by the names of old gods, crushing the wine glass in his hand into a mound of dust. He saw through the eyes of his servants that the fledgling hunters had survived their first battle.

But they had not won.

He commanded the gathering horde of monsters to let the young humans go. Perhaps they would cross the bridge and return home. Perhaps they would be foolish enough to try and cross the Otherworld by way of the Graveyard. Or, perhaps, they would attempt the long way around the island, past the Sagemistress.

He was counting on it.

The varcolac sent orders to his subjects to set the trap.

Chapter 22

They ran for what seemed like an eternity, past the bridge, and further past Basilisk Pit. It was as if time, space, and the terrain itself were warping and expanding as they retreated. The group lost sight of where they were going, and stopped running when they felt their legs begin to ache.

Looking around, they had no idea where they were. Darcy reached for her necklace, but there was no time for that.

New lines of monsters closed in on three sides, with another turbid river pinning them in on the fourth side. These were not small groups of boggarts or giants, either. These were organized, militant lines of the Dark Prince's minions marching against them.

The monster hunters were outmatched and outnumbered.

Nash stomped once, twice, but the monsters were too far away, and too many to make any difference. Charlie held his friend back, concerned about preserving Nash's energy.

An opportunity presented itself as a long, wide boat drifted over the river. Charlie shoved everyone onboard. The boat was a trap, he knew—what else could it have been?—but the alternative was worse.

The boat was wide enough to ferry across twenty or more people. A figurehead of a skull with menacing eyes protruded from its bow, and it felt like they had entered a cold, empty death the moment their feet stepped onto the deck. With only the thought of escaping the approaching company of flesh-starved monsters on land, they began a frantic search for oars, or anything they could push off and paddle with.

"*A PAYMENT IS REQUIRED, FOR PASSAGE.*"

A cloaked figure materialized from the stern of the boat and they jumped, unnerved at the sound of his raspy, grating voice. The others could not see his face, but Charlie could. He didn't like what he saw under that tattered black and gray hood.

"*PAYMENT, OR LEAVE.*"

Trembling, Lisa reached up to her right ear and removed a silver disc earring, and extended a tentative hand to give the ferryman his due. To their collective horror, the cloaked figure took the piece between two fingers of bone, and then reared back his head into the light. He placed the earring between his two skeletal jaws and swallowed, before looking at Lisa. His eyes were empty sockets but for the faint glimmer of blue-gray fire.

"*THANK YOU.*"

The skeleton ferryman rowed the thick, creaking boat across the river, just as some of the monsters had begun to reach the riverbank. When the beasts saw the fledglings were on board, they turned and marched for Blood Castle.

It was an eerie ride across the waters, with a skeleton for a guide and with Charlie's eyes blazing a violent red. He spent the trip staring into the restless water like something was ready to emerge and devour him. The five were relieved when they heard the bottom of the boat scratch along a rough-sand beach and stutter to a halt on the bank of an island. Each in turn, they hurried to step ashore.

"Where are we now?" Lisa asked, stretching her wobbly legs.

"Hold on, I'm trying to find out," Darcy said, thumbing the

sequence of colored gems on her necklace.

"Um, where'd the boat go?" Nash asked.

Sure enough, it was gone, leaving a swirling mist in the image of a skull in its place.

Liev looked over the water. "Creepy."

"I agree," said Nash.

"I have it," said Darcy.

Darcy hesitated, staring at her map. Charlie nodded, seeing the look on her face.

"We're trapped," he said. "Right where he wants us."

Darcy's heart filled with dread. "We're on Witch Island."

Chapter 23

Nash looked to the twins.

"That's bad, isn't it?"

Liev and Lisa grimaced.

"Well," said Lisa, "it really depends. Witches can be dangerous —"

"— deadly —" said Liev.

"— but some aren't very powerful. Let's hope the one that lives here isn't one of the stronger ones."

"The witch here is strong," said Charlie, seeing the magic that saturated the air. "And I think there's more than one."

They all looked toward the woods blanketing the inland center of the island.

"Then yes," said Liev. "It's bad."

"Let's circle the bank," Charlie said. "Maybe we can find a way off this island without having to deal with anything. . . bad."

They didn't get far. Ahead, a line of trees overtook the ground, which had become higher and rockier. It became evident that the island had been designed so that no one could tread this land without passing through the mangled webs of the trees.

"I guess we go in," muttered Darcy. Charlie spared her a look before leading into the thicket.

Navigating the ground was difficult to itself, without having to crouch through dense trees and tangles of webs and vines. A thin layer of dirt mingled with rotten leaves, covering rocks and tree roots. Every few steps someone would trip over the uneven floor. It became more frustrating, and dangerous, the deeper they trekked.

When the whispering began, it became terrifying.

Voices spoke amidst the trees — wretched voices and fair voices — voices soft, menacing, kind, and harsh. All of them barely audible; enough to cause a person to listen close and lean into the darkness of the weald, hypnotized. The five stared into the clotted forest, looking for unseen faces.

The voices whispered things to them, and about them, and many things they simply didn't understand. Curses? Spells? They couldn't be sure. Ancient words lingered on the mist, just out of reach, yet willing them deeper toward their call.

As the five hunters grew closer to the center of the island, the whisperings grew loud enough to hear.

"*She has the Amulet,*" whispered one voice.

Another one answered, "*This one has the Sight.*"

Two more voices spoke in unison, "*These two act as one, they are —*"

"*Haha, look at this one!*"

Charlie was frightened. He searched with his Sight, yet the witches remained unseen. It was the first time his gift had failed to reveal what he looked for. Shadows of doubt and fear gripped his heart and mind. *I can't lead them. Who was I to think that I could do this? I'm a loner! A loser.* He allowed his thoughts to distract him, and weigh him down.

Charlie shook his head, seeing a pale tendril of yellow magic reaching for him. The witches. They were planting doubt in his mind.

"*What weapons. . . ? What gifts. . . ?*"

"*Fools, all of them, they will not —*"

"*The Sagemistress says they might —*"

218

"— *no, they are fools, you hear? Fools!*"

"*Children, easy prey. . .*"

"*No challenge, so disappointing—*"

"*. . . tender, too, and tasty. . .*"

"*Ah, look at this one, you see?*"

"*Yes, we see him. . .*"

"*He has the Sight, doesn't— ?*"

"*Yes, the boy with the Sight. . .*"

"*. . . the one the Prince wants. . .*"

"*. . . their leader. . .*"

"*He has led his friends astray.*"

Charlie began to run, as a faint laugh mingled with the whisper-ing woods. It was a clear laugh, not like the other voices. He knew whose voice it was when the varcolac spoke in his mind.

"*Hello, boy.*"

He ran harder. Cold sweat beaded across his brow, and his breath came in ragged gasps.

"*You failed to heed my warning. Have you figured it out? Which of your friends will die that horrible, threefold death? Would you like to know?*"

Charlie shook his head and clenched his eyes shut, tripping over an upturned root. He fell headlong to the ground.

"*There's still time, boy. Turn around, go home.*"

Charlie realized the voices had stopped. The ground beneath him was soft, free from roots and rocks. He opened his eyes and found he had made it to the edge of a clearing. The others had followed and helped him to his feet. He staggered forward, trying to put distance between him and the horrors of the trees. They shared nervous smiles, thinking they had made another narrow escape.

But they looked and saw something in the middle of the clearing that tensed their spines with foreboding panic. A large and crooked black house loomed, surrounded by a fence topped with flaming skulls. It took them a moment to realize the pickets of the fence were constructed with bones too.

The front door opened, and an old woman hunched with age, stepped out. She took the porch steps with a quiver, causing the tea tray in her hand to tremble and rattle. From beneath her shawl, she gazed at them with electric-blue eyes. She smiled, causing laugh lines to stretch her crinkled face, revealing a mouth of pristine, straight teeth.

"Welcome, children. I've been expecting you. Tea?"

She held up the tray for them to see—tea cups, biscuits and sugar squares were laid in a meticulous and appealing presentation—and then moved to set the tray down. Though he knew she was a witch, Charlie worried she would drop it, her frail display convincing. But a black, mist-like stream of magic flowed upward, congealing into an intricate table where she set the tray. Six chairs formed around the table in the same manner.

Charlie could see an air of magic about her, yet he didn't see anything else. Unlike the boggarts, this old woman seemed to be exactly what she looked to be.

Charlie scoured the tea with his vision. "No, thank you. We're not here for tea."

"Sit, children. No harm will come to you."

"And we should trust you because . . . ?" Darcy asked. "No offense, but we don't trust monsters, even if they're dressed up like my grandma."

Something flashed across the witch's face—irritation, pride, but more than emotion. *Magic, then?* Charlie couldn't put his finger on it.

220

"Ah yes, the huntress' daughter. I can see her in you. It's a pity, what happened to your mother. You humans just keep throwing your lives away."

Darcy felt her legs buckle. She fell backward, the twins catching her.

Charlie understood what the witch was doing to them. He tried to command the situation. "We don't trust you, and we don't have time for games—"

"The Prince has requested that I turn you away from this fool's errand peacefully, before more of us get hurt. That includes you. We'll let you cross through the gateway without pursuit or attack. But you must return from where you came."

"Can't do that," said Charlie, matter-of-fact. "You'll come through the portal and attack our town as soon as we're gone."

"Yes and no. Hunter's Grove will fall, but your families will be spared. Think what you might, but this is not a trick. I'm prepared to swear by blood and magic." A black dagger appeared in her hand, which she held to the skin of her left wrist.

Charlie could see she was serious. If she swore an oath with magic, he was sure he could spot any lie or deceit with his Sight. Couldn't he?

"I don't get it. Why now?" he asked.

"Your presence is an inconvenience to him. You cannot survive this journey, although you can weaken his forces. Still, the Prince would rather you not destroy so many of his ranks. Consider this a compromise."

"We know what he's up to," said Lisa. "We can't let him resurrect the Ancients."

The witch laughed long and hard; a forced, lifeless laugh. Her

221

face changed again, like the ripple on a pond, and Charlie began to understand what he was seeing.

"What you fail to understand," said the witch, "is that the resurrection of the Ancients is inevitable. They will come. Whether now or in the future, by the Prince's hand or by the hand of another. But if you turn back now, the Prince has offered to spare you, and to guarantee your safety when the Ancients take back the human world. It is a small price to pay for your lives."

She looked at Charlie, sending a shiver up his spine. *She knew about the thrice death*, he comprehended through unspoken communication. *Is it possible for all of us to get out of this alive?* Charlie searched for answers.

The others looked at each other. The witch's proposal was tempting, considering their families, their homes. If they failed, everyone in Hunter's Grove — and humankind — would be consumed by the Dark Prince's insatiable hunger and whatever horrors would be unveiled with the Ancients. If they accepted this offer some, at least, would be guaranteed to live.

It was Nash, trembling, who spoke first and cleared their senses. "So we act like cowards and you'll let us live, while everyone else dies?"

The witch's face rippled again. "Did you not hear me, boy? The Ancients are coming and when they arrive, your human world will fall. This is your only chance to survive under their rule."

The five shared glances that they understood. It was surprising to them how well they had learned to communicate with a single look.

"Sorry," said Charlie. "But we're not here for tea, or compromise. We're here to stop the Dark Prince."

The witch smiled, though it was not a comforting gesture. "I thought as much."

What happened next surprised them all, even Charlie. He should have been able to see the witch—really see her for what she was—but her glamour was strong and deceptive.

The witch stood, throwing the shawl from her shoulders. It evaporated in fire, along with the table, chairs, and everything on the tea tray. What addressed them now was not a fragile old woman, rather a tall, frightening crone radiating with centuries of unnatural power. Her eyes projected an electric-blue glow that revealed an existence seated somewhere between timeworn wisdom and utter madness.

The Sagemistress pointed a long, taloned finger at them, as a line of witches marched forward from the trees. These were not the green-skinned, pointy-hatted characters Charlie and his friends were familiar with from childhood stories. These were warrior women, wielding hidden knowledge and harnessing the power that existed within that knowledge. They carried daggers and sickles, and staffs inlaid with archaic symbols and gemstones. Their presence indicated that they were ready to end this fight here, now, on Witch Island.

Darcy slung her crossbow forward, firing at the Sagemistress. It looked like the shot was going to hit its mark, but then they saw the arrow floating in the air, inches from the Sagemistress' forehead. The venerable witch smiled and plucked the arrow from the air, dissolving it to ash in her hand.

Lisa and Liev stepped forward, thinking as one.

"I won't be easy to kill," the Sagemistress said, looking at Darcy.

"Who said anything about killing you?" shouted Lisa.

The twins cast a net of white-black energy toward the enchantress. It was the first time they used their gift in the Otherworld, and despite the distance, they were able to entrap the Sagemistress. The witch screamed in fury.

The entire island shuddered as the coven of witches charged, daggers gleaming, sickles raised for the kill.

"Protect the twins!" Charlie cried. He ran forward as a witch brought her scythe down, aiming for Lisa. With an uncharacteristic battle cry escaping from a deep place of resolve inside him, Charlie raised Loch's spear—his spear—blocking the witch's blow.

Charlie pushed with his spear, sending the witch backward in forced retreat. Not a moment too soon, he swung the blunt end to batter another enemy coming from his right. The iron ball hissed on impact.

Behind him, Charlie heard S.M.U.G.G.'s bellowing fire as salt grapeshot tore into the advancing witches. He and Darcy stood next to Nash, ready to face any witch that got through his salt barrage, as the twins wrestled the Sagemistress into submission.

Despite the danger of salt, the witches pressed forward, intent on releasing their mistress. They continued to fall as Nash levied heavy fire against their ranks.

"STOP!" cried the Sagemistress.

The witches flew back, letting S.M.U.G.G.'s fire fall short. Charlie placed a hand on Nash's shoulder, signaling for him to ceasefire.

"That's enough," said the Sagemistress, agonizing against the currents. The twins' bonds singed her flesh. "Leave this island."

The hunters stared at her, dumbfounded.

"Just like that?" said Darcy.

The Sagemistress scowled at the twins. "The Prince is a fool. I will not watch my coven destroyed when he refuses my counsel. Go home now, or go to your death. Either way, we will not stop you."

The twins looked at Charlie. He nodded.

"Drag her to the water."

"What?" cried the Sagemistress. "I've given you what you wanted, now let me go!"

"We will, as soon as we're off this island."

"We're not idiots, you know," Darcy added for good measure.

The coven recoiled as their leader was dragged over the ground, toward the trees. They inched forward, until the Sagemistress shouted at them with harsh language none of the hunters recognized. The witches stepped back and, with hesitation, threw their blades to the ground, then turned and flew into the trees.

"Get it over with," said the Sagemistress, clenching her teeth. Charlie, Nash, and Darcy formed a circle around the twins.

"Sorry," muttered Liev as the Sagemistress' head bumped into a tree.

The group dragged their prisoner through the woods, sweating as figures flitted through the trees. They were being watched and Charlie could see dark, hateful magic dancing in the air, waiting to attack them.

Nash slipped, stepping shin-deep in water. Charlie held out his spear and pulled him back, fearing what was in the water. Darcy was alone to guard the twins.

They took defensive stances, expecting the witches to emerge from the trees and overtake them in their moment of weakness.

The Sagemistress chuckled madly. "Do you think so little of us?"

Charlie ignored her, staring over the waters. "Call the ferryman."

"Very well. Kerinnon! These children wish passage of your river!"

Materializing through a heavy fog, the ferryman appeared at the riverbank. "*YES, SAGEMISTRESS. YOU SHOULD KNOW,*

YOUR MASTER IS NOT AT ALL PLEASED."

The witch huffed.

"Lisa," said Charlie, "could I ask—?"

"No problem. Darcy, can you get my other earring?"

Darcy edged between the twins to remove Lisa's other earring. She and Nash hopped onboard the ferryman's vessel, giving the ferryman his due and helping the twins aboard. Charlie jumped on last, sure that they were safe.

"So what's it to be, boy?" the Sagemistress asked, eyeing them with hate. "Do you return home now, or make your way further to the death that haunts you every night when you close your eyes?"

"What's she talking about?" asked Darcy.

"We go forward," said Charlie. "There's no going back. Kerinnon, take us there." He pointed to a small mountain standing in the distance, deep in the belly of the Otherworld.

Kerinnon nodded. *"AS YOU WISH, PASSENGER."*

The ferryman set his macabre vessel to motion, navigating downstream. The twins held the Sagemistress for as long as they could. When they felt the energy slipping, they released her, panting. She spat on the ground, pointing a dirty, crooked talon at them.

"You go to face the prince, and—I swear it is the truth!—one of you will die. I have seen it. So has the boy you look to as your leader. I warned you, just as I warned the woman who came before you. Remember my words, children."

Her voice drifted away as Witch Island disappeared into the mist.

The Sagemistress watched as Kerinnon ferried the five human fledglings away, her blue eyes aflame with anger. Still, despite the pain in her arms and legs, she smiled.

These were the ones. They were strong enough, and cunning. Perhaps even lucky enough.

She felt the Prince poking around inside her mind. The Sagemistress recited several vindictive curses and wards in her ancient tongue, blocking the varcolac's long nose from spying in places it should not be. She heard him cursing in his Great Hall before fading away. She grinned, reveling in her spiteful authority.

The Sagemistress watched as the monster hunters were swallowed by the mist rolling across the same foul river the varcolac used to imprison her coven.

She turned, retreating to her stygian home among the knotted forest.

"Is it true?" asked Darcy, looking at Charlie—all eyes were on him. "Have you seen one of us die?"

Charlie looked from the stony face of Wyvern's Peak, to his shoes, and back again.

"Yes." He turned to face them. "It's a nightmare that has plagued my dreams for some time."

"You should know," cried Lisa in frustration, "after all we've been through, even nightmares should be taken seriously!"

"I do take it seriously!" Charlie countered. "But what would you have wanted me to do? I can't see who it is. I've tried, but I can't.

I've had these dreams long before I knew any of you. Should I have warned you all that one of us might die? You already knew that! I already knew that!"

The boat skidded to a halt. Lisa stormed onto shore, followed by the others. Kerinnon watched them exit his craft with his fiery eyes, then turned without a word and rowed into oblivion.

"Listen, we've already talked about this," Charlie said. He was pleading, more with himself than with them, tears coating his red eyes. "We knew the risk, and we know what will happen if we don't take that risk."

No one said a word. Hardly a breath was shared between them. Charlie continued, looking at each of them in turn.

"If any of you want to leave, go home, I won't stop you. No one will stop you."

Nobody moved.

"I don't want to be here anymore than you." he waivered, trembling with the grave understanding that there would be loss. The only thing certain in his heart and mind going forward was that death was inevitable. He would bear that burden alone if he could. "This is something I have to do. I have to at least try to stop this monster and his army. It's the last chance to stop the varcolac from crossing into our world."

Charlie faced them one more time, then turned and began to climb Wyvern's Peak. The weight of his words pressed against the others, testing their resolve. One by one, they lifted their heads with the knowledge that one of them would never see their home again, and began the steep hike.

It was a silent climb, lonely, filled only with sounds of exertion, and the occasional slipping of feet and loose rocks tumbling. They were so immersed with the events that had just transpired that they forgot about the danger ahead of them. Bearing the name Wyvern's Peak, the twins, at least, should have been wary of the landmark's draconic christening.

Even when they reached the top, and walked past the ominous cave to their right, they were, again, distracted. At the summit of Wyvern's Peak, they could see the entirety of the Otherworld they had yet to cross. And it was a view that was crawling with monsters.

Giant tarantulas, trolls, manticores, boggarts, nelapsi, harpies, hundreds — thousands — of monsters, organized and gathered for what looked to be an invasion. Pacing at the rear of the formations were giant wolves, hellhounds twice the size of horses — gray, black, white, and brown, all prowling in anticipation. Rising into the purple sky behind all of them, surrounded by a filthy black moat, stood the black fortress.

Blood Castle.

The monster hunters were speechless, terrified, unmoving.

Darcy broke the line and plopped to the rocky ground. "How are we going get through that?"

No one answered. Tension thickened the air as the hunters felt eyes on them. The hair on the backs of their necks were sharp, causing the sensation of tiny pins stabbing the length of their arms and backs. Someone, or something, was watching them.

They had forgotten where they were, until now. Wyvern's Peak. *Wyvern.* That formidable and nasty species of dragon from history books, which the twins knew liked to snack on large elephants. They were careful not to share this trivia with the others.

Together, the group made a slow turn to their right, now fully appreciating the ill-boding cave that was home to the great sentry, the wyvern, which watched over Blood Castle from its peak.

Any conflict with a dragon, or any sudden or loud movements on the crest of this mountain, would alert the monsters below. Everything they had struggled through would come to a premature, futile, and rapid end.

The bushes at the mouth of the cave rustled, and the small trees jutting out of the crags rippled a slight sway. No longer concerned for the army of beasts below, the hunters scrambled for their weapons. Still ravaged by the day's events, and overcome by the panic of a close-range introduction to a fierce dragon, they fumbled with loading and aiming their weapons before the foliage revealed its mystery.

Which was a good thing.

Dräng, Chief of Assistants to the Dark Prince, lollopped from the bushes unaware of the frightened teenagers training their defense against him. Coming to an abrupt and fearful halt, Dräng crouched and covered his head with bony fingers, expecting blasts of iron, salt, and all manner of discomfort to befall him. He could not only see, but feel their anger, shock, and unbridled astonishment.

Darcy, having been bitten by the little monster, was especially sour. "You!"

"Oh, good," said Liev, lowering his aim. "I thought it was a dragon."

Ignoring him, Darcy raised her crossbow and centered the little monster in her sights.

"Please, no! Wait! If you only wait, yes wait, I can show you. I have a heart of change. Am here to serve you, to help you! Being a friend to the fledglings."

"Help us? You marked us! You marked our friends and our family.

You're the varcolac's assistant!"

Charlie restrained Darcy, and motioned for the others to lower their weapons.

"Hang on! There's something different about him. I don't know why, but I feel he may be telling the truth. Let's hear him out."

Nash stepped in. "You've got to be kidding me. We have no reason to trust him."

"Nash, wait! Tell me, Dräng, you must have some proof." Charlie knew something was different here. "Give us one reason to believe you and let you live."

"Because he's telling the truth!" A rusty voice broke through the entangled shrubs and twisted vines. "You should listen to what he has to say."

The proprietor of that rusty voice emerged from the foliage, rabbit foot and all.

Chapter 24

The bushes shuddered, releasing one Fish McCollum. Before he could get to his feet, one Wardley Dink rolled out and over the top of Fish.

"I am so sick and dang-blasted tired of these ridiculous woods around here. Can't take a single step without falling in something that stinks or getting tied up in vines from the belly of Hell itself! Ain't never seen so many scraggly weeds!"

"Fish! Dink!" cried Nash. He looked at Dräng, confused. "You?"

"Yes, me, now please believe and do not execute," he said, slicing a worried finger across his neck.

"Your little friend here told us you were in trouble," said Fish. "He helped us get into this world. Now we're here to help you."

Fish was covered in all sorts of charms. He wore his usual rabbit foot necklace, but was also now wrapped in two strands of garlic, rosary beads, and wearing a bracelet of painted pebbles. An iron horseshoe hung from his left pants pocket. Anyone else would have looked like they needed intervention, but with the intense, honest expression Fish wore — not to mention the hunting rifle, silver dagger, and two ammo belts he carried — he looked dead serious and very much in control of his faculties.

Dink, on the other hand, fashioned a simpler get-up. He carried a shotgun. And a fishing pole.

Nash nodded to the field of monsters. "We could sure use the help."

Fish and Dink scanned a critical eye over the battlefield.

"Right," said Dink. "You all take the ones on the right. I got the ones on the left."

Darcy looked at him out of the corner of her eye. "I don't think that's going to work, Dink."

"It could," Liev whispered, grinning.

"And that fishing pole might not do you any good down there."

"Well, you know," Dink said, holding up his fishing pole with pride, "I thought, since we were coming to another world and all, I'd check out what kind of fishin' they got here. Got to be thinking about the important things in life. You'll see when you get old and crusty like me."

Charlie gave a grim chuckle, surveying the battlefield. "You don't want what's in the water here, Dink."

As the others discussed the best approach, Darcy sat down on a small boulder a short distance from everyone else. She was the first to offer her opinion in most cases, whether it was wanted or not. But now, she was haunted by what the witch had said about her mother. She was fidgeting with her necklace, when she had an idea.

Dräng raised his scrawny arm to speak, but Lisa had already started to ask a question.

"How many do you think you could take out with your stomping from here?" she said.

"From here?" asked Nash. "None. It doesn't reach that far. But if I was able to get closer, maybe a bunch. I haven't had much opportunity to test it."

"I could probably knock out a couple hundred," said Liev, waving his grenade launcher.

Purple Monster, Yellow monster, Brown monster, three, thought Darcy, *Why are you jumping on my bed?* That part was easy enough to figure out. Purple, yellow, brown.

"But then they would know we were here," Charlie was saying.

"That might be a good thing," Fish said. "They would rush up here, and we'd be fighting from higher ground."

Blue monster, Black monster, Purple monster, see? Now I am stomping on *your heads. It has to be offensive,* thought Darcy. *Right? Stomping heads sounds offensive.*

Charlie nodded, agreeing with Fish. "We'd have a strong defensive position on the peak."

Liev enthusiastically cocked the hammer. "Locked and loaded! Just tell me when to fire."

Lisa rolled her eyes.

Charlie was still thinking. "Hang on. Darcy, Lisa, when Liev fires off the first round, be ready to pick off the front line coming for us. You too, Nash."

"I'll be ready," Nash said. He activated the pressure from S.M.U.G.G.'s vest.

"Good." Charlie looked at Fish and Dink. "I don't know what regular weapons will do against monsters, but I guess it can't hurt our chances."

"Don't worry 'bout us," said Dink. "Fish set us up somethin' special."

"Silver buckshot," Fish said, pointing his thumb at Dink's shotgun. "And I've got my own rounds. My da used to tell me stories of his homeland. Taught me how to protect myself well enough."

"That's great," said Charlie, ignoring Dräng, who was still trying to speak. "All right everyone, are you ready? Darcy, did you hear?

Darcy?"

Darcy wasn't listening. She was thumbing her necklace. And walking downhill.

"Darcy! What are you doing?"

Darcy was, in fact, pressing the gems on her necklace according to the macabre nursery rhyme her mother used to sing. A few of the monsters noticed her, and a shudder of activity rippled over the battlefield.

Then Darcy stopped and, where she stood, pressed the last gem—purple—pointing the necklace toward the beasts in the field. There was a loud roar, like a jet engine at takeoff that traveled through the lines of monsters. A beam of white-hot light lit up the battlefield, engulfing most that were gathered in the center of the field.

The hunters felt chills run up their arms and legs as the light from Darcy's necklace sucked the life out of the air, wherever it touched. Charlie gasped, seeing the powerful, dark burst of purple magic inside the light.

When the light faded, they could see an army of confused, irritated monsters. They were still standing, and now all of them were aware of the hunters on Wyvern's Peak.

Darcy felt the blood drain from her face and limbs. She was wrong. That nursery rhyme was not meant for an offensive attack. Now she became the main target of a horde of bloodthirsty creatures. Darcy kicked herself mentally. *What was I thinking?* She backed away, trembling like a leaf in a summer storm.

Before she could get far, the nearest monster, a hideous centaur with one red eye and no skin to cover its pulsating underflesh and organs, turned to a monster on its left, a green troll with a curtain of ragged hair. The centaur grasped the troll by its hair, threw it to the ground, and stomped its head with a slimy hoof.

"Well," said Liev, watching from the peak. "That was unexpected."

Dink nodded with raised eyebrows. "Suppose they didn't like each other very much, then."

It didn't stop with the first two. Another monster stomped on the troll's head, and then another stomped on the centaur's head—an unpleasant sight, considering its lack of skin.

Deadly scuffles erupted in the center of the monster army. Any being that had been touched by the light from Darcy's necklace fought viciously under its spell—stomping on whatever head was nearest to them. The effect was widespread and unsightly.

Darcy watched the scene and felt the corners of her lips tug upward. It was a macabre humor, but the nursery rhyme suddenly seemed funny, and useful. Charlie's beckon from the peak interrupted her thoughts.

"Darcy!"

She looked and saw he was pointing to something. It was the aggregation of monsters who had not been hit by the light. They came marching, crawling, flying, skittering, and slithering toward her without delay.

"Use the necklace!" Charlie was calling. "Hit them with it."

Darcy raised her necklace, struck with both panic and exhilaration. *Take that, monsters.* She repeated the coded series, thumbing the gems like sending a text on her phone...

...but nothing happened. There was no sound. No light.

She tried it again, then a third time. Nothing.

Darcy's courage bottomed out. She ran up to where the others stood at the top of the hill, tripping and scrambling up the loose rocks. Liev covered for her, firing off a couple of grenades. There were distant explosions and angry howls as Lisa and Dräng pulled Darcy the rest of the way.

"Why won't it work?" Lisa asked, frantic.

"I don't know!" Darcy cried.

"It doesn't matter now," Charlie said. "We need to level as many as possible before they get here!"

Two more explosions resulted from Liev, as monsters, arms, legs, and other pieces flew from the fresh points of impact.

"Hey Dink!" Liev said with his mischievous grin. "Better get ready to use that fishing pole!"

Nash stomped as hard as he could, sending relentless crackles of energy over the front line of monsters, buying as much time as he could. He loaded several canisters into S.M.U.G.G., and discharged them against clusters of monsters.

Darcy and Lisa swung their crossbows forward and watched for the closest threats to emerge before firing. Fish stood tall, relying on his hunting instincts to remove some of the bigger, more threatening monsters. Charlie saw one of Fish's rounds hit a troll in the neck before its head and shoulders dissolved. He wondered what exactly Fish's secret recipe for ammunition consisted of.

Dink positioned himself a short distance down the hill, where his weapon was within effective striking distance. His silver buckshot didn't dissolve the monsters like Fish's ammo, but it did send smaller monsters flying through the air, often in pieces. He dropped an imposing six-armed giant with a flush shot between its three eyes.

Even Dräng helped. He would pick up small stones, muttering words that infused them with light and life, before lodging the stones into the fray. Charlie could see the magic that would gather, swirling, around each stone. The diminutive monster's makeshift projectiles would hit their targets like a boulder — not mere stones — sending throngs of monsters crashing down.

Charlie, the only one without a long-range weapon, brought his spear down and forward, walking close to Dink. He stood there, waiting.

Dink smiled at him between shooting a goblin-hybrid and a screeching harpy from the sky. "Hey there, Charlie. How ya doin'? Ain't this fun?" He let loose a hearty, and goofy, giggle and nudged Charlie's shoulder.

The five monster hunters and their friends kept the monsters at bay, but they couldn't stall forever. The Dark Prince's army was too big. Sooner than later, they would be overrun.

A stilt-legged monster with a tiny body and bulbous head made it through the barrage. It fixed two large eyes at Charlie and thrust a long stinger toward him. Charlie ducked with swift precision, positioned his feet for a counter attack, and answered with a swipe of his spear, hitting the creature in the legs. It fell to its back, long legs scrambling to get to its feet. Dink planted silver buckshot in its sideways head as they found themselves fighting off another lumbering giant.

"Charlie, Dink! Heads down!"

A volley of lightning from Nash thundered its way over their heads, striking the giant, toppling it onto several monsters in its wake.

Flying over the chaos, a banshee opened its blackened mouth, revealing circular jaws lined with jagged teeth. She wailed, piercing the sky and shaking the hunters to their bones. They cowered and covered their ears from the shrill. In their moment of weakness the monster army moved in to eliminate the bothersome humans.

A familiar shriek rocked the air, rivaling the banshee's own cry. Monsters and humans alike looked up to see the banshee's limbs being ripped from its core by a dragonesque gargoyle. Each rip from the banshee became wisps of smoke and dirt, until the ghostly spirit was vanquished.

The gargoyle flew upward into the purple sky, screaming victorious—a cry both fearsome and invigorating. Then, twisting in the air, it plummeted headlong toward the hillside of Wyvern's Peak. Claws extended, wicked beak open, and its stone tail thrashing, the gargoyle decimated untold numbers of monsters before swerving back toward the sky.

Charlie stood, gasping for air. Eyes wild, he knew what needed to be done.

Inspired by the gargoyle's arrival, Charlie raised his spear and ran forward yelling the first word that came to mind.

"CHAAAARGE!"

The others fell behind him in a wedge formation. The team of eight sprinted down the hill, drawing swords, daggers, rapiers—and fishing poles. Any monster Charlie failed to down with his spear, the others would finish in his wake. For a boy who was clumsy in training, Charlie cut an impressive, bloody swath on the battlefield. The gargoyle helped, assaulting aerial threats like a skyward assassin.

They ran fast and hard for Blood Castle. Charlie knew they were cutting themselves a path, but the monsters not slain would soon regroup behind them, and his team would be surrounded.

They reached the foot of the hill and neared the black moat. The battlefield was grim; the teens now understood why war was Hell. They trudged through the charred bodies of Nash's handiwork, and stepped around creatures with Dräng's magic stones protruding out of their flesh. Under the watchful shadow of Wyvern's Peak, scores of monsters lay on the ground with their heads crushed, and pockets of survivors still clamoring to stomp on one another.

Charlie angled for those monsters still under Darcy's spell, seeing an opportunity. "Don't attack them!" he huffed over his shoulder.

The others didn't argue, and soon saw his reasoning. The monsters chasing them from behind got caught up with the monsters under Darcy's spell, causing a blockage.

Charlie looked back and smiled, but grimaced as the movement caused his chest to burn. He was growing tired, even with the Otherworld's energizing atmosphere. He looked at the others and saw their faces — weary, pained, and in need of rest.

"Stay strong!" he yelled. "We're almost there!"

They nodded at him, ready to persevere, survive, win — no matter the cost.

Charlie saw a large force of red manticores lingering to their left — their human faces sneering — and remembered seeing Manticore Den on the map. Something about the lion-like cross-breeds brought the onset of a headache.

Liev saw them too, and shot two grenades into their midst, sending up torrents of salt, silver, and dirt.

On the other side, Nash followed Liev's advance. He stomped, attempting to stop an incoming force on their right. Charred bodies were flung into the waters near Banshee's Stay. Pale arms eagerly wrapped around the bodies and dragged them into the sloshing water.

Nash turned to their rear and decimated the closest of the monsters chasing them. Dink clapped him on the back before picking another harpy from the sky. He unloaded on it a second time, after it crashed to the ground.

"Dang things," he muttered. "Ugly as heck, too."

"Not as ugly as that," Fish said, pointing to a scorpion-centaur mongrel. The shot only bounced off its snapping claw.

Fish fired again into the monster's armored abdomen, its chest, and its neck. It was wounded, but kept coming. Dink's buckshot, however, shattered a claw and cleared a space between its ears.

Dink nudged it with the tip of his fishing pole.

"Crazy things just don't want to give up, do they Fish?"

"Not so easy, my friend." He turned to see an incoming goblin riding a giant spider, and held up a string of garlic. Marching forward, he commanded, "Be gone, foul rider of evil household pests!" With a lunatic laugh, he plunged forward to face the foul devils.

The battle raged on, and the hunters continued their march of destruction. For the moment, they had the upper hand and forward momentum. But they were still outnumbered, and tired. It was a matter of time before their defenses would be breached—or before everyone ran out of ammo.

And yet, they were close. So very close.

Ahead of the group, Charlie speared a lone goblin before coming to a sudden halt, causing Darcy to topple into him. Blood Castle stood in front of Charlie like an angry fragment of Hell. He stared at the line of werewolves standing in front of the fortress, glaring at the approaching hunters with primitive, murderous eyes. Charlie's vision blurred and he was struck with sudden sickness. He felt he had been here before.

Something was wrong.

Before he could do anything about it, Dräng grabbed Charlie's hand and pulled him toward the back of the castle, to where the river ended, and where Demon's Gorge began.

"What are you doing?" cried Charlie, seeing they were headed for a thicker line of wolves, their hackles raised. The Alpha was among this group.

"Secret way," puffed Dräng. "I've been trying to warn you, you cannot enter front door, silly human! But here, we may enter."

The others followed, hesitant. Dräng was marching them to the edge of the Otherworld, where many of their enemies — stronger enemies — stood waiting for them, guarding the secret entrance to the castle.

"Nash!" Charlie yelled. He pointed at the wolves and other monsters waiting there. "Little help here?"

Nash complied and peppered the line with S.M.U.G.G., helped by Liev's grenade launcher. Bodies flew like bowling pins, clearing space for them to get through.

"That was easy," said Liev.

Lisa nudged her brother, moving her crossbow to face the monsters drawing near. "It's not over yet."

Hiding among his fallen brethren, the alpha wolf snarled. He survived the barrage, foreleg charred, but already beginning to heal. He was no small creature to be shot and discarded from memory.

"It is here," Dräng said, clapping. He rushed forward and pushed back a mat of vines and moss, revealing a stone trapdoor. "Here! Come, silly human, help me."

The hunters gathered in a semicircle, giddy, tasting victory. They continued to hold off monsters while Charlie and Dräng tried to lift the stone door. Charlie faltered, glimpses of his visions becoming clear. Too clear.

A splash from the moat announced the wodnik had heaved his great, fish-like body onto the battlefield, croaking threats against the humans. Dink saw him first.

"Bless my overalls! Fish, do you see that?"

"I do indeed."

"How many filets you reckon I could get out of that thing?"

"Not sure I want to find out, Dink."

The wodnik reared his slimy arm and clawed at Dink's shin, shredding his pant leg. Dink yelped, slamming the butt of his fishing rod into the wodnik's squishy face. Grandfather Bilibin slipped back into the moat, unconscious.

"Dang." Dink inspected the waters. "There goes that catch."

"I'm sure you'll find another."

Darcy and Lisa's supply of crossbow bolts dwindled, as did Nash's salt grapeshot. They became picky with their targets, leaving Fish and Dink to do most of the shooting. Still, it was easier here, on the edge of the Otherworld. Their enemies approached from one direction, allowing them to concentrate their defense, making it easier to guard Charlie and Dräng.

"You done yet?" Nash yelled over the ruckus.

"Almost! Almost!" Dräng answered. This escape passage was never used, and it opened with the greatest reluctance. They had opened a space large enough for him to fit through, but not large enough for the humans.

Nash finished the last of his ammo, and the line of monsters came too close for Liev to continue using his grenade launcher for fear of hitting his teammates.

Darcy gave the rest of her arrows to Lisa, and began slipping through monsters, confusing them. She used her dagger and foil to slice into startled wolves, trolls, and goblins before they could retaliate.

A manticore broke through, its red body bounding forward, mane and hackles pulsing, scorpion tail slicing the air. It leaped—claws narrowly missing Charlie and Dräng—and landed in front of Liev. The manticore clawed once, snapping at him with its three rows of fangs.

Liev landed two successful stabs into the beast, and laughed at his own skill. He didn't see the poisonous barb that shot from its tail, until it had landed in his thigh.

Four shots came from Fish and Dink in succession, mortally wounding the manticore. Together, they drove the dying creature into the moat while Lisa ran to her brother's side. She knew what the poison of a manticore would do to a human being.

"Liev," she said, panic rising in her voice. "We've got to get that out *now*. It will kill you!"

Liev broke off the end of the barb and waved her away, hoisting his grenade launcher onto his shoulder. His face grew pale, and he was no longer laughing. He could feel the poison spreading from the wound; a hot, itching pain crept up his leg and through his torso. Grimacing, he tried to ignore it.

The hunters became desperate, as monsters swarmed them with vengeance. With Liev's injury, and the entire team reduced to close-quarter combat—and no end in sight to the throng of monsters closing in—it seemed they'd lost.

A chunk of earth grazed Charlie, causing him to drop the trap-door precious inches. A troll had thrown a ball of compacted dirt and clay, and was now advancing on him, ready for the kill.

To Charlie's relief, Darcy intervened, stabbing the monster's leg with her foil and—when the troll bent, yielding to the pain—piercing its soft skull.

A few feet away, a banshee bit into Fish's shoulder. While he struggled with the ghastly spirit, a wolf slipped through a gap in their defenses, tackling Nash. It bared its razor-sharp fangs as Nash hit the animal with a burst of lightning before it could tear into his shoulder.

Just when it seemed they'd taken too long, that too many monsters were breaking through, Charlie and Dräng threw the trap door the final inches. It fell over with a thud.

"Everyone in!" barked Charlie.

He didn't have to ask twice. The hunters ran to the tunnel, guarding one another as they staggered in.

Lisa realized something was wrong, looking up for her best friend, and brother. Charlie saw it too, then heard Lisa scream.

"*Liev!*"

Liev was engaged in fierce contest with a great wolf. The Alpha.

The beast singled Liev out as the weak link in the group, springing from his cover to attack. Now, Liev had only his silver blade to keep the monster at bay, but was fast losing the fight.

The gargoyle returned like heaven's fury, crushing several monsters under its heavy body, but those monsters were of less concern. It rose behind the wolf and slashed the Alpha's back with its stone talons, giving Liev enough time to disengage and catch his breath.

The wolf roared in agony and spun, honing its sights on the stone guardian. For a moment, the hunters thought the gargoyle would crush the wolf with a swift blow, but the scales of Destiny would tilt to feed their distress.

The gargoyle snapped at the alpha wolf with its beak, missing by inches. The wolf crushed a heavy paw against the gargoyle's side, leapt onto its shoulder and, to Liev's shock and dismay, ripped a sculptured arm from the gargoyle's torso. The wolf used the gargoyle's own arm as a weapon against him, beating the statuesque protector until its body began to crack.

"Stop!" yelled Liev, with all the authority he could gather. He flung his dagger into the wolf's shoulder, turning the Alpha's attention back on himself. It was a noble mistake.

The enraged werewolf launched from the gargoyle's back, as an arrow zipped through the air, piercing the wolf's side. The beast stopped and clutched at the wound when another shaft flew into its clawed hand.

Lisa marched forward, shooting twice more as the wolf turned. One arrow found its way to the wolf's bicep, another to its abdomen. The hunters could see Liev's relief as the wolf fell backward, toppling toward the moat. They could also see a witty retort already forming on his lips. But he never got the chance.

"Liev," cried Lisa, "look out!"

As she screamed in warning, the wolf clawed out for something to hold onto, nails raking across Liev's back. Liev howled in pain as the savage grabbed hold of Liev's shredded shirt, pulling the pale twin down with him. The wolf latched onto him with its claws, grasping for life, and sunk its teeth into Liev's shoulder in spite.

The brother and the wolf disappeared over the edge of the moat.

"No!" screamed Lisa, rushing forward. But she was too far away. The gargoyle, broken and dismantled, dove into the moat trying to save Liev, still trying to protect.

Lisa reached the edge of the moat in time to see the gargoyle and the wolf being dragged down by the rusalkas. Liev's body was nowhere in sight.

"No!" she cried again. "No, this can't happen. *No, no, no, no!*"

She pounded the ground with her fist, her emotions rupturing inside of her. Liev was gone. Her lifelong friend and companion.

Her brother.

Dead.

The others called for her, but she didn't—couldn't—care. Weeping, she punched the ground until her knuckles were raw and bleeding. Sorrow mixed with anger, racking her body and punishing her thoughts.

A strong arm dragged her back. It was Nash, pulling her to the tunnel, grabbing Liev's grenade launcher as he did.

Lisa's body ached from sobbing, her mind slipping from consciousness, bearing the weight of her brother's death. Her heartache turned into anger, and losing control of her thoughts, Lisa used her gift to strike out. She wanted to hurt the monsters, hurt them as much as she could for taking Liev away.

Jagged tendrils of energy—pure black energy, no longer sharing Liev's white glow—flew from Lisa's hands, cutting through monsters like matchsticks in a firestorm. This was not the flowing, netlike manifestation of her gift—it was irregular and serrated, a wrathful weapon Lisa was subconsciously creating.

Nash flinched as one of the tendrils singed his forearm. His small movement sent Lisa's delirious aim in a wide arc over the monsters. It bludgeoned, sliced, and scorched everything it touched, buying Nash enough time to clear the secret door into the tunnel.

Lisa's throat was raw from screaming. Strands of black energy recoiled, seeping back into her shaking form or blinking out altogether. She curled into a ball in Nash's arms and cried into his shoulder. He glanced at where he last saw Liev standing before carrying her deeper into the tunnel where the others watched and waited. Tears flooded every face.

Their pain was palpable, their fear tangible, and they were caught between the two emotions. Not a single monster attempted to follow them inside, which made them all the more nervous.

Charlie let Dräng lead. He didn't feel like playing leader anymore. He could have prevented this. If he understood the Sight better—if he'd paid attention—Liev would still be alive.

He walked several paces behind everyone else, dragging his spear and watching the rear.

Charlie took Liev's grenade launcher from Nash, who carried a catatonic Lisa. Liev had loaded a final grenade before dying. Charlie bit back tears and aimed the gun toward the entrance to the tunnel, and pulled the trigger.

The explosion rocked the walls and floor, and a cloud of dust bellowed through the tunnel. Earth and stone crumbled, sealing the tunnel entrance shut and delivered them into darkness.

Charlie laid the gun down, and walked away.

The Dark Prince watched the battle, furious.

The young hunters had made a mockery of his army. Worst of all, they were now inside his castle, being led by his treacherous Chief of Assistants.

The varcolac's Lesser servants fled the Great Hall, terrified. He tore his robes as pillars shattered and the marble floor cracked open.

The great fireplace no longer blazed, the hearth crumbled into ash.

The Hall was covered in darkness, reflecting the mood of its master.

One of their ilk had died, fulfilling the thrice death prophecy as the varcolac had foreseen. It tore the hunters apart. Even now, he watched them walking through his escape tunnel. They were disorganized and weak, no longer the powerful hunters they had believed themselves to be. Now they were mere children, mourning their fallen friend. Their leader, Charlie, broken.

This soothed the Prince.

He stood from the ruins of his throne. Despite the progress the hunters had made, his plan was coming together. They had lost the upper hand. Now they were in his domain, and his grasp. The next move was his to make.

As the hunters drew near, the varcolac prepared for a final play that would eliminate their nuisance, this time for good.

Chapter 25

The Way of Mirrors—a labyrinth of looking glasses snaking through the underbelly of Blood Castle. The intricate maze of rooms was something of a fascination for the varcolac—a place where his reflection was forever absent, but where his enemies could be stored, hidden. The monstrous prince had spent centuries creating the elaborate layout and mechanics of this network of rooms and mirrors. He considered it a crown achievement, merging artistic play and life-sustaining function into the very heart of his domain.

Now, the team of monster hunters stood at its threshold, waiting for their cue to enter.

Inside the Way of Mirrors, one particular reflective panel began to move. It sunk backward into a wall with a mechanical click as hidden gears rumbled, causing the mirror to slide away. A secret door opened.

A short monster with bulbous black eyes and a crooked smile poked his head out of the wall, looking left and right before hopping out. Six humans followed him into the expansive Way of Mirrors. They shivered, overcome with the smell of blood and the sense of hatred in the room. They felt eyes on them.

Centuries ago, the Dark Prince imprisoned captured hunters here, turning them into mindless slaves, and forcing them to build his maze. In a gruesome display of cruel boredom, the Dark Prince then used the brainwashed hunters as finishing touches to his masterpiece. Dräng decided against explaining the morbid history of the Way of Mirrors. He scrambled to his feet and beckoned to Charlie with long hands.

"This way! Come this way!"

Charlie let the others pass, still not in the mood to be in front.

The hunters had to break into a jog to avoid losing the little domovoi. The mirrors were disorienting enough without getting lost in them. Nash and Darcy pulled Lisa along as she stared dispassionately at the dank flagstones.

Charlie started sweating. Not from exertion, but because of his Sight. He could see all manner of dark magic lingering here. Worse than the magic, he saw ghostly silhouettes suspended inside the mirrors.

These were the varcolac's old drudges. They stared out at Charlie, their black sockets drawing him forward with silent screams, beating their fists against the inside of the mirrors. Charlie became entranced and reached out for the mirrors. Their screams became deafening inside his head.

Someone jerked Charlie away from the glass, hard. Shaking from his stupor, he looked down to see Dräng holding his arm. The monster shook his head.

"No looking at mirrors for very long."

Charlie nodded, finding it difficult to break from the hypnotic pull the mirrors had on him.

"Ugh, we don't have time for this," Darcy complained. "Nash, can you smash through these mirrors with your storm-stepping thingy?"

"I could try."

Dräng tensed, opening his mouth to speak, but Darcy spoke

faster and louder.

"We need to get out of here and get to the Prince, now. The longer we wait, the closer he is to getting through the gateway."

"Yeah, good point. Here, hold Lisa."

Nash raised his foot, and Dräng felt as if his small heart might pop. Charlie jumped forward, forced back to reality by their conversation.

"No, don't—!"

He threw himself in front of Nash, nearly tackling him. Nash scowled.

"Charlie, what the heck is your problem?"

"Don't break the mirrors," said Charlie.

Darcy snapped. "And why not? Is this another one of your freaky Sight things?" her voice escalating.

Charlie spun on his heels, glowering over Darcy. "As a matter of fact, it is!" His eyes deepened into a darker shade of red as he seethed through his frustration.

The others watched as the two stood, glaring at each other, Darcy slowly realizing she was no match for Charlie's gift of Sight. Lisa looked out from blank eyes as Nash and his two woodsmen friends waited for the tempers in the room to cool.

Dräng coughed, raising a finger. "The boy is right. To break the mirrors would be bad, very bad. The prince's slaves live inside. They are not . . . happy things."

Darcy turned from Charlie, to Dräng, and back to Charlie. She flung her arm out at Dräng as if to say, *Go ahead then.*

Crisis averted, the group fell back into a steady, tense cadence of twists and turns. Fish squeezed his rabbit foot for good luck.

"Almost there," said Dräng in an excited pant. "There! There is door!"

He ran to the door and pushed with all his might as a brilliant, purple light spilled into the room. It danced around the mirrors, momentarily blinding the hunters. After adjusting to the refracting light, they saw the Way of Mirrors surrendered to a large courtyard. The purple sun of the Otherworld was setting, plummeting over Blood Castle's black stone wall.

The spacious courtyard hosted a handful of grid-inlaid, wood and metal doors and two foreboding gates. Through the gate to their far left, they could see Wyvern's Peak and the battlefield, still teeming with monsters.

"Why are they out there?" asked Nash. "Why don't they attack?"

No one answered because, deep down, they knew why. The Dark Prince was allowing the hunters unhindered passage through the castle.

"Not far. Not far now," said Dräng. His voice was raspy. "The Great Hall is close."

He led them to the other gate, leading into Blood Castle's towering keep. Through the gate was a large, formal entryway lined with long-dead skeletons. They sat in swinging cages or, worse, hung from tall spikes nailed to the stone walls.

"This is wrong," said Nash.

Dräng nodded, having resigned long ago to the horrors that Blood Castle prized. He simply focused on the open doorway ahead of them, and only when they reached it did he allow himself to look around.

In front of them, a hallway split, with limited vision as to where it led.

"Which way?" asked Darcy.

Dräng shrugged his shoulders. "Matters not. Either way leads to the Great Hall."

"We'll go right, then," said Darcy. She glared at Charlie expecting a challenge, still upset about earlier. He didn't argue.

As they walked, the hallway curved in a giant half-circle. Which meant the Great Hall was housed inside a massive circle hallway.

Dräng confirmed that fact a few minutes later. "This is bad," he said. "This place is a giant circle used for defensive magic. It should have come to life by now. We should be dead, or in very much pain."

"So," said Nash, "we're alive and unharmed. This is bad . . . how?"

"Seriously, you little imp! Were you leading us here to kill us?" Darcy fumed.

The others in the group tensed at the thought.

"No! No! But, if the magic is not alive by our presence, it means the Master made the magic here to sleep. He let us through for bad purposes."

A hush fell over the team and they continued forward.

They came to a pair of large doors to their left.

"We are here," said Dräng. "Here is the Great Hall."

"Then what are we waiting for?" asked Darcy, impatient. "Let's go."

Dräng stopped her, gesturing to another set of doors on the opposing wall. His ears drooped, and he seemed to cower beneath them as he spoke.

"Before facing his majestic evilness, there is something for you to see."

Fish and Dink braced against the obsidian doors with their shoulders and heaved with all their strength. As the doors parted, the group wished they had remained closed. The smell of death wafted past them, along with a cold, dank wind.

Fish grabbed one of the torches from the wall, offering it to Charlie.

"Lead the way," said Fish.

"I—I can't."

Fish sighed, his shoulders slumping. Darcy grabbed the torch.

"Come on," she said. "We should hurry."

Together, they forged into the dark.

Dink tripped over something, causing a clatter. "Can't hardly see nothin' in this—"

He clamped his mouth as Darcy lowered the torch and they saw what he had tripped over. The femur bone of a human skeleton lay at their feet.

"Yeesh!" cried Dink, leaping away from the remains. He shivered from head to toe.

"Yeesh?" teased Fish.

Nash bent over to look at the skeleton. It looked like it had been leaning against a cage before being tripped over.

"What is this place, Dräng? Why did you bring us here?"

"It's a dungeon," said Charlie. He was looking around the room, being able to see all-too-clear without a source of light. It was filled with cages that hung from the ceiling or bolted to the floor. Tables covered with wretched, unpleasant tools were scattered throughout the room. Charlie tried his best not to look for long at any of it.

"Oh no," he whispered as he saw the first person, and ran forward.

"Wait!" cried Darcy. "What is it, what do you see?"

They shuffled toward Charlie, trying to avoid tripping over each other, or colliding with torture devices. The more their eyes adjusted, the more they saw hiding in the dark—and the worse they felt for seeing. Then they found Charlie.

He was standing in front of an older man dressed in rags. The man's arms were held up with chains from the ceiling with a heavy collar around his neck, weighing him down. Charlie couldn't see the man's face hidden behind his long, dirty-white hair and beard. He tried brushing the hair to reveal a face.

"Sir? Are you...?" He searched for a word. "Are you alive?"

Blue-green eyes stared empty from behind the curtain of matted hair. The man didn't answer Charlie.

"I think he's dead," said Charlie.

"No. He is alive," said Dräng. The little monster pointed to ragged bite marks on the man's shoulders and arms. "He is a slave to the prince now. Long ago, my master would eat them all, but food supply is low now. He keeps them like this; imprisoned with old magic, unable to live or die without his command. He controls everything about them."

"Like some sort of canned food," said Nash, angry.

Dräng nodded, saddened by this fact, and that he's had a part in this evil for so long.

"Are there more?" asked Charlie.

"Yes. He keeps them close together, to compare them."

Darcy brought the torch forward. Not far from the old man was someone who looked to be an Asian monk wearing tattered clothes from the turn of the century, if not a century before. He was rigorously suspended in midair by a wooden board and chains.

"Guys," said Charlie. "Look at this."

As Darcy's torch swept across the room, they all gasped. Fish whistled.

"They're all here, aren't they?" asked Dink.

Locked behind cages or in chains, were all the missing people of Hunter's Grove.

Darcy's eyes watered and she nearly dropped her torch. "Mom!" she gasped.

She shoved the torch into Nash's hand, rushing to where her mother stood, haggard and frozen in time. She reached out to touch her face.

"Mom. She's alive."

"I count ten," said Charlie, scanning the dungeon. From Elizabeth Witherington to Robert Wickles. Mr. Tonson the locksmith and Elijah Silverstien the carpenter were also there. Little Bobby Muldor sat curled in a ball, dirty, with an infected bite mark on his forearm. He saw everyone who had gone missing, except one. Eleven total had gone missing.

Nash realized what Charlie was about to say. He handed the torch off to Fish, scouring the faces imprisoned around them. He looked a second time, closer.

In a fit of rage, Nash grabbed Dräng by his torn robes and lifted the monster into the air.

"There was another," he growled. "An old woman. Why isn't she here? Where is she?"

"T-t-there was one more...like you say," sputtered Dräng. His robes bunched under his chin, making it difficult to breathe. "The female...she didn't...."

"Didn't what?" asked Nash, though he knew the answer. Mrs. McBranson, his friend and wily mentor didn't survive. He wasn't willing to accept that truth.

"Nash," said Charlie. "Let him go." He placed a hand on Nash's shoulder, but Nash recoiled, ignoring his friend.

Dräng gasped and coughed, struggling to inhale small pockets of air. "She was too frail. She didn't...please, please put me down—"

"Didn't what? Say it!"

"Nash! Put him down before you kill him!"

Nash spun, eyes searing into Charlie. It wasn't Charlie's blood-red eyes that forced Nash's compliance, rather that Charlie was right. Nash dropped the former Chief of Assistants and fell against one of the cold metal cages.

"The aged female was too weak," Dräng rasped. He rubbed at his sore throat and shoulders. "She died with little suffering, little pain. I...I am sorry." He cringed, expecting Nash to pummel him.

Nash just wiped his eyes and nodded. "Thank you...for telling me. Is there a body?"

Dräng shook his head.

"What about those who are still alive?" asked Fish. "Can they be saved?"

"Sever their tie to the Prince. It will be hard."

"Does that mean we have to kill him?"

"It is preferable."

"It's on our to-do list," said Charlie. "Let's go."

Darcy took one last look at her mother before Dink patted her on the shoulder.

Dräng scrambled to keep up with Charlie. "What if you silly humans cannot kill him? What if you fail miserably? What if you die, or worse, are captured?"

"Have a little faith, Dräng. We got this far, didn't we?" Charlie was as nervous as he was confident.

"No. The Dark Prince is unlike any monster you have faced,

Lesser or Greater. If you fail, all is lost."

"I know. Thanks for reminding me."

They poured back into the circular hallway, leaving the dungeon and all of its death behind. In front of them—the doors to the Great Hall. The Dark Prince was beyond this final threshold. This same monster, who had terrorized their community, around which their town was built, and which had haunted their fears since Hunter's Grove was founded, sat on his pompous perch, waiting for them to crash through the doors to his throne room. The time had come to set free, or to doom, Hunter's Grove—and the rest of the world—once and for all.

Chapter 26

Charlie knew what waited behind those doors. He had foreseen the Hall too many times in his dreams.

He turned to face the group of hunters, his allies. His friends. He met their eyes, even Lisa's, whose blank stare had turned to fiery determination once more. Speeches and commands were unnecessary. He simply nodded, and sucked in the deepest breath he could.

The doors buckled under a wall of lightning from Nash's feet, and the monster hunters burst into the Great Hall with a righteous fury, followed by their fishing pole and rabbit foot-bearing friends, and one increasingly hesitant Lesser monster.

Lisa was first up the steps leading to the court of the throne, growling under her breath, "For Liev!" She outran the others, like a disease-maddened hound on the trail of its prey.

"*Where are you, blood pig?*" she screamed.

Her voice echoed back, louder and distorted. It repeated over and over until changing to a voice that was not hers—a deeper, richer voice. Her words blurred together, becoming perturbed laughter.

"*WHERE AM I? WHERE AM I?*"

The Dark Prince mocked Lisa.

Charlie looked throughout the Hall with his Sight. He could not find the varcolac. The Prince chuckled.

"LITTLE ONES. I'M RIGHT HERE!"

A burning chunk of marble flew at them. They ducked aside escaping the projectile, except for Darcy. She stood her ground, using her gift to become dense, too dense for the object to harm her. The flaming debris cracked into hundreds of pieces. Some of it flew past her, falling down the stairs. Other parts fell to the ground near her, catching fire to a rug. She took off her jacket and added it to the fire in hopes of increasing its light.

With Fish and Dink at their backs, the four remaining hunters moved further into the darkness of the immense room.

"STUPID HUMANS. SCORES HAVE COME BEFORE YOU. THEY COULDN'T DEFEAT ME, DO YOU, CHILDREN, THINK TO DO BETTER?"

Charlie tried a different approach. He reached out with his mind, trying to see through the varcolac's eyes. It worked.

"Nash! Over there!"

Nash looked to where Charlie was pointing and stomped.

"You're dead, monster!"

A fusillade of electricity flew to the ceiling, disturbing a cloud of red-eyed bats from their roosting place.

With great pain of heart, Lisa released a flickering black web of energy as the bats tried to escape, catching them in midflight. The bats gathered into a shadowy mass before melting into the shape of a man. Lisa's crackling web became tighter and tighter, ropelike. Motivated by revenge, she emptied her will into making the net a burning, destructive weapon of might. Everything within her wanted the varcolac to feel her pain, to experience the rending of her heart.

"You killed my brother!"

The varcolac laughed and broke the web. He took hold and flicked it like a whip, sending Lisa flying. He chuckled again as he blew his singed hands.

"No, your brother ruined himself by petting the Exsecrifer on my diary. I have to admit, I never thought any of you would make it this far."

The Dark Prince was tall and broad-shouldered, well-built and imposing. He wore hooded, red robes hanging majestic over a black suit of armor—fit for a king, and for a blood bath. His face, glowing from the fire that had spread at the front of the Hall, was chiseled to perfection. Too perfect, as if the varcolac had chosen this face above all others.

As he looked upon them, a demonic smile cut across his flawless lips.

"But you did make it. Such a pity, too. You will, however, make fine additions to my blood cellar. Especially you," he mused, cruel red eyes aligning with Darcy. "The blood of a young, generational hunter. Precisely what I need to raise the Ancients."

He turned and held out his hand. With a magnetic draw, Dräng flew from behind a pillar, landing in the varcolac's grip.

"No doubt this traitor has shown you my blood cellar. Am I correct, apostate?"

He threw the grieved monster with malice, turning back to smile at Darcy.

Darcy leveraged a threat in her eyes, remembering her mother, alive and yet, without the breath of life within her. She launched herself forward, making herself as dense as she could, and threw a solid punch at the varcolac's ribs.

Her hand connected with his side. *CRACK*. She fell to the

ground, cradling her fist in pain. The varcolac extended his leg and nudged her with his toe, sliding her several feet away.

With a clear view, Fish and Dink opened fire. Their hand-crafted munitions bit into the prince of beasts, forcing him abaft. In the shadows, they could see chunks of material and flesh disappear from his black silhouette with each shot. Soon the varcolac was reduced to a mess of holes, but Fish and Dink kept firing, until their weapons were empty.

The Dark Prince's ragged form shuddered, twitching and shaking until his silhouette became whole again.

The hunters watched in horror as the varcolac stepped forward with hellfire eyes and a malicious grin. He held out his hands, and Fish and Dink looked down to see they were no longer holding weapons, but they had transformed into large snakes. They cried out and threw the metal-scaled snakes down, stomping their heads.

Nash let another tumult of lightning fly. The varcolac held up a hand, and the energy flew into his palm. Congealing into a glowing orb, it flickered into a ball of smoke and fire.

The Dark Prince returned the energy and fire at Nash, catching his jacket on fire. Nash flailed, removing the jacket and escaped the flames.

Charlie looked around. They were being defeated on their own terms, with their own grudges. They were, as the varcolac had said, children, divided and full of rage. They needed a leader.

The varcolac watched Charlie, eyes like burning coal.

"Would you like to try your pathetic gift against me as well?"

Charlie didn't have time to respond before he felt the monster inside his own mind. He saw the varcolac for what he truly was—not a handsome prince, but a decrepit and twisted rejection of all that was good. This was no storybook vampire, as the twins had suggested, but an abomination.

He dropped his spear, burying his head in his hands as images badgered his mind repeatedly — visions of the varcolac's true form, his nightmares, Liev's death . . .

Amidst the chaos of painful images, Charlie could see the truth behind his nightmares, prophetic in vision. Liev was gone, and it was Charlie's fault. And, now, the varcolac was on the verge of victory. His plan would unfold, without hindrance, and the world would be lost.

Tears stung Charlie's eyes as the varcolac reminded him of Liev's thrice death. Poisoned by a manticore, wounded by the wolf, and dragged to the depths and drowned by murderous rusalkas. The varcolac forced Charlie to remember the night they'd found the diary, when the Exsecrifer bit into Liev's thumb. Liev had been cursed to die in that moment.

"You knew, in your soul, that Liev was cursed by the Exsecrifer," said the Prince. "How does it feel? Knowing your friend was cursed, and that you still put him in harm's way? Blinded by your own ambition, you let him take the fall."

The Dark Prince stopped talking, and the painful images stopped flickering through Charlie's mind. He heard scuffling.

Charlie looked up to see that Dräng had launched himself onto the front of the varcolac's intricate armor. Chunks of glowing marble were in both of the creature's hands. He was beating his former master relentlessly. The varcolac shielded his face, torn and bloodied with each impact of Dräng's magic-enhanced chunks of stone. Under Dräng's barrage, the Prince's face shifted from bloodied flesh, to a hairy and snarling snout, and back to chiseled perfection. Dräng laced his physical attack with elements of spelled confusion, spoken runes, and unbridled anger, unconcerned for his own safety or well-being.

It was the moment Charlie needed. He stood, shaking with exhaustion, and looked around at his fallen friends, teammates, and fellow hunters. *They needed a leader.*

"Get up," Charlie urged, helping Darcy to her feet. "Get up! We have to fight him together. We can only beat him if we work together."

Emotions flickered over each face — sorrow, anger, duty. They looked at each other and found themselves again.

The moment was interrupted, hearing a pained screech and watching as Dräng's small body collided sideways with a broken pillar. He fell to the ground, unmoving.

"Now!" screamed Charlie.

The four hunters lurched forward, wounded and spent, to where the varcolac stood holding his scarred face in its true form — fur, horns, tusks, and fangs. With his back against a toppled mantle, he summoned glamour to reveal a handsome, princely visage again, but it was too late. The four hunters cornered him.

"Together," Charlie said with grave intention.

As Lisa's net of black energy pushed through the air, Charlie remembered Loch's last words before stepping into the gateway.

"Charlie, wait!"

"Yes?"

Lisa pushed with all her might, pinning the varcolac to the mantle. A small streak of white current flickered through the bonds, as if Liev were helping his sister one last time.

Lisa saw the white spreading, and her heart jumped. She pushed with a power beyond herself — the memory of Liev. She focused as Loch had taught her. Her stream became a solid, inflicting chord against the varcolac.

The varcolac felt his skin burning, and he squirmed in agony.

Loch passed the box to the boy. "Inside — don't open it! Inside is a . . . mirror of sorts. A looking glass, if you will."

Darcy moved forward, condensing her mass and throwing punches at the varcolac through Lisa's bindings. The Prince's bones shattered and tried to heal themselves, only to be broken again by the girl's determined beating.

Nash was nervous about hitting Darcy, but stepped forward and brought his foot down hard. The electrical-charge jumped to its target mixing with Lisa's stream, striking the monster in the chest, where his black heart held no beat.

Charlie replayed the full conversation with Loch.

"A mirror?"

"Yes. You may not be able to kill the varcolac. He's a powerful Greater. If you can't kill him, show the mirror to him, but don't set eyes on it yourself! This mirror will show the Dark Prince his reflection, and it will bind the varcolac within the glass. With this, you'll have an advantage the first hunter's didn't have. But whatever you do you — and this goes for those blockhead friends of yours as well — you must not look at the mirror yourself. The mirror is facing the bottom of the box, so you know. Do you understand what you have to do?"

Charlie reached into his jacket pocket for the box Loch had given him. He closed his eyes and — though his mind was fragmented with pain and his nose began to bleed — summoned the images of as many people in Hunter's Grove as possible, seeing through all of their eyes at once. An ocean of images roared through his Sight, threatening to tear his mind apart. With these images, he pushed with his mind and sent the tormenting cacophony of visions into the varcolac's head.

"For Liev," whispered Charlie. "And for Hunter's Grove."

The varcolac screamed. The visions consumed him, and the bonds with which he imprisoned slaves began to slither around his spirit and choke his very existence. He had never felt this much pain, never been weakened by an opponent like this. The fear he felt exposed him. His beauty and his princely robes fell away to reveal a hideous beast covered in coarse fur, with horns, dry flesh, and shriveled wings. He cried out, begging for mercy, for release, for anything but *this*.

The three hunters brought their assault to a halt at Charlie's command. Broken and smoldering, the monster fell forward, slumping to its knees. Unrecognizable, the only resemblance of its former countenance were his hell-burning eyes. The beast looked up at the hunters, lost and devoid of cohesive thought.

Charlie held the mirror forward, and they all looked away.

The varcolac squinted at the four blurred shapes standing before him. His sight cleared enough to see the reflective object Charlie held toward him. *What magic is this?* Two red dots stared back at the varcolac, and then . . .

There was no longer any reflection. He found himself staring at his Great Hall from within a glass prison.

He pressed against the glass but it didn't bend. His broken body healing faster now, the varcolac pounded against the clear surface, only to realize it wouldn't break. The room fell away and was replaced by the velvet lining of the thin box in Charlie's hand. The varcolac roared in silence from inside his mirrored prison, and his vision went black. Charlie had sealed the mirror-box.

The Dark Prince was defeated, confined to the reflective chamber.

Charlie rubbed his face as sections of Blood Castle's ceiling began to cave. His nose was no longer bleeding, but a cake of dried blood formed down his face and jacket front. The others were talking to him, but their voices were distorted. The loss of blood and the mind-splitting effort of looking through so many eyes at once toppled Charlie.

Nash caught him before Charlie's head met the marble floor. Destined to carry yet another of his friends that day, Nash hoisted Charlie's smaller frame over his shoulder and nodded to the others.

"This place is falling apart," said Fish, pulling Dräng out of the rubble. "We need to get out of here."

"We've got to get my mother first!" cried Darcy.

"We'll get them all out, but we need to move."

Nash jumped over the flames at the Great Hall's entrance, Charlie in tow. Darcy and Lisa followed, and Dink after them. Fish took up the rear, holding a conscious but wounded Dräng.

They escaped as the hall collapsed in ruin.

The Sagemistress watched with her coven of witches from Wyvern's Peak as the tallest tower of Blood Castle crashed into dust. She smiled, knowing the fledglings had succeeded. The Prince was finished, and his accursed, binding magic was crumbling.

She watched as the varcolac's army began to disappear from the Otherworld.

The wolves howled, released from their master's bonds and

vanishing into swirls of light, returning to their long-forgotten homelands.

Banshees and boggarts faded into mists of freedom, returning to green coastlands.

Everywhere the Sagemistress looked, the same. The Prince had been overthrown, and their vows to him were broken. Unknowingly, these new hunters had released monsters back into the world, to their places of origin and homelands.

Howls and roars and screams of celebration rose into the air, and then faded into eerie silence.

The shockwave of wind rushed upward to Wyvern's Peak. The Sagemistress cherished the moment, and her coven of witches simmered in excited chatter.

She raised her head and closed her eyes as the wind surged around her. Sweet release.

The Sagemistress vanished.

They ran through the hallway, pushing and pulling the former prisoners along the path. Charlie was awake, but needed help moving forward as well. Nash pushed from the rear with Fish and Dink, making sure no one fell behind. He carried little Bobby Muldor, whose little legs wouldn't have been able to outrun a collapsing castle. Fish and Dink helped the two centuries-old prisoners keep up.

They reached the courtyard and took no pause. With towers and buildings collapsing around them, they ran for the open gate, through the portcullis and across the lowered bridge.

Fish and Dink were the last to jump from the bridge to the empty plains of the Otherworld. Blood Castle gave a final heave and the outer walls fell. The bridge and gate crumbled under the strain, crashing into the void waters of the moat.

Exhausted and strewn, they all sat staring at the shambled remains of Blood Castle.

The hunters and their friends fell against the ground, taking the first chance in a very long day to rest and breathe. Those who had been imprisoned by the varcolac took the opportunity to massage sore joints, and move without hindrance.

Somewhere in the midst of it all, the two Witheringtons — mother and daughter — found each other and embraced in a long-awaited reunion. Silence and tears spoke all that words could not.

Darcy buried her face in her mother's shoulder. "I missed you so much."

"I missed you, too, my beautiful warrior. Let's go home."

The humans and their newly adopted, brave, little monster marched unhindered through the Otherworld, and into the smoky light of the portal. For better or worse, all were free. Humans and monsters alike.

The four remaining hunters would soon face the consequences of the Dark Prince's defeat. But for now, they could return home and enjoy what centuries of former monster hunters had not been able to accomplish.

Chapter 27

Loch perched on an old lawn chair in the Key's garden, cradling his runic shotgun like a pillow. One eye was blue, the other a glassy red as he kept a watchful eye on the bridge. The magical membrane protecting it had deteriorated hours ago. He would either welcome back his five young students, or give the Dark Prince all the fight he had left.

His young monster hunters departed not long after sunrise, and now the sun was in its descent. He feared it would be the hunters' age-old adversary who breached the earth-side portal, not Charlie and the others.

Loch stiffened, his aim at the ready, when the gateway regurgitated several figures onto the bridge. More than double the number that had crossed over returned, tripping and fumbling over each other, attempting to recover from the dimensional jump. Something else came in behind them—something big—moving quickly to hide itself in the shadows of the garden.

Loch was more concerned with the humans rolling around like worms on the bridge. For a moment, he was too shocked to speak.

It was done. They had actually done it.

Loch stood up and shook his head, regaining his crotchety composure. He crossed his arms and gave his most disapproving scowl.

"I hope I never looked this bad crossing a gateway."

Among the newcomers, Elizabeth Witherington winced.

"Hush, old man! I didn't see you there when the varcolac's castle fell."

"Elizabeth! It's been too long. I was hoping you'd come back in one piece."

Loch moved to help her.

"Not sure about one piece," Elizabeth grumbled.

"Wait," said Darcy. "You knew? You knew my mother was over there and you didn't say anything?"

"Slow down, girl. I wasn't sure she would be alive. I only knew when this one came back and told me," he said, thrusting his thumb toward Dräng. "I would've strangled his scrawny neck then and there, if he hadn't introduced me to Fish and Dink. Good friends to have, these two."

He held a hand out to help them.

"The victory's even sweeter," Loch continued, "seeing just how many others survived the Dark Prince. I'm sure this will restore the life and joy in Hunter's Grove."

"Not everyone," said Nash.

A deep sadness settled over the group.

"Mrs. McBranson didn't survive. And. . . ."

It hit Loch with a crushing weight. His shoulders slumped as he realized there were only four of his young hunters — their white knight was not among them.

"Where's Liev?" he asked, his tone downtrodden.

A small whimper escaped Lisa. She hid her face from the others as Darcy drew her close.

Charlie stared at the ground.

"Liev . . . didn't make it," he managed.

Loch nodded. "I'm so sorry. I wish … oh God, I'm so sorry."

274

Lisa shook her head. She understood why Loch was apologizing—he felt responsible. But she also knew Liev better than anyone. Had her brother known before hand, he would have made the same choice. Remembering his bandaged thumb, some part of her wondered if Liev had known. The thought ruined her, and she pushed it out of mind.

"Why don't we get inside," Loch suggested in a softened tone. "We can have some hot cocoa and talk where it's warm."

He ushered them inside, turning back to the garden before going inside himself. He walked over to where the big stone beast hid, taking in the miserable creature.

The gargoyle was damaged badly. It carried its right foreleg in its beak, laying it down at Loch's feet. There were several cracks along its body, and several pieces of its face, including a horn, had broken off during battle.

"You're in a bad state, aren't you, my friend?"

The gargoyle quietly bellowed in response. Loch caught eyes with the construct and was taken with shock, realizing the moisture darkening its stone face was, in fact, tears. No one had ever heard of a gargoyle crying—constructs were not built with those faculties.

Grating against itself, the gargoyle fell over. Loch was worried it was dying, but then realized it was trying to hand him something with its one good foreleg.

Loch held out his hands, his heart breaking at what the gargoyle was giving him. It was a shirt, shredded and lacking form. It had been white at one point, but was now bloody and marked with dirt and grime.

"You stayed with him till the end," said Loch. "Didn't you?"

The beast nodded, letting its head fall to the ground.

Loch bent down to pet it, reassuring the guardian.

"You did your best, and you got the other four of them home safe, and alive. There is nothing to be ashamed of. Rest now. I'll make sure you're fixed up, nice and smooth again, after you've been static for a while."

The gargoyle nodded, aching with sadness. It took back Liev's tattered shirt in its big claws, and lay down as comfortably as it could manage before drying up and becoming an immobile stone form once more.

Hot cocoa was nice, but after spending weeks, or years, in the Otherworld, the missing people of Hunter's Grove were starving. With the help of Fish and Dink, Loch covered the dining room table with microwaveable dinners: Salisbury steaks, mac and cheese, and nuggets—presumed to be chicken. Loch would have been upset that a month's worth of food stores were being eaten, had it not been for a good cause.

The small crowd moved fireside in one of the Key's better kept parlors. As they discussed the events that had transpired in the Otherworld, Darcy and Nash took turns telling stories, with the help of Elizabeth Witherington and Robert Wickles, Donnie's "crazy" uncle. Lisa and Charlie focused on eating, neither feeling the need to recount their time away from home.

Loch praised them for their accomplishments and left it at that. Coming to grips with their sacrifice—Liev's sacrifice—would take time.

Dräng chugged down his hot cocoa, furiously licking the bottom of the mug for any residual chocolate. Slurping and snorting, he looked over the top of his mug to the silent group of humans watching him.

He might have been a monster, but he had also served royalty, acted as a diplomat, and overseen scores of castle servants. He realized how rude he was being and raised his mug in explanation.

"This," he said sheepishly, "is not customary from where I come. This *ko-ko-a*, as you call it, must be from that heavenly time before the Ancients. A most pleasant communion."

"It's called hot *cocoa*," said Loch. "Might want to wipe off your muzzle, though."

Dräng crossed his eyes to see his nose, lapping his forked tongue up and around. His eyes rolled back, tasting the cocoa lost on the tip of his nose, and sighed.

"Ahhh. Yummy, yummy delight."

Everyone got a good laugh at the silliness of a cocoa-loving monster. Even Lisa allowed a grin to crack one side of her mouth. She remembered it was just days ago she was trying to catch the little domovoi with her brother.

"What about this little domovoi?" she asked. Her raspy voice silenced the room. "Where does he go from here?"

Loch pursed his lips and took a deep breath as he gazed upon Dräng.

"He could stay with me," Lisa continued.

"We'll see. He has a home here or with you, regardless. He's shown his colors true. We'll need to consult with your parents, especially considering. . . One step at a time." Looking at Dräng, Loch nodded. "Either way, your home is with us for now."

"Home," Dräng whispered to himself, "I have a home again. I am full of happy! It has been many, many years since I have been home."

Everyone grinned, and the room seemed to warm a few degrees.

"Please, if I may ask of you or you," he said, looking at Loch and Lisa. "No matter where I live, will we be certain to have more of this?"

Dräng lifted his mug and smiled impishly.

Laughter again broke through the quiet, if for a moment.

Loch turned to the two unknown prisoners, whose captivity was a mystery to him. They had been given new clothes, and now sat devouring their second and third platefuls of food. Neither looked to be in good shape, even with the new clothes they'd been given. "And what about you two? What's your story?"

"Priest," said the older of the two men, still concerned with his meal. "My name is Priest." He swept his dirty gray hair out of his face before taking another bite. It had been so long since he'd eaten, sustained only by the Dark Prince's will.

"I am Chen," said the other. His hands were shaking. "The Dark Prince took us shortly before the others could finish building the Key."

"Finish the Key? Surely, you don't mean finish building Hunter's Key? How long have you two been in the Otherworld?" Loch asked.

Priest allowed his eyes to drift upward, breathing slow and heavy through his beard. "I noticed things look a little different than last time we were here, but. . . What century is it?"

"Twenty-first."

Priest dropped his head in a slow nod.

Chen's hands stopped shaking in a moment of dour reflection. "Then it has been two hundred years," he said. "Two hundred years since we began building the Key."

Darcy's jaw fell, and Charlie shared raised eyebrows with Nash and Lisa. These men were part of the group that had first built Hunter's Key. They were true elders in a long line of monster hunters.

The residents of Hunter's Grove looked at each other in awe.

"I'm sorry," said Loch. "I'm sure this is all very strange to you. We'll make sure you're taken care of, but right now we need to get these people get back to their homes."

"Please do," said Chen.

Priest agreed. "The Good Lord knows their families have missed them," he said.

"Right," said Loch. "I'll be back in a while, then, and catch you up on, well, the past two centuries."

Everyone hurried out of the room, anxious to return to their homes and families.

As they walked down the front steps of Hunter's Key, Loch pulled Charlie aside, urgency arresting his words.

"Did you kill the varcolac, or capture him?"

"He was too strong for us. I used the mirror."

"The mirror, then. Do you have it?"

Charlie nodded and revealed the thin black box, handing it over without delay.

Loch stowed it inside his coat with care. "He's in here?"

Charlie nodded again. "What are you going to do with it?"

"I'll put it somewhere safe, like the diary. Just more junk to be hidden away under the protective watch of the Key. You did good, m'boy."

"It wasn't just me."

"It wasn't at all. But every group needs a leader. You are their leader. You'll need to put your mind to learning what I know, for the next time you face the supernatural."

Astonished and confused, Charlie looked up with wide eyes.

"What do you mean? Didn't we just stop the varcolac?"

"You did, but there are always threats out there, Charlie. And I'm afraid there will be even more threats in our world after today."

"What? How?"

"Centuries ago, the Dark Prince gathered a large force of monsters and moved to a small, concealed section of the Otherworld—the same you and your friends just came through. For years, hunters around the world have kept the monster population in check in our world. But after the Dark Prince was defeated, all of his servants would have been released from their obligation."

"I still don't understand what this has to do with us."

"When you defeated the varcolac, Charlie, where do you think all those monsters went? They didn't just disappear. They went back home."

Realization dawned on Charlie as a white truck interrupted their conversation.

It sped around the dusty courtyard of the Key, driven by an emotionally distraught William Witherington. Unable to bear the loss of his daughter any longer, the mayor intended to have it out with the current inhabitant of Hunter's Key and find out where she had gone.

The truck came to a screeching halt, and out plopped Mayor Witherington. He rubbed his eyes, and refocused his vision. "Impossible!"

He saw Darcy, and he gasped in relief. She smiled and waved to him. Then he saw the woman standing beside her.

William Witherington ran — stumbled — weeping and yammering with arms outstretched, until he collided with his family. The three melted into a synchronized hug.

From the steps, Loch and Charlie watched, weary despite the team's victory.

"We'll talk later," said Loch. "Right now, we have some people who would love to see their families."

Hunter's Grove rippled with excitement. Tears, laughter, and more joy than anyone could remember in recent years swept through the close-knit community.

Mayor Witherington called for a celebration and set about organizing a party the entire town could enjoy. A feast was prepared, evergreen boughs were hung in as many places as they could be hung, and music and dancing were the top order of the evening.

The mayor delivered a welcome home speech, and was sure to honor both those who had returned, and those who had fallen. Against his better judgement and wishes, Loch was introduced to the town and Charlie, Darcy, Nash, Lisa and Liev were recognized for their bravery and sacrifice.

With these recognitions, the people of Hunter's Grove were introduced to the idea that monsters were, indeed, among them, and that a very different world swirled around them. Murmurs and hush-hush conversations dotted the social landscape for weeks to come.

And for as much joy that was spread throughout the nestled little town during the festivities, it was punctuated with the memory of two of Hunter's Grove's dearest residents. In their memory, white bows were attached in each place where evergreen was hung, and Mayor Witherington made a declaration in honor of Mrs. Ellie B. McBranson and Liev Vadiknov.

Each year on this day, from this time forward, the lights of Hunter's Grove were to be illuminated for a week's time. Special strands of clear, white lights were cast throughout the town, and it was declared that every building and street light were to remain lit during the annual memorial. The residents took it upon themselves to add to the remembrance by leaving their porch lights on for the week's length.

People would never forget the ultimate sacrifice paid in an unseen war between two worlds. These two fallen souls were hailed as heroes, and would be forever remembered as *The Lights of Hunter's Grove*.

Epilogue

O n the night of the celebration, Lisa slipped out the back door of Town Hall. Her parents had returned home, leaving early to mourn their son. Lisa couldn't bear to go home without Liev, so she hung back.

Wandering, she found herself plodding uphill to Sanctuary Gardens, a public garden known for its panoramic view of Hunter's Point and the town below, even more so for its breathtaking view of the sunset. The owner of the land the gardens were on kept it as a hobby, changing the flowers through the seasons, and keeping the place tidy during fall and winter. It was open year round, available for anyone who needed to enjoy quiet time in a peaceful setting.

Tonight, Lisa was one of those people. The further from the celebration she climbed, the harder it was to hold it all in. She didn't know how long she could live like this — without Liev.

She was empty, broken. Her twin, her best friend, was dead. Now that the adrenaline of the return home, and the buzz of community gathering, was wearing off, her thoughts were consumed with the loss of her brother. Her heart felt like it was being seared with a hot iron. Tears began to break through.

She worked her way through the gardens to the center, where stone benches welcomed weary travelers. She sat, and finally let it flow, holding nothing back. She wept and wept.

Lisa asked herself if there was anything different she could have done so that Liev would still be here.

Every second of their experience in the Otherworld replayed in her mind as she searched for clues. There was no comfort to be had.

Except...

She remembered that while they were battling the varcolac, there was a faint white flash that filtered through her own dark energy bands. As far as she had experienced, that only happened when she and Liev used their gift together. It was the only time after he fell to the wolf it had happened. Every other time, her power was black, dark—void of light.

Her excitement dampened as she wondered if the glimmer of white had been from Nash's current joining hers. They had all been using their abilities at once, as a unified force. Liev hadn't been there to help them. Hope evaded her thoughts.

The weight pushed her down. Her brother and friend was gone, and there was nothing she could do about it.

Lisa folded her knees under her chin, wrapping her arms around her legs, and sobbed again, soaking the sleeves of her shirt with tears. She peeked up and over her elbows to the setting sun, blurred by the salt and water in her eyes, realizing this would be her first sunset without her brother.

"I miss you so much, Liev. Goodbye, brother. I love you."

Her tears became too thick to see, and so she lowered her face once again.

Lisa heard a rustling on the stone-pebble path behind her and wiped her face, taking a deep, steadying breath. She looked over her shoulder to see who was approaching. No one was there.

She stood and turned, allowing her senses to adjust to the failing light, opening her mouth to call out when an impish creature stepped from behind a rose-covered lattice.

"Dräng! What are you doing here?"

"Please, if I may, sad human. I have come to be a friend. I mean no harm."

"I know you mean no harm. How did you find me?"

"I followed you. I, too, once lost my family. To the Dark Prince, I lost them. And I thought, perhaps . . ."

"Thank you, Dräng. It's good to know you care. I'm . . . sorry about your family."

"I am sad. But I am here and hear the future calling. We can answer it together if you like."

Lisa smiled and nodded. She bent down to hug her little friend.

"For now, sad human, there is another family waiting for you."

Dräng smiled, pointing over his shoulder.

"Okay, I'm coming. And stop calling me sad human. It makes me sound pathetic."

"Forgiveness, please. Now come and see."

Lisa took a moment to dry her eyes again before following. Dräng looked back from time to time as they trod through the gardens, making sure Lisa was still there. They approached the edge of Sanctuary Gardens, where the hill descended toward the town. At the bottom of the hill stood Charlie, Nash, Darcy, Fish, and Dink. They were there to let her know she wasn't alone.

Dräng hopped in a circle, looking back at Lisa. He cocked his head to the side, like a puppy, and grinned at her. She was certain that if he had a tail, he would be wagging it.

"Let's go," insisted Charlie. "We all need a good night's rest."

"Definitely sleeping in tomorrow," said Nash.

"Forget that," said Dink. "I'm going fishin'! Have you seen this weather?" He looked up with his arms spread open wide. "You ain't keeping me indoors tomorrow, no sir!"

They all laughed at Dink's weather forecast, and turn back toward Hunter's Grove.

Except for Lisa. A thread of hope lingered, and she had to see for herself.

She let the group continue on several paces ahead before turning to face the sun, which was now only a sliver of burnt orange, melting the skies in the distant landscape. As quiet and controlled as she could manage, Lisa cast one small thread of energy.

She gasped. It was there! A glimmer of white in her black cord.

Her mind raced, and hope stirred inside her.

Still walking toward Town Hall, Charlie's eyes turned the slightest shade of red, and he smiled.

Across an ocean, a howl pierced the night sky, mingling with the full moon's light. Scores of crimson, hungry eyes seethed in the dark, and an ancient terror took a small village by the neck for the first time in two centuries.

A letter was hastily scribed and sent off with a horseback messenger. They were taking a risk, but what else did they have?

A message had been sent to the monster hunters of Hunter's Grove.

About the Authors

D.C. McGannon is co-author of the *Charlie Sullivan and the Monster Hunters* series of books, and one-half of the humorous father/son duo known as *The Monster Guys*. When not travelling to conventions and talking about Japanese and Steampunk monsters, he can usually be found moon-gardening, hiking, or searching for his next cup of coffee.

D.C. is confident he can still breakdance with the best of them, but realizes his writing and speaking schedule is probably taking too much of his time. This is good news for all other break-dancers.

He is married to Holly, father to Michael and Nathaniel, and they all hang out together somewhere in the Midwest with their little Maltese puppy, Jewel.

C. Michael McGannon is co-author of the *Charlie Sullivan and the Monster Hunters* series of novels, and is one-half of the humorous, father/son duo known as *The Monster Guys*, mixing humor, horror, and all manner of comedic improv to special events. An expert in all things "monster," he brings an "academic humor" to the subjects of folktales, urban legends, and storytelling.

Michael is a fan of stories, of libraries, of books, and of Japanese and British humor. He is particularly fond of ginger beer, as well as chocolate darker than that one Pink Floyd song. When not writing or attending conventions, Michael is usually recovering from all-night gaming excursions.

For this and other exciting titles, visit:

www.WyvernsPeak.com

@WyvernsPeak

Sign up for our newsletter, get free stuff, and be the first to know when new books from your favorite Wyvern's Peak authors are released.

Follow us on Twitter
@DCMcGannon
@MichaelMcGannon

Like us on Facebook
www.facebook.com/DCMcGannon
www.facebook.com/cmichaelmcgannon